Sausalito Nights

MONTGOMERY BEAUTY SERIES, BOOK 1

STEPHANIE SALVATORE

Sausalito Nights
by Stephanie Salvatore

Sausalito Nights (Montgomery Beauty Series: Book 1)

Edited by: Jessa Dahmes
Cover design and formatting by Just Write Creations and Services

Printed in the United States of America
First Printing: December 2018
Independent Publisher

ISBN-13: 9781790598298

Author's Note: This book may contain triggers for some people. Due to the nature of the book and characters, certain scenes contain amounts of violence and graphic sex. If while reading this book you find yourself disturbed by its content, please take a break from reading and pick it back up when you feel ready again. Thank you and enjoy your journey.

– Stephanie Salvatore

This book is dedicated to Jill Horle.
Thank you for being there from the beginning, rooting me on with your pom poms, and cussing me out for making you wait for the next chapter.

Table of Contents

The Unexpected Journey

Christopher

Summer

I WOKE TO the sunlight shining through the bedroom window. No noisy, annoying alarms to tell me it was time for another day of high school. My eyes fluttered open as a sinking feeling crept through my mind that this summer wouldn't be the same as the past.

The doorbell rang in the distance and I decided to lay low and wait to see who it was.

"Good morning," an elderly woman spoke. It was my Nana Rosemary. Stretching, I sat up to listen in.

"Good morning. Come in, Nathan is just finishing up in the kitchen for breakfast."

"Sorry for just popping in, we were in the area."

Mom paused before she spoke. "A visit from you is always welcome, Mom."

I furrowed my eyebrows. I knew better. They weren't just here for a visit.

"Actually, there is a reason for the impromptu visit," Papa spoke this time. They were both here?

Footsteps clicked against the wooden floors toward the living room. "When I called the other day, Nathan was telling me about the struggles he's having at the construction business." I imagined my parents looking at each other, and back to Nana and Papa.

"We want to help," Papa said after a moment.

Mom sighed. "You know we'd accept your help, but I don't think moving again is an option right now."

"We know the number of times you've had to move is significant, Grace," Papa said. "If you'll hear us out, the offer we have in mind might be beneficial for all of you."

"How?" She asked.

The downhill battle for construction work in Oroville and its surrounding areas was competitive, and in my opinion rather scarce.

"Well. We have an extra house, in Sausalito," Nana said.

"Sausalito sits just outside of San Francisco, on the north end of the Golden Gate Bridge," Papa added.

"So, this would be an opportunity to be close to a bigger city," Dad said.

"Yes, Nathan. This move would bring you to big city living; but rest assured, Sausalito won't give you that feeling."

Silence remained in the room before Mom spoke once more. "Okay, but Christopher is in his last year of high school. Shouldn't we wait?"

"We considered that and saw the summer as an opportunity for the transition. We know it's not exactly ideal, but three months is plenty of time to readjust your surroundings," Papa said, and his words were genuine.

"He will miss out on graduating with his friends, but if this is what's best for the family…"

"We wouldn't be persistent unless we saw the pros outweighing the cons," Nana said.

"Where is the house located exactly?" Dad asked.

"It's located at the Castillo Yacht Club. One of the top elite communities you could live in the Bay Area," Papa said.

"I brought pictures, Grace," Nana added.

There was a pause before Mom commented. "It's beautiful; but I think one of my concerns is the cost it's going to take to live there."

"If you take this offer, we wouldn't charge you anything to live there, and we would pay for Christopher's tuition at a prestigious private school," Papa insisted.

"We want you to focus on getting the construction business back on its feet," Nana said.

"I agree with your Mother," Papa said. "You have an opportunity to save the business and, hopefully, pass it on to Chris one day. Plus, we're getting older, and the winery is getting to be a lot of responsibility."

"We understand," Mom said. "I would love to take your offer. I honestly think it'd be for the best."

"I agree," Dad said.

This sounded like a done deal to me, and I wasn't sure how to feel about it.

"Then it's settled." I could hear the satisfaction in Nana's voice.

For as long as I could remember, my Dad's parents were the only active grandparents involved in my life. They weren't just there for the big events; they made weekly visits from Napa, or they would invite us out to the vineyard on the weekends to unwind from a long week of work and school.

I tried to absorb what I'd just overheard. I was unsure of how I should feel. As the construction business in the area dried up, there simply wasn't enough work to go around. My parents never used to fight, but in the last year I had overheard many conversations about bills turning into arguments. If this move stopped that from happening for good, this summer could hold a solid promise for the Montgomery family's future.

Three weeks later

I found myself packing up the last of my belongings. Soon enough, I would be bidding Oroville goodbye, maybe for good. I couldn't say I'd miss it. This place filled my head with memories including the struggles of moving from one run down house to the next as my family attempted to keep afloat. Sausalito held the promise of unknown possibilities.

Crawling into the back of my closet, I opened the door in the wall that led to a storage crawl space. Inside, I spotted a single wooden floorboard with a nail sitting on top and picked both items up. I stared down at the tally marks carved into the old wood. As a kid, I found the loose floorboard in my bedroom at my first home and I would tuck my favorite toys into the floor at night before bed. It happened to be my earliest childhood memory, and I couldn't let it go, so I used the floorboard to keep track of the moves we made.

Picking up the old nail, I used the shadow of light peeking through as I started scratching in the fifth line across the second set of five tally marks. I backed out of the space and into my room, where I slid the floor board into a box full of books, taped it up and stacked it on top of the other boxes that were ready to go. Turning to look around, the rest of my room was bare. Moving day had arrived and I was more than ready to see where this journey would lead me.

Castillo Familia Rituals

Lorelai

I PACED MY bedroom as I waited for my older sister to remove herself from the bathroom. I groaned as I stopped and hit my fist on the door. "Luciana! Hurry up! I need to get in there before Papino summons us to this Godforsaken family meeting!"

I heard her singing to the music blaring in the background and rolled my eyes when a light bulb went off in my head. I stomped to her bedroom door which was unlocked and walked into the bathroom, turning her obnoxious music down.

"Hey! I was listening to that! What the hell?" She turned and glared at me.

"I need to shower and you're hogging the bathroom. We share this bathroom, remember?" I crossed my arms and scowled.

She scoffed, turning around to continue applying her classic Marilyn Monroe Red lipstick. Her hair was down in curls, and she looked perfect per usual. I rolled my eyes at her and went to get into the shower. "So, what is this meeting about anyway?"

"I believe it's that time of year again." I waited for her to continue as the warm water ran down my body. "You know, where we catch up on the family business and bid on summer jobs."

"Not sure why I'm still included in these meetings. Papa knows I'm only going to work at the yacht club."

"Well, maybe it's time to come onboard the family business. You're seventeen, and you're a Castillo, Lorelai."

I stayed silent as I lathered the soap into my hair. "You know how I feel about the family business. The Yacht Club is where I draw my lines."

"I'll never understand your thought process, Lor. It's in your blood."

I finished up my shower in silence and stepped out, wrapping a plush towel around my body. "I have my reasons," I said simply.

"Fine. On another note, when are you going to deal with Santino? You know Mom and Dad are going to find out about him sooner rather than later." She eyed me in the mirror.

I sighed, "Maybe it's better they do, so he'll leave me alone."

She rolled her eyes. "He has a thing for you, Lor."

"He has a funny way of showing it," I fumed.

She was silent a moment as she finished applying her mascara while I went to find clothes in the walk-in closet attached to the bathroom. "Well, if you don't tell Papino, Armani will take matters into his own hands; and we both know how that will end."

I pulled my clothes on while I tried to think of something to say. The truth was, Santino was one of Papino's second strings in the family business. He'd been after me for years. I had no interest in him, but he wouldn't take no for an answer; and his advances toward me had been getting out of hand lately. After my older brother Armani caught wind of it, I feared that if Santino didn't back off there would be bloodshed. My stomach churned.

I sat in the plush chair at my vanity and grabbed my brush. "Hopefully, it won't come to that," I said.

"Suit yourself, Lorelai. You know the risk you're taking without letting our Father handle it." Her tone was cold, and I looked back at her as she started cleaning up. "We're supposed to meet at the vault in a half hour. Don't be late."

I was quiet as she finished up and left the bathroom. Deep in my own thoughts, I met my reflection in the mirror. There was no right answer. Whether I involved my parents or let it go, lives were at risk. Who the hell was I kidding? Lives were always at risk at the hands of a Castillo.

Entering the kitchen, I watched as my mother stacked aluminum foil tins full of food. "Morning, Mama."

"Lorelai. I'm so glad you decided to join us. Your Papino is already down in the vault making sure the agenda is perfected."

I rolled my eyes. Before I could respond, the door shut. "Familia?" My best friend, and cousin, Marie called from the front door.

"In the kitchen!" I responded, and she bounced into the room.

"Mom sent me over early to see if I could help with anything."

My mom smiled brightly. "Lorelai? Maybe you and Marie could take the breakfast trays down and set the buffet up?"

"Sure, Mama." I picked up the trays and waited for Marie to grab the others before I led the way down to the lower level of the penthouse and stopped at a wall of family portraits. I set my hand on the centered portrait of my father. His dark hair and stern eyes, with the stiff jaw line and pressed lips made him appear powerful; and I knew he did it on purpose. Pulling on the edge of the portrait, it opened to a hidden keypad. I entered a code and the wall slid open. Marie and I passed through a dimly lit tunnel and descended a flight of stairs with an almost eerie illumination. I came to another wall where I pressed my fingertip. A pair of double doors slid apart on the wall and I entered the stadium style seating vault where our family meetings always took place. "Morning, Papino."

He looked over, and a smile rose on his lips. "Good morning, sweet pea. Have you given any thought to starting your training this summer?"

I eyed him carefully and shook my head.

"Still haven't changed your mind, huh?"

"No, sir." I went to set the trays down with my back toward him when Marie spoke up.

"Lorelai and I are the odd balls out, Uncle Armani. Didn't you know?"

He chuckled. "You're exactly like your mother, Lorelai." He looked at Marie. "Sweet niece of mine," he pleaded. "You don't want to come work for your Uncle?"

"Hell no! I already completed my sworn secrecy, Uncle."

The sworn in secrecy was a big deal, and I hadn't done mine yet. The decision to train and learn the life of what it was like to be a Black Diamond was forced upon us before we turned eighteen. If we chose to walk away from the family business, we were not cut off completely. I knew that Marie's parents would give her a trust fund when she turned eighteen, but she was to never be caught in Black Diamond Headquarters without permission from one of the elite members. If she ever broke those rules, the consequences were extreme, and would not rule out death depending on the rate of deception. What our parents didn't know was that Marie and I made a pact to never enter the family business when we were thirteen and old enough to figure out what it all meant. Hell, I didn't even tell Luciana or Armani about the pact; but growing up watching my parents disappear all the time and relying solely on my siblings for my needs never sat well with me.

My father looked back to me as Marie and I completed our assignment. "Lorelai? If you're opting out, we need to complete sworn secrecy," he paused, "today."

I darted a look at him at the change in his tone, and nodded slowly. "I understand."

He nodded, his face turned stone cold as he stood up without another word. He left and I met eyes with Marie. We both knew our parents meant business, but this was a pretty big reality. Papino had looked extremely pissed off when I gave him my final word. Both of my siblings opted to follow in his footsteps, and I think he was hopeful that he would have all of his children there to back him up. I sighed, not knowing what to think about his reaction; but I knew I had already made up my mind. There was no turning back.

When breakfast was set Luciana and Armani joined us, and once we were all seated, Papino looked at me over his glasses. "Lorelai, I have some bad news for you."

"Lay it on me." I hated when he beat around the bush.

"We hired a new chef for the yacht club and he came equipped with his own top of the line staff. All good for the club, but your job has been eliminated from last season."

I pursed my lips. "Okay. So, what are my options?"

"Well, I took some time to think about it. You like the hospitality work, so I'm going to put you and Marie in charge of the boathouse rentals."

I exchanged a smile with Marie. "I can handle that."

He slid two packets full of responsibilities toward us. "Moving on to the next order of business…"

I ate my food as I looked through the job description and realized this might not be so bad. The rental boats were never fully booked, which meant I could escape and be hidden if I needed too.

When the meeting ended, Marie left and I stayed behind while my parents left abruptly. Luciana and Armani stood and moved in front of me with their arms crossed. "What?"

Armani sent a daggered glare toward me, wrinkles creased up his forehead, his dark brown hair falling back and to the side. "Did you tell Papino you weren't joining the family business?"

I nodded slowly. "I did. Why is this coming off as a surprise?" I sat back in my chair, crossing my arms to match theirs.

"We can't protect you when you bow out, Lorelai." Armani snapped.

Luciana rolled her eyes. "Armani! She's not going to be excluded from the family or the protection we can provide. Don't listen to him. He clearly didn't read the clause correctly."

"We don't turn our backs on family, Luciana. Turning the business away is doing just that…" Armani snapped back, the fury in his eyes intensifying.

The door opened, and our father appeared in a black robe with my mother. "It's time Lorelai." I stood up to follow my parents to their office. My father unlocked a secret door in his bookshelf that led us to an enclosed staircase. When we arrived at the bottom, we were outside one dock away from the back entrance to the Black Diamond Club. Swallowing hard, I looked at my mother, fear filling my eyes.

"It's okay, Lor. Go ahead, I'm right behind you."

I did as I was told until we reached one specific yacht. Boarding, I was led inside to the lower level. Every passageway we went through required a code to enter. My father had this operation under lock and key, but somehow, I wasn't surprised.

Arriving at the unknown destination, Mother maneuvered me behind a removable wall, stripped my clothes, and placed me in a silk red robe. Then she took my hand, bringing me out to a wooden circular table. Candles were lit around the contract handwritten by my father on an off-white scroll paper, burnt at its edges. I shuddered at the image, the burns of the paper told me one thing, this paper was fireproof. There was no burning of this agreement.

Picking up the calligraphy pen slowly, I bit my lower lip before I signed my name. I dotted the I's and crossed my T's as if I was really crossing my heart and hoping to die if I acted out of conduct according to the contract.

"Let's get started, shall we?" My father paused. "This agreement says that you, Lorelai Sienna Castillo, have agreed to distance yourself from the Castillo Syndicate. If you change your mind, you will have to plead your case before the members. There is a Castillo family ritual ceremony. Now that you have signed the contract, I must burn this black iron stencil of flocking birds into your right forearm, followed immediately by a tattoo of these same birds on the opposing arm. It's how we've identified family members for centuries. Once the ritual is over, you aren't to step foot into Black Diamond territory under any circumstances unless you are with a member or it's approved prior to the visit. Anything you've witnessed up to this point will not be spoken of to anyone outside of our family, do you agree to these terms Lorelai?"

I was absolutely horrified that this was even proposed as a family ritual. If you were in, you still endured the pain; only after it was over, you were entered into a brutal training course. I had to take on the pain and the emotional toll of walking in an unknown direction. No matter what path it was, I would have to walk around for the rest of my life with a scar of flocking birds on one arm and a tattoo of them on the other, and I didn't get a choice in the matter?

How was this happening? I hesitated as I felt my parent's eyes on me. They would have loved nothing more than for me to give into their lives, but I couldn't. To my parents, I knew that the family business was a lifetime commitment. They had organized crime down pat, paying people a percentage of the money coming in and a set amount for each task a member completed. Between Uncle Thad, my dad, and Marie's father Lorenzo, they were three of the richest men in the world, building their fame off of the world class Black Diamond Casinos. I knew the major details, that the business went widespread in Las Vegas with my great grandfather. I also knew the Black Diamond name brand was spread to strip clubs and into the Castillo Yacht Clubs, which had also spread throughout America all the way to the East Coast. I knew being a Castillo would get me out of trouble if I ever got into any and that we had connections to pull strings in high places, but I didn't want any part of their connections. I wanted nothing to do with the organized crimes; because in the end, I would get pulled down with them when they were finally caught. My brother was educated well on the business and his claim was that we had family on the inside of the law. Uncle Matteo, the youngest of my father's brothers, was only ten years older than me and hit the ground running with his law firm because of our last name.

Coming back to the present, my parents still stood looking at me. "Yeah. Let's get this over with..." I whispered.

My father nodded, moving to gather his supplies. I tried to ignore what he was doing as I knew what was coming. Mom took me to the gurney bed and sat me down.

"Lie down," Mother whispered. She sat next to me on the bed. I remember Armani and Luciana telling me not to look when the ritual was happening and that the smell of the burning flesh alone would make me want to run screaming.

I watched my father put on the proper protection and open the incinerator built of hot flames as he clamped the iron bottom to the flat magnetic field on the end of the wooden stick. Armani was right. I couldn't look. The more I realized that this was going to hurt, the more nauseated I became.

Mom pulled the restraints around my chest, legs, and my waist before attaching a ball gag to my mouth to muffle the inevitable screams. Anxiety and vulnerability came down all at once, and my breath caught in my throat. I inhaled deep breaths through my nose and closed my eyes as Mom tied my arms to the railing of the bed, and I grasped the bars. I barely heard my Papino's footsteps coming toward me. His hand slid over mine, and he whispered, "Take a deep breath, Lorelai," before he pressed the iron stencil against my skin. Gasping loudly, I gritted my teeth into the gag as the iron burned into my skin, quickly followed by the extremely foul smell of my own burnt flesh filling the room.

A panting cry left my throat as my mother tried to comfort me by rubbing a hand up and down my thigh. "Shhh…it's almost over."

I opened my eyes to watch. I didn't want my parents to think I couldn't handle it; but when I saw the heat rising from my skin, that's when the realization of humiliation and disgust kicked in. This was the exact reason I needed to do this, so that someday, when I met the man of my dreams, my children would never go through this. I would protect them from my parents, siblings, aunts, uncles… hell that pretty much covered it. No one associated or related to the damn Castillos would come near my family and this was my only option to ensure their safety.

When he lifted the iron stamp, he proceeded to spray the burnt skin with a spray that seemed to take the immediate sting away and wrapped my arm in gauze. Once the burn was wrapped, he placed my arm back at my side and removed the ball gag.

It hurt like a son of a bitch and how I would hide the burn now crossed my mind. My panicked state of mind intensified. What would the kids at school think? I couldn't wear a bandage or long sleeves every day. I would have to suck it up, act as if it wasn't there, and play dumb if someone asked. I wanted to run and hide, never to be seen again, but I couldn't. I wasn't that much of a coward.

'It's a birth mark…' Like anyone would believe that.

"Good. I'll give you a few minutes to rest while I get the sketch together." Papino spoke quietly while Mom moved to the other side of the bed to set up the supplies he would need.

Mom removed the restraints, and gave me a glass of water, rubbing a hand on my back. Lying there waiting for this entire process to be over, I thought about the life my parents led. They were the jack of all trades, but not heroes in the least bit. They ran a military for organized crime; and you were either a thousand percent in, or you weren't, the in between was an ugly death.

As the roaring buzz of the tattoo gun came to life and pierced my skin, I watched as he carefully outlined the flocking birds and realized that this had always been an easy decision for me. The risk of taking on a role in the family business meant I would have to marry an underdog working under my father, we would follow into my parents' footsteps, and there wouldn't be an easy way to escape without bad blood shed. I knew I didn't want that. I would take my chances by flipping the coin to the other side into the unknown, unplanned future.

What did I want? I didn't know for sure, but maybe this summer or the year coming up would allow me to figure it all out.

Once the tattoo was finished, he sprayed the anti-sting spray and wrapped it up. "Your mother will give you instructions on how to take care of that, and once she does, you're free to go."

I nodded and watched him leave without another word while Mom cleaned up after him. In some ways, I wondered if she was happy with it this way. Throughout the entire process my mother had remained quiet. She did as my father said, without a question. If I didn't know any better, I'd say she kept her mouth shut to keep him from becoming angry, or she feared him herself.

Sitting up after she walked away to go clean the supplies up, I followed after a moment. "Mama?" I asked quietly.

"Yes, Lorelai?" she said as she discarded the bloody gauze and used needles into the proper container.

"Are you happy with Dad?"

She turned to look at me sharply. "Of course, I am. Why would you ask such a question?"

I opened my mouth to speak and a sudden stab of pain caused a muttered groan to leave my lips. Inhaling a deep breath, I tried once more, "This life you live seems to be one-sided, with dad making all the decisions."

"What your Papino says goes, Lorelai. I don't question it, and neither should you."

I guess I had my answer. She was obedient and stuck in her ways with him, and nothing would ever change because it was all she knew. Or, perhaps it was the luxuries that came with being a Castillo wife. She tagged along, and learned the ropes so she could be a trainer, go to all the black-tie events they hosted, and be the gossip queen of their kingdom here in Sausalito. I rolled my eyes at the thought. I silently made my way out as I realized that this could be one of the last times I was allowed in here, but I knew what I wasn't getting myself into. Now it was time to find out what Lorelai wanted and gun for it.

Three

New Beginnings and a Coffee IV, Stat!

TODAY WAS THE day. The Montgomerys were leaving Oroville to start a new adventure. Dad drove the family car while Nana and Papa followed, and the moving truck trailed behind us. As our moving train worked its way through the town, I reflected on the fact that I had very few attachments to this place and the people in it. Memories of growing up here brought a great deal of stress over the struggles my family had faced throughout the years. However, as I watched out the window, I took in the scenery of the trees and the bridges that crossed over rivers surrounding the only town I called home. I realized that I would miss the weekends spent at the Bidwell Canyon Campground, fishing with my parents, taking in the view of Lake Oroville with the mountain views surrounding us. Now that we were leaving it all behind, I saw beauty beyond the nightmares and struggles. I saw a place that would remain in my past that I could never forget, no matter how hard I tried, because it was also a part of what made me who I was today.

Upon arrival to our new home at the Castillo Yacht Club, Dad began shooting directives at the movers as they carried boxes off the truck. Stepping from the car, I walked toward my mom. "Should we just follow the movers?"

"I have a map Christopher… we'll find our way. Don't worry."

Lorelai

Exiting the building, I walked to the end of the walkway to meet Marie. "Ready for day one of work, partner?"

Marie's facial expression dropped at the thought of day one. I couldn't blame her, we had to rely on my mother guiding and bossing us around, which meant no time for goofing off in our normal day to day routines. "Sure. Can we please get coffee first though?"

"That's a given. I'll take five gallons, please." I nudged her with an elbow.

"You should just have a continuous IV drip to walk around with," she teased.

I widened my eyes at her with a smug smirk. "That would be freaking fantastic! You should invent it… we'd make millions!"

She shook her head and giggled. "One rich, but wild and strung out, Lorelai and Marie coming up!"

"We would have those boat houses cleaned up in no time," I pointed out. "To be fair, we're already wild and strung out."

"True story! For now, I say we order the gallon and make sure to ask for extra cups, cream and sugar. It's going to be a long day," she replied, and I saluted her as we giggled our way down the boardwalk.

Retrieving our coffee and a dozen donuts, we headed down toward the boathouse rental headquarters.

As we were about to cross the boardwalk, a group of men came through with carts full of boxes. A teenage boy followed them with an older woman that appeared to be his mother.

Marie's head turned as her eyes remained glued to the perfect strangers. "Who… is that?" she asked.

My lips parted as I stopped in my tracks, staring at the newcomers walking in with suitcases. "Did you hear anything about a new family moving in, Marie?"

I could see her shaking her head in my peripheral vision. "Nope. You?"

I pulled the cup of coffee to my lips and sipped the hot caffeine. "Why are we always the last to know?"

"Because we're too busy gossiping about everyone and everything else," she paused. "How are your arms by the way?"

"The burn is killing me, and the tattoo itches. Makes no sense. Why do we have to endure double the torture?" I asked, watching as the young man and his mother walked closer to where we were standing.

"We all go through it, including the members. Have you ever gotten close enough to see Luci or Armani's marks?"

I shook my head. "Not really. What are they?"

"Crowns over a black diamond." She said with an edge in her tone.

I nodded, reading her silent message. Loyalty was royalty. I sipped my coffee. "We should get a move on. Mom will be waiting and make us work ten times harder if we aren't on time."

"You don't want to follow the new neighbors?" She said as we started walking.

"And do what afterward? Act as if we've become lost?"

She grabbed my arm and pulled me forward. "Just walk. Chances are he could walk back this way."

I glared at her. Now wasn't the time, and she knew why. I followed her lead, and we walked past the house. The door was open as his father and the movers brought the first load in. I watched as the new mystery boy came walking out to help unload boxes; and when he glanced our way, I flashed a small smile at him. To my surprise, he flashed a smile back.

As we made it out of earshot, Marie looked at me wide eyes. "Someone call the fire department, because he is on fire! Lorelai! You must use your owner's daughter card and go introduce yourself."

I bobbed my head back and forth thinking about it and bit my lower lip at her reaction. "I could… or, I could let us meet naturally and wait until he comes out to explore."

"Absolutely not! If you don't do it, I'll welcome him and set you up on a blind date."

She clearly was not taking no for an answer. "Fine." I groaned.

She smirked. "You'll thank me later, I'm sure."

Christopher

After helping Dad and the movers with the last load, I stepped out on the deck looking over the view of the bay and the mountains. I placed my hands on the wooden fence and took in the smell of fresh mountain air mingled with the scents of salt and seafood. The water was serene, and I took in the rows of houseboats surrounding us in the bay. There were multiple rows of houseboats as far as I could see, and the wooden docks gave way to each section of the housing community. Taking a deep breath, I thought back to the girl lingering on the dock while we were moving in, and I wondered who she was. Did she live in this sector with the boathouses? More importantly, would I see her again? I heard Mom's heels clicking against the wood as she came to stand next to me. "What do you think, Chris?"

I stayed quiet for a moment before I looked at her. "I think this is going to be better for our family. I know you're worried because it's a big move before I go into my last year of high school, but I'll be okay. It's not like I was all that into participating in school events anyway, and my true friends will keep in touch."

She smiled my way. "I'm glad you're taking this move so well." She looked back at the house. "It's bigger than the last place we were in."

I turned to look up at our new home. "It is, isn't it?" I paused for a moment. "When we lived in Oroville, and Dad constantly placed his all into the construction business and taking care of our family, he seemed to be in a constant state of frustration. If this move helps Dad succeed and move to higher places with the construction company, then nothing else matters."

She smiled at me and narrowed her eyes as she looked me in the eyes. "You are wise beyond your years, Christopher. No other seventeen-year-old would've taken all the change we put you through as well as you have."

I smiled at her as Papa Nick stepped out on the dock. "Well, what do you guys think? Million-dollar view?"

"It's definitely something, Papa Nick."

He laughed and came over to wrap his arm around my shoulders. "You were actually just who I was looking for."

"Oh yeah? Why is that?" I stared off at the reflections of the other houseboats on the water.

"Your dad and I talked. He said you passed your driver's test last year, but he couldn't afford to buy you a car and then I realized something."

"What's that?" Papa's ideas usually always came out of left field with a pot of gold to accompany them.

"Well, your nana and I barely drive the Mercedes, so we want to give it to you so you can get to school and grow some independence." He sounded serious, and I was shocked.

"That's very generous, Papa. You don't have to, though."

"I know I don't have to, Christopher; but I want too."

I smiled. "Thank you, Papa!" I reached over and gave him a gentle hug.

He hugged me back and patted me on the back. "We'll come back later this week to go get the plates changed over, and get you signed up at Pennington."

"Is that the school I'll be at?"

"Yes, it is. You'll gain a good education for your last year in high school."

I smiled. "I'm glad, Papa, and thank you."

"The Montgomerys stick together. We never stray too far from the sidelines of loved ones. We stay close and intervene when the opponents of life intercept or do one of our own wrong."

I smiled and looked back out at the view. The feeling of happiness that began when we left Oroville was growing; and while we hadn't been here long, I had a good feeling about this place.

Later that night, I was helping Mom unpack the kitchen items, putting the dishes up on the shelves of the cupboards how she wanted them when there was a knock on the door. "I'll get it. Scope out a spot for these serving dishes?"

Mom ignored me as she stared at my father. "Nathaniel! You're spacing out again! You do this every time I need your help. Pay attention."

Dad was messing around with the cell phone Nana and Papa gave him as a welcome home present. "What? I do not. What is it, dear? This new technology is a damn brain teaser."

"Put the damn phone down and help me find a place for the serving dishes."

"Honey, the kitchen is your spot, the workshop which I no longer have is mine. We've been over this a million times."

She shook her head. "You're getting a damn workshop. We'll scope out an old warehouse where you can carve your arts and crafts soon enough. Can you focus for five minutes?"

I laughed a bit at the bantering they had going and opened the door to find the same girl that walked by earlier standing at the door with a gift basket. I smiled warmly at her, unable to contain my excitement. "Hello. Can I help you?"

Time seemed to freeze as our eyes locked and she turned her bright smile on me. "Hi. My name is Lorelai Castillo. I'm the owner's daughter and I wanted to bring this welcome gift for you and your family."

My Lord. This girl belonged in a beauty pageant. Hell. She could have won Miss USA against all the Queens in the world. I flashed another smile toward her. "Awe. That was very sweet. Thank you." I reached to take the basket from her. My fingers swiped against her soft hand, tingles traveling up my arm as I locked my own eyes on her baby blue hues.

"You're welcome. What's…your name?" She asked.

"My name is Christopher…but you can call me Chris," I said. I didn't know why I had to tell her my full name.

She laughed softly. "Well, it's very nice to meet you, Christopher."

Great, now she was going to use my full name every time we crossed paths. "Nice to meet you as well, Miss Castillo."

She smiled at me once more before she took a step back. "I… take care of the rentals around here. So, if you ever need anything, I'm always around."

"Actually, there is one thing I could use."

"And what's that, Mr. Christopher?" Her face lit up with excitement.

"A tour of this place. It seems really big, and a little confusing," I said.

"Oh, well," she paused, "I could definitely help you with that. I'm actually getting off work here soon. Why don't you meet me at the end of the docks by the mainland in about an hour, and I'll give you a personal grand tour of the yacht club?"

I paused for a moment. "That sounds like an offer I can't pass up, Miss Castillo." I smiled and winked at her. "I'll see you then," I spoke quietly, and waved at her as she turned to walk off the porch.

"See you then," she murmured.

I watched until she disappeared out of sight and closed the door.

Damnit, she was beautiful, and my parents were still bantering about those bloody serving dishes.

I set the basket on the counter as I took a seat at the island. "We received a welcoming gift," I said as they turned their attention toward me.

"That was nice. Who was it from, Chris?" Mom asked.

"The owner's daughter. She's going to take me on a tour around the yacht club. Do you two have a handle on the rest?"

"Yeah. You go. Have fun. Your Nana and Papa are ordering in dinner."

I stood up. "Don't wait up, I'll eat when I get back."

One hour later, I stepped off the docks onto the mainland and found a bench on the boardwalk where I could wait.

Lorelai came into sight a moment later. She wore a white summer dress and her hair looked like it had been freshly blown out. She had gauze wrapped around her arms, and I wondered why, but I couldn't bring myself to ask such a personal question this early on. The glow of the sun shined brightly from the sunset and distracted me rather quickly, she looked…illuminatingly beautiful. No makeup necessary, simple natural beauty fell over this girl and I was floored. I couldn't find words.

"Christopher? Why are you looking at me like that?"

I snapped out of it and stood up. "What way? I wasn't looking at you in any particular way. I'm ready to head out when you are."

She smiled and held back a laugh. "You're sure? You look like you just saw an alien."

Whatever the reason behind the gauze, she didn't seem bothered by it. I chuckled. "I definitely wasn't thinking that you look like an alien."

She laughed, turning her attention to the men hanging up the 'Annual Castillo Yacht Club Summer Bash' banner between the posts at the entrance of the docks.

I looked at the sign and stood up. "Does this place have a lot of parties?"

Her tone changed to a serious one. "My father will find reasons to throw a party."

I arched an eyebrow. "Interesting. This place does kind of look like a good place for parties, though."

We began walking down the boardwalk. "Our community is a very rich one. We have your typical born from the womb snobs that travel from San Francisco on the weekends, the rockers slash motorcycle gang groups, and then we have the elderly that just come here to retire and want to be left alone with their books and long walks in the sunsets."

"I've never really been the party type. I was always too busy with school or helping my parents around the house, going to work with my dad, or visiting with the grandparents out in Napa."

"Yeah? What's your dad do for a living?"

"He's in construction, which is why we moved here. The work in Oroville was scarce."

"I'm sure he won't have a problem here. The San Francisco area is constantly growing," she said as she stopped about halfway down the docks.

I stopped and stood facing toward the buildings behind us and saw two men standing across the street looking my way. I attempted to ignore their intimidating stares as I flashed a smile at Lorelai. "That's what we're hoping for. Mom helps out with the numbers and booking jobs; but I think my grandparents want me to take over the construction business once I finish college. They're getting older, and they own a winery; but the responsibilities and upkeep are getting to be too much on them."

"Hmm… so what's going to happen?"

"I've learned the ropes about construction from my dad, and he will eventually hand it down for me to take over, so my parents can help take care of the winery."

She nodded as she took it in. "Family business done right."

I chuckled. "Sounds about right. The Montgomerys don't back down from a challenge, no matter what."

Her brow rose, "Really now? I'll have to remember that." A lighthearted laugh left my lips. "You better," I teased.

"Considering a Castillo never takes no for an answer, you should. I know you mentioned you weren't the partying type, but you should come to the party on Friday. I'll be your guide and break you in." She flashed that beautiful smile at me again.

"Yeah? I might just accept your generous offer. Just don't break me too hard." The sarcasm broke sooner than I expected; but when my words sent her into a burst of laughter, I knew I wasn't in too much trouble.

I laughed at his joke. "No worries. I'll be gentle."

Chris rose an eyebrow toward me. "I'm holding you to your word."

Four

Jumping Lessons 101

Lorelai

CHRISTOPHER HAD CAPTIVATED me from the moment I set eyes on him; but after even such a short time together, the need to know him multiplied. His dark brown hair, tan skin, and piercing grey- blue eyes caught my attention like a fresh pot of coffee brewing in the early morning. I got the impression that he was a very caring and giving guy. Clearly his family meant a lot to him. He hadn't mentioned a girlfriend and I was suddenly desperate for him to be single. I wanted him for myself.

He paused as we walked on and looked back at the banner.

"What is this Summer Bash exactly?"

"It's one of the many parties my family throws. We eat, drink, mingle and set sail out on the bay."

"I'll accept your invite, but I have one condition."

I froze, trying to hold back the excitement rising in my throat, and laughed. "Oh no. A condition. That sounds scary. Alright. Lay it on me, Montgomery."

He looked out at the water as one of the fancy yachts sped by and met my eyes once more. "I apologize in advance for the torture you might endure, but I'd like you to go as my date."

I pursed my lips as I thought about it. "I think I could deal with that level of torture."

He stared at me for a moment before his eyes moved up and down. Was he checking me out? Did he notice the gauze wrapped around my arm? Would he ask questions? The healing process wouldn't be done for a while. If I were in his shoes, I would be asking questions, and that's exactly what I feared.

"I can't see a better way to break myself in than to show up to this party with the owner's daughter." He didn't flinch or stutter. This Montgomery guy was confident, and reeling me in like quicksand.

I cocked an eyebrow at him. "If that's what you want to call breaking gentle…That's a pretty high jump, Montgomery."

A smile cracked through his lips revealing his pearly white teeth.

"I'm not afraid of heights."

I smiled back at him. "Are you jumping in with two feet?"

He chuckled. "I think I am."

"Then it's a date." I smiled at him as we walked. "You see those turquoise buildings along the street?"

"Ooh. A date? What's that?" He looked at me after purposely ignoring my question, and smirked.

I stopped to look at him, and my eyebrow rose, "Well, it's when two people have a mutual interest in each other, and they go on a magic infested adventure in a faraway land to see if their connection manifests to a level where they can take the world on together." I managed to keep a straight face as Christopher's eyes widened as he stared at me with his intense hues. I knew I ran on the off-beaten path. The million-dollar question was, could he keep up?

"A magical infested adventure? This adventure? It doesn't involve riding unicorns down glittering rainbows, does it?"

"You bet it does," I whipped back.

He shook his head. "I don't know about all that."

I frowned with a puppy pout. 'Well… okay. But what if I said it could conclude with a kiss?"

"It's a date." His low tone and quiet stare made me wonder what it would be like to have that kind of attention on me all the time. "I see the buildings, Lorelai," he continued, "what about them?"

It took me a minute to remember that I was playing tour guide. "My parents own those buildings, as well as the Yacht Club. I live in the penthouse of the biggest building in the center. As for all the little shops along the boardwalk, the owners are contracted in with the rental space. The big building just past the shops, that's the clubhouse where the fitness center is. There is also a spa and a five-star restaurant in there. My family has brunch in there on Sundays, but the buffet is open seven days a week."

Chris looked around and took it all in. "So, this place is a pretty big deal in Sausalito?"

"We've been here longer than my siblings and I have existed. My family is very well known in this community, as well as the city."

His eyes widened a bit. "So, what you're telling me is that your family is a pretty big deal?"

I pursed my lips. "They like to think so." I laughed. "But really, we're just a really crazy Italian family with bad tempers."

He laughed. "Kind of sounds like my family. My dad drives my mother crazy. They'll be working on a house project, and my dad gets distracted and my mom gets frustrated with his short attention span."

I laughed. "Never a dull moment, huh?"

He shook his head and laughed. "In the Montgomery house? Never."

I giggled nervously to cover up the dark secrets my family made me hold in. "I can completely relate." I stopped walking as we got to the end of the boardwalk. "Without staring, look to your right."

He followed my instructions and looked back to me. "Okay. What about it?"

"Did you see a sign that says Black Diamond Club?"

He nodded. "Yeah…why?"

"Whatever you do, never go back there. It's off limits," I said, hoping he didn't notice the tremor in my voice.

"Aye aye, Captain. Is there a reason for the restriction?"

"It's for elite members only. Don't question it, Montgomery."

He nodded. "Noted."

"I didn't mean to snap, but it's vital you don't go back there."

He shook his head. "This is your family's home and business. You have my word that I won't wander back there."

I couldn't help but worry that he was curious, and telling him about the family business was not a topic of conversation I was going into right now.

"Come on, let's head back. The rest of the place is pretty much free range."

As we walked back down, I showed him where paddle boards and other water sport rentals could be found, and then took him back toward the rental boathouses. "This is where I'll be most days. Starting at the third dock of this sector are all rentals that members own and rent out year-round. I clean them and restock linens, and all that fun jazz."

He smiled at me. "Is that a hint for me to come find you?"

"Hm, perhaps?" I winked at him. "There's plenty more to discover with San Francisco and the area we live in; but we'll leave that for another time, if you want that is."

"Well, I definitely don't have a clue about anything in this area, so my mind is yours to fill with knowledge."

A laugh escaped my lips that seemed to be contagious as he joined me. We exchanged smiles as we paused and locked eyes.

I took both of his hands intertwining my fingers into his as I walked him backwards.

"Fine…but I'll have to take a rain check and head back for dinner."

My heart sunk, as our time was being cut short. "Of course. The yacht will be anchored just against the boardwalk…You won't be able to miss it."

"I'm sure I won't. Thank you for showing me around." He smiled at me before he slowly drew his fingers from mine and winked at me.

I sighed softly as he walked off. His smooth words, teasing tactics, and confidence staggered me. My heart ached, I needed more. When he was out of sight, I realized that it would be a few days before I was guaranteed time with him again. Friday was simply too far away.

Stepping from the limo after a long day of relaxing and primping with my mother and Luciana, we finally arrived to the rolled out red carpet where our awaiting guests stood behind the black velour ropes. Gliding down the entryway in a floor length sparkling red evening gown in my heels, I looked for Christopher in the crowd. A nervous feeling crept into the pit of my stomach as I passed the one person I didn't want to see.

Santino. Son of a bitch! What the hell was he doing here?

The tall man with dark blonde hair and entrancing green eyes with a permanent smirk etched over his lips stood at the front of the crowd. My eyes quickly met Luciana's as she grimaced. Trouble settled into the atmosphere, and there was no escaping it.

As we made our way into the main entertaining space of the large yacht, soft piano music played in the background. I looked around seeing a scarce number of familiar faces before I escaped to the top deck and stood at the railing in the middle of the large vessel. Scanning the guests arriving from below, I froze. A smile lifted against my lips and I sighed in relief as I spotted Chris on the bench we sat on the other night.

"Montgomery!" I yelled. I caught his attention and inclined my head.

He stood and locked his eyes on mine, walking toward the crowd and winking at me as he waited to get in. I nonchalantly wandered over to the snack table and popped a piece of cheese in my mouth, standing at the opposing railing looking out at the view of the San Francisco skyline beyond the bay. The sky was filled with wispy clouds, the colors turning pink and purple as the sun set behind the mountains. Chris would be up in a matter of moments. I couldn't have been bothered to think about the risks to be seen with him publicly because all I wanted to do was spend more time with him.

I felt a hand grasp the side of my waist and pull me out of my thoughts. I jumped slightly, slowly turning around to see Santino standing behind me. "What are you doing? Get your hand off of me." I narrowed my eyes at him.

He chuckled lowly. "Oh, come on, gorgeous. Did you really think we wouldn't see each other tonight?"

The last encounter we had started just like this and ended when I pushed his unwanted hands off of me. "What do you want, Santino?" My tone was cold.

"You know exactly what I want, Lor. You know we have something. Why don't you just accept it?" He placed both his hands on my hips and backed me up against the railing.

I looked away from him trying to keep my emotions together. "And if I said I disagreed, then how does this end?"

He chuckled. "I think you're in denial."

I rolled my eyes, scoffing. "No, because I'm not interested. Why can't you accept that?"

His hands returned to the sides of my waist, his eyes were intimidating and a smug smirk was on his lips. "Cause I know what I can give you. A life full of luxuries you couldn't dream of. Our families have the same values and standards. You don't even have to be in the business, Lor. You can be my sweet baby mama, and I'll spoil you. Besides, your parents love me and I'm sure your father would approve."

"Yeah, well. I don't approve. Move out of my way." I snapped. Santino didn't know I completed the family ritual, and the red glamour gloves to match my dress hid the evidence.

"What is your big rush? Are you going to meet that new kid?"

My lips fell open as I realized that he had been watching me. He saw me with Chris. I did not like this, a horrible feeling settled in the pit of my stomach. I needed to get away from him, but he was stronger than me; and frankly, I was afraid of what he would try if I made a scene, but he wasn't giving me much of a choice at this point.

I pushed him away. "You were watching me?! Santino, this is the last time I'm going to ask you nicely. Leave me the hell alone."

Before he could say another word, my brother came flying in from the other side of the yacht, taking Santino down to the ground. "I told you to stay the fuck away from my sister!" he said before he punched him square in the jaw.

My eyes diverted off toward the water, as a crowd moved in around Armani and Santino fighting before a pair of arms pulled me out of the line of fire. I turned to meet Christopher's striking eyes.

"What happened? Are you okay?" he whispered.

"No, and I really don't want to talk about it. I need to get away from here." -

He pulled back to look at me and then to the men being pulled apart by my father and Matteo before he glanced down at me once more. "Of course. Come on." He left an arm around me and led me down the staircase.

We walked downstairs, and up the side corridor to the back of the vessel, finding a semi-circle couch to sit down on. He wrapped a gentle arm around me and we looked on as we moved away from the setting sun painting the colors pinks, purples, and orange swirling through a layer of clouds sitting on the horizon.

His thumb brushed against the back of my shoulder. "I know it's a little soon to talk about what just happened, but can I ask you a question?"

I looked back at him with anxious eyes. "Of course, you can."

"I noticed the bandages on your arms the other day when you were showing me around. I…just wanted to make sure you were okay."

I swallowed hard. This wasn't going to be easy to explain, let alone open up about. How could I explain it without actually exposing the syndicate?

"Coincidence of bad luck. I bought my first tattoo this week, and the other is a burn I got from splashing oil from the fryers at the club house restaurant."

"That's too bad. I'm sorry. Are you okay?" His tone lowered, and he sounded almost sad.

"Yeah… I'll be alright. Thank you for checking on me though."

Inhaling a soft, sharp breath, I exhaled slowly relieved that he didn't push the subject about the tattoo and the burn. I was safe for now, but I wouldn't be for long. His caring demeanor told me that he could very well follow up on this later, and there simply was no good way to explain the mirror images of burn and tattoo. I wasn't ready for that, and I hoped I wouldn't have to explain myself. I needed to be as discreet as possible about the family business. I didn't know much; but I knew that organized crime was illegal, that my father went to great lengths to protect our name, and the massive income that came along with his title as a fucking mob boss.

I feel the hot Italian blood in me boiling. This was the exact reason I wanted out. I didn't want to be the poor soul that sold my family out. Looking at Chris watching me with those big gentle eyes, I feel myself come down. It was too soon to tell if it would happen, but I wanted him to be the one that saved me from the lonely path I'd be taking when this last year of high school was over… and it had not even begun.

Why did I do this to myself?

Chris and I stayed as far away from the other guests and my family as possible in the hour after the fight between Armani and Santino. We talked about early childhood memories, favorite foods, holiday traditions and the conversation flowed. I was surprised that he allowed my excuses about my arms go so quickly, but it showed he had respect, and perhaps that I could trust him? We might need more time on the trust, but his respect hit a high chord of positivity for sure.

Leaning into Christopher's arm that was still wrapped around me caused a desire to ditch the party; but before I had the chance to ask him, Papino waltzed into our view. "Lorelai… a word…" He was quick to disappear and he didn't look happy.

I looked at Chris and mouthed an apology to him before I followed him around the corner. "What is it?"

"Who is that boy and why are his hands all over you?" he snapped.

"His name is Christopher Montgomery. He just moved here. He's very nice, Papino."

He shook his head. "He needs to leave. You are not to see him again. Do you understand?"

I furrowed my eyebrows at him. "But…"

"I don't want to hear another word. Dating of any kind is off limits, young lady." He walked away as I turned back to Chris and found my brother escorting Christopher toward the exit. Tears welled in my eyes and I couldn't believe that my family had reacted so harshly before they took a chance to get to know him. This would not end well.

I needed to see him again, no matter the cost.

Precarious Business

I WALKED DOWN the ramp back to the boardwalk and looked at the man that escorted me out as we docked. I was able to get a closer look at him as he stood in front of me. He towered over me in height but had a slim build and striking combination of dark hair and blue eyes. It was impossible to miss the similarities that his features shared with Lorelai. Couple that with his protection of her and I knew he had to be her relative.

He placed his arms across his chest. "Look. I don't know you and I'm sure you're a nice kid; but I have to look out for my sister, and you can't come around her again."

Her brother? Great. He would more than likely pound me like he did the other guy coming onto Lorelai if I didn't back off. I pressed my lips together as I tried to hold back frustration and stared off for a moment. "Alright. Alright. I get it. Can I go now?"

He eyed me carefully with narrowed eyes. "This is the only warning you get. Don't cross the lines or you'll regret it." He stepped back, dropping his arms, revealing a decent sized tattoo of a crown hanging over a diamond. He walked backward before he disappeared and left me outside of the yacht on the boardwalk.

I ran my fingers through my hair and blew a breath of air out of my mouth attempting to wrap my head around the events that took place over the last hour. She wasn't safe from the man that had pinned her against the railing, and now I couldn't even see her to find out how she was. What was the deal with this Castillo family? Were they just power hungry? What the hell was it that made them so successful? Maybe I was better off not asking questions. I felt like the less I knew, the safer I was.

I didn't need, nor want, another Castillo in my face. A sharp pain pierced my skin as goosebumps rose over my body. I continued down the boardwalk with my head down and my mind spinning as I ran my fingers through my hair and forced myself in the opposite direction of the yacht. The short-lived memories of my time with Lorelai raced through my mind. Everything about her flashed through my head like a film strip. Her smile, the bright blue eyes that resembled the very stars in the sky above her hometown. I found another bench and took a seat leaning back as I stared off into the darkness feeling defeated. Perhaps I should take her brother's warning and accept that this wasn't meant to happen.

A group of men in suits surrounding Lorelai's brother and Santino came into view, breaking through the paralyzing indecision in my head. Six men surrounded them, three on each side, and all eyes turned to look at me. Were they signaling one last final warning meaning business? Looking at the ground after they passed, I turned my head slightly to the right and watched as they continued under the Black Diamond Club arch.

I inhaled deeply. There was no doubt in my mind that there was a dark cloud hanging over this place. A sick, twisted feeling stirred in my stomach. I remembered Lorelai's warning from a few nights ago, and I wouldn't dare go back on my word. This was clearly none of my business and I normally didn't care to stick my nose where it didn't belong, but the heavy realization that I would not be able to see Lorelai tugged at my heart strings further. Her father and his minions were everywhere.

As I made it past the yacht, I looked out at the moon reflecting on the bay and spotted a large sailboat with a lantern on it. I narrowed my eyes as a petite figured shadow in red came into my vision.

"Psst…Montgomery!" A soft female voice called out.

I walked down the dock. "What on Earth are you doing?"

She flashed a smile at me. "Going for a ride. Care to join me?"

"I… was told I cou-"

"I know what you were told." She cut off my rambling words. "What they don't know can't hurt us." She spoke softly, her tone sounded almost devious.

I walked closer and looked around at the setup. The blue-eyed brunette was ready to set sail.

"Come on, join me! Besides, our date at the Summer Fest was a blowout. We can finish it up on Cakes and Pies." Her playful tone returned and I couldn't help but smile back at her.

I chuckled. "Cakes and Pies?" My eyes were drawn to the name painted on the side of the vessel in hot pink.

"Yeah. What's better than Cake and Pie?" She stood at the stairs leading onto the boat and reached her hand out, staring at me with a playful smirk tugging at her lips.

I hesitated as I thought about the warning I was given. The call was tough, and apparently the universe was testing me.

I inhaled a deep breath before I stepped off the dock onto the vessel and took her hand. "How can I say no to cakes and pies?"

She giggled and placed a hand on my chest. "You simply cannot," she whispered.

I chuckled softly as my hands found her hips. "You're absolutely right. I can't. We should get out on the water before someone spots us."

"You worry too much. I am going to break that." She winked at me before she went to pull the rope off the dock and threw it to the floor before she started the motor, and we made our way out on the water.

Looking around, I was calm enough to take in the large size of this sailboat, and I realized this wasn't your average sailboat. It was the size of a yacht, with a motor on it. Considering where she came from, I wasn't too surprised. I sat in the chair across from her and placed my ankle on the top of my leg. "How long have you been sailing?"

She looked at me. "I've been on boats my entire life; but Armani, my brother, started giving me lessons when I was seven, so about ten years."

I raised an eyebrow. "Armani? Is that who escorted me out earlier?"

"That would be the one. He's the first-born son named after my father. Junior is four years older than me and thinks he's the king. I also have a sister; her name is Luciana. We're fourteen months apart. She walked in with me and my mother, Amelia," she paused. "Do you have any siblings?"

I shook my head. "Nope. It's just me and my parents and Nana and Papa. We have a small family, but we stay close."

She smiled at me. "You're lucky. I have a very large, temperamental Italian family that is spread out all over the world."

I stayed quiet for a moment. "Temperamental? I couldn't tell."

She laughed softly. "Italians? Temperamental? Never." She flashed a smile and the remainder of the ride remained silent.

Allowing the sound of the vessel moving through the water to calm my anxieties about sneaking off with her, I could see why she loved being out on the water so much. "Where are we going?"

She glanced at me as we turned to dock. "It's a surprise," she said as the vessel came to a stop, and she turned the engine off. It was dark except for a light on the back of what appeared to be a houseboat.

I watched as she tied the boat to the dock and stepped out. "Come on. Cakes and Pies will be here when we get back."

I chuckled and went to exit as I saw her reach a hand out for mine. I smiled as I took her hand and followed her lead. She pulled a ring of keys out and opened the door before she led us inside and put on the lights before she dimmed them and looked at me. "Don't worry. It's vacant for the week. No one will find us here."

I smiled at her. "Well, I can't deny your logic."

She laughed and walked into the kitchen and spotted a bottle of wine. "Do you drink?"

I shook my head. "Not unless I'm at the vineyard."

She gasped. "Vineyard? Tell me more."

I laughed. "My grandparents own a vineyard as part of their winery up in Napa; and for some reason, my crazy family thought it would be a wise idea to start me out early on wine tastings."

Her eyes sparkled under the dim lights as she popped the cork from the bottle. "Your family has eclectic tastes in how they raise their kid. Wine is my best friend."

I chuckled. "Really now?"

She poured the white zinfandel and handed me a glass.

"Absolutely. I'd like to propose a toast."

I leaned against the counter and crossed my arms holding my glass. "Alright. Let's hear it."

"To your first summer in Sausalito. May it be adventurous, thrilling, and safe with a certain brunette that has had her eyes on you since the moment you moved in."

I smirked. "To the long nights that I won't sleep because sleeping with one eye open isn't actually possible."

She clung her glass to mine and took a sip. "Who said anything about sleeping? These rentals book way in advance, and the owners close down the reservations after a certain point. I can guarantee we'll have a place to hideaway if you wanted to see me again after tonight."

I looked at her after I sipped my own and chuckled. "Are you trying to tell me you're going to corrupt me, Miss Castillo?"

She took a step toward me, a foot of space left between us as she looked up at me. "Absolutely, so you better embrace it Montgomery."

I slowly reached my hand up to cup her cheek. Her fingers grasped around my wrist as I pushed soft curls behind her ear. "Embrace it I will," I whispered as I took the initiative and inched toward her. She met me halfway and froze with her eyes focused on mine, our lips inches apart. I'd never experienced a moment that felt so charged with anticipation. I moved in slow motion until my lips pressed against hers; and, was incredibly thankful when she returned that sweet kiss. Dainty hands grazed over my chest snaking around my neck.

Without breaking the kiss, I grasped the sides of her waist and pinned her back to the wall. My carpenter hands grazed the sides of her waist. Keeping a gentle hold on her with one hand, I cascaded my fingers over the slim curves of her waist and chest, cradling my hand against her cheek gently as our lips parted. Her chest heaved up and down before I tasted the heady mixture of chocolate and coffee gloss on her lips. A volt of energy surged through my veins as our lips locked with one passionate kiss after another.

Her hand cupped the scruffy facial hair against my cheek as I grazed her lower lip with my tongue and slipped it into her mouth. For a moment I felt a gentle sucking sensation before she entangled her tongue against mine. I sucked in soft breaths between pressing my lips against hers. Caressing finger tips traveled over her waist, accidentally finding the line to the zipper on her gown. A smile curved my lips, as I traced the line to the top and tugged gently.

Pulling the strapless top to the evening dress that hugged her every curve, the satin gown pooled around her feet. I dragged my hands down the contours of her slim curves. Breaking the kiss, I moved my fingers through the soft curls, bunching the dark brunette locks between my digits. My lips found her neck planting suckle kisses against her silky skin. Soft cries of pleasure fell from her lips as she pressed her body against mine. I could only imagine that her mind was racing much as mine was in this very moment. Pausing, my lips remained an inch from her neck, the tiny hairs standing up on her skin. Pressing gentle individual kisses, the sensation of buttons coming undone on my shirt traveled down my chest and abdomen as she fought with the shirt to remove it from my body. I shook the sleeves, and grasped a hold of it in one quick move, letting it drop to the floor. Pulling her close, I grasped her thighs, sweeping her off her feet and groaning as I felt her legs tighten around my waist. Her blue eyes locked on mine as she cupped my cheeks, her touch feather-like, as if she feared that if she touched me with further force, she could break me. Tackling her lips once more in another deep, passionate kiss, I proceeded blindly out of the kitchen bringing her to what I thought might be the couch, where I set her down, hovering over her for a moment. Breaking away from the kiss, I drank in her milky skin, placing my knees on either side of her body as her hands played with the button on my pants until they came undone. I placed gentle kisses from her jawline to her neck and collarbone. Breathing heavily against her skin, I pressed the bulge in my pants against her groin, the counter reaction coinciding with a gasped moan against my ear which caused the blood to rush toward my cock.

"Christopher…" She whispered.

I hesitated as I met her eyes, placing my hands at the side of her waist grasping at the skin gently. "Lor…"

Her lips curved into a gentle smile, and she placed her hands over mine, moving them over each of her breasts. "Don't hold back, I want this as much as you do…" Her hand slipped through the open button on my pants.

Sucking in a deep breath, I exhaled a groan, and smoothed my hands over her waist and up her back. Undoing the clasps one at a time before sliding the material away from her, I tossed her bra to the floor carelessly as her fingers slipped around the pulsing erection pleading to escape.

"Ffff-…." I growled and captured her lower lip between my teeth, tugging gently, scathing my teeth across her soft pink lip. "-uck…" I grasped my hands around her ample breasts squeezing and massaging gently as I took in the feeling of her hand pumping the erection to life.

Leaning back, her eyes filled with lust as she bit her lower lip. A smile crossed my lips as I massaged her breasts and leaned in pressing gentle pecks down her neck, moving her into a horizontal position on the couch. I scaled my fingertips over her slim body down to the elastic band on her panties, pushing my thumbs under the strap. Pulling at the stretchy elastic, I leaned in and, pressing my lips against the opposite side of her neck, snapped the bands to her panties. With each kiss I pressed to her skin, the inhaling and exhaling of her breaths became deeper. A smile crossed between my lips as a harmonious moan trembled between her lips.

I smirked and continued pressing gentle kisses down her neck to her collarbone, taking her nipples between my thumb and forefinger, applying slight pressure before twisting at the hardened tips of her breasts. She wasted no time unzipping my pants, and pushing them to my knees. I stood slowly and kicked them off. Towering over her, I took in the sight of her voluptuous body. She leaned against the back of the couch, her lips parted as she reached up to trace her freshly manicured nails over the defined lines of my abdomen.

Digging my teeth into my lower lip, I reached back for the elastic on her panties and snapped them against her skin once more before I pulled them down her long silky smooth thighs, tossing them to the heaping pile of clothes.

She was completely laid out in front of me, naked. We both knew what was to come, but the look that fell over her face crossed between deviance and seduction. A crooked smile rose against my lips, as I tried to keep my excitement to a subtle level. I knew better. I shouldn't have pushed this, but she appeared to want me as much as I wanted her. Who the fuck was I argue?

Addicted

Lorelai

THE SMIRK THAT fell over his face made my insides hot, sending shivers up and down my spine. The way his hands slid over my body, grasping in just the right spot turned me into putty, and he was molding me to his own liking. I dug my teeth into my lower lip as he towered over me. Reaching forward, I wrapped my dainty fingers around his long, hard cock and grazed my thumb over the head. I watched as his head fell back as he inhaled a sharp breath, and exhaled a groan of pleasure. Moving my hand up inch by inch, I felt the growth harden and expand. Sitting up, I looked up at him and felt his fingers graze through the bottom of my curls, grasping a firm hold. I breathed against the head as I wrapped my lips around the girth that entered my mouth.

I slid my lips down the length allowing the tip to hit the top of my throat. He grunted, grasping a firm hold against my shoulder. Before I knew it, my back hit the soft couch cushion. While I moved my mouth up and down the length, a strong hand moved over my breast grasping, and kneading in a massage. I moaned against him, sending vibrations against his length and smiled as he groaned loudly. Fingertips fell over my body, inching between the top of my inner thighs. I felt the soft cushion of the couch brushing against my bare skin as my legs were spread apart one at a time with his hand.

Fingers grasped through my hair as he pulled my head back. I bit my lower lip as he smirked and kneeled, hovering over me while his fingers slid up my inner thigh. Inhaling a deep breath, I laid my head back, shutting my eyes as I felt his lips press against my collarbone and pulled back.

"God, you're so damn beautiful Lorelai…"

I smiled and opened my eyes, looking down at him and sinking my teeth into my lip. "It's my pasty skin, isn't it?"

He chuckled and paused as his hand continued sliding up my inner thigh coming dangerously close to the wet lips between my legs before I felt myself being lifted into his arms, and I quickly wrapped my legs around his waist before I lost my balance. My arms found their way around his neck. I pushed my fingers through his chestnut brown hair; a soft gasp left my lips as I felt his lips against my neck and I closed my eyes taking in the feeling of his soft, succulent lips pressing against my neck while he carried me to the bedroom. The door shut; and no sooner than it had, my back hit the door as he gripped my wrists gently, pinning them to the door.

He lifted his head, pressing his forehead against mine. "I want to kiss every inch of your pasty skin…" His tone was husky, a bit dark and serious against my ear. I felt the heated moisture grow between my legs. He was driving me insane, but I loved every second of it.

I couldn't help but giggle softly before he nipped at the sensitive cartilage of my ear, brushing his lips down my jawline, pressing a deep passionate kiss to my lips. I pushed playfully against his hold on my wrists as I returned his continuous deep kiss.

I smiled at the thought of Christopher's response to my terrible sarcastic banter and quirks, even through this heated moment that he took seriously as he broke the kiss leaving me breathless before he moved the deep planted kisses to the contours of my neck and body. I set widened eyes on his as he moved to his knees and his lips covered my aching clit. Arching my back, I moaned softly and placed my hand at the back of his head. The tip of his tongue flickered back and forth as he wrapped his strong arms around my slender thighs. His digits slid within the slick surface between my legs.

Pushing my fingers through his full head of dark wavy curls, I grasped a tight hold as his fingers penetrated my entrance. His tongue swirled against the sensitive button as his fingers moved through the inner folds, cries of pleasure left my lips, my hips gyrating gently against his movements. The pleasure built quickly, his fingers were quick and continuous. A coat of sweat covered my body and I thanked a higher power that he had a tight hold on my legs. Leaning my head back against the door, I moaned my way through hot pleasure that took over my entire body.

"Fuck!" I yelled out, breathing heavily before an orgasm fell from my hot core against his lips.

I bit my lower lip as I felt the sucking sensation of his mouth around my lips. His tongue slid up separating the folds between my legs with his tongue, being sure to lick every last drop of my orgasm clean. I met his eyes and smiled as he planted gentle kisses against my skin making his way back up between nipping and sucking at my hips, stomach, and breasts. Standing back to his feet, I felt his hands grip my hips. He turned me around, walking me back toward the bed, and pushed me back on it gently. Standing at the end of the bed, I watched intently as he drank in the image of my naked body laid out in front of him.

A smile fell over his lips as he hovered over me, leaning down and placing his lips against my forehead. I placed my hands to each of his cheeks brushing my thumbs over his scruffy manscape. He planted a few more gentle pecks before he moved to the bed and laid beside me.

Turning my head to look back at him, I studied his eyes staring back at me, and bit my lower lip. He grazed his thumb over my top lip before he wrapped an arm around me and tugged me close laying his forehead against mine. "When can I see you again?" He whispered.

"Soon. I hope." I whispered back

"How will we stay in touch?"

He brought up a valid point. "Cakes and Pies has a mailbox. Perhaps we could communicate long hand? Or, I could come up with something else, but it's not a for sure thing."

He pulled me in close, enclosing my waist with his arms and smiled. "I suppose I could handle that, but if you can't read my chicken scratch… it's not my problem."

I giggled placing my hands against his chest. "We should get back to Cakes and Pies so you can get home."

He grumbled. "What time is it anyway?"

I leaned up on my elbow. "Almost eleven…"

I felt him sit up and slide his arms around me as he leaned in to press a gentle kiss against my shoulder. "I should get back before my parents send out a search party."

I looked back at him with gentle eyes. "My parents don't care to check in on me; but the moment they discover me doing something they don't approve of, it's all hands-on deck."

He paused for a long moment, his hands slowly falling away from me as he stood up and brought our clothes back from the living room. "I'm sorry to hear that." He separated the clothes. "Come here."

I stood up walking to the end of the bed where he re-dressed me and pushed the now messy curls behind my ear. "I care about checking on you. How will I know when I can see you again?"

I bit my lower lip. "You'll just have to trust my word. Let's meet tomorrow morning, say around eight a.m. in the parking lot? We can go adventuring together…"

His eyes lit up, but he held in a bout of excitement. "I'll be there."

I leaned up to peck his lips before I left to utilize the bathroom and fix myself before we made our way back to Cakes and Pies, hand in hand. I stepped over the threshold, keeping my hand in his as he followed.

Powering up the engine, I started back toward the main marina. Upon arrival, I wrapped the ropes around the bow tie anchor posts, and returned to Christopher and reached for his hand.

He took my hand in both of his looking up at me from his seat. "I'd walk you home…but, it'd be a risk being seen with you."

I bit my lower lip as I met his gentle gaze. "I understand," I whispered, leaning down to meet his lips. He returned the kiss, pulling me down into his lap. I held onto the sweet kiss, allowing the taste of his lips to linger on mine before I opened my eyes to him looking back up at me. "I'll walk you out…"

He grazed his lips against mine once more, his hand finding mine. I watched as he climbed out on deck and waved him off before I disappeared into the cabin shut the door and leaned against it, a shit eating grin crossing my lips.

If I wasn't smitten over Christopher Montgomery before, I most certainly was now. Replaying the night through my mind as I walked back to the bathroom to do something with the Montgomery hand-tangled hair-do I was now sporting, I sighed happily. How the hell had I gotten so damn lucky to set my eyes on him before another girl snatched him up? Would I cross his mind as much as he did mine? He wanted to see me again, and this was good and bad. Good, because he asked when he could see me again and that showed interest. In a matter of an hour, he managed to sweep me up into those strong arms and show me that our bonded connection could be heightened with heated passion. Bad, because I needed more and my father wouldn't like it as he already had him removed from the party earlier and banned me from seeing him.

This was my life and I'd be damned if his power-struggle affected me more than it already had. I sighed as the sting from the burn and the itch from the healing tattoo reminded me that he was still in control, and continuing to see Christopher would have to be orchestrated carefully.

Christopher

Walking back home, I entered quietly and closed the door. The house was silent. I safely assumed my parents retired to bed. Looking in the fridge, I saw a box of food with my name on it. I checked inside, my stomach gurgled and shouted at me as I inhaled the chicken parmesan dinner. Transferring it to a plate, I stuck it in the microwave.

Retrieving a large glass of milk, I settled myself out on the patio and realized that I had Lorelai Castillo imprinted in my mind. No matter where I went, what I did, she was always on my mind; but after tonight and a promise to see her first thing in the morning, I could survive until then even if I didn't want to leave her alone. I looked up across the bay. Lanterns lit up the docks, strings of white and multi-colored lights decorated the perimeter of the sailboats reflecting on the water. I caught sight of the turquoise buildings behind the boardwalk in a distant view beyond the marina. Ground level spotlights shined up on the center building where Lorelai resided. I couldn't get her out of my head. Her soft feminine tone, her brilliant blue eyes, the curls laying perfect in her hair, the way she pushed every emotion she could muster into the way she kissed me. She took a high risk calling me out on the boardwalk. One of her family members could've been watching from a far and we wouldn't have known it. Her free-spirited personality was as striking as her beauty and, in my opinion, a rare and special find.

As unsure as I was about this move, I realized after meeting Lorelai that Sausalito was written in the stars. She was a rebellious beauty and if sneaking around to see her was what we had to do, I was fully prepared and I'd be the knight in shining armor waiting to sweep her away with a sweet escape.

Seven

Spill It, L. Castillo!

Lorelai

THE HAPPIEST OF sighs left my lips as I stripped my clothes off and waltzed into the bathroom with an extra pep in my step.

A panicked scream echoed through the walls of the spacious bathroom as I caught sight of a figure in my mirror. I fumbled to grab a towel, wrapping it around myself.

Turning around slowly, I set eyes on my best friend sitting in my cozy chair at the vanity. A blast of gold glitter and white and pink pieces of paper clouded my vision as she pulled the string on a confetti popper.

I moved a hand over my heart as it attempted to erupt from my chest.

"Did the welcome party wagon get shut down, Lorelai?"

I crossed my arms. "Clearly not, Marie. Cause here you are."

"Mhm. I came over after the party ended to get all the gossip."

I inhaled a deep breath as my heart was still beating rapidly and proceeded to go start my bath water as she went on talking at a million miles a second. "Fair enough. However, you showed up just on time for new and improved 'Lorelai Castillo's Talk Show'."

"Ooh? Well, you best get your pretty little butt in that tub and spill then."

I saluted her with two fingers. "Aye aye, Captain."

"Speaking of Captains. Why aren't you at Cakes and Pies?"

"I just came from there. Did you end up going to the Summer Bash?"

She shook her head. "I was given a choice this time. I decided to stay home and rest. It was a long day of check-ins for the house-boats."

"I bet. Sorry I wasn't there to help."

"It's okay. I understand family obligations."

I rolled my eyes. "I'm over the Castillo Family obligations. I hope I start getting a choice of whether I can attend or not. But I do have an update about the new family that moved in."

"Ooh! Tell me!"

"Apparently the boathouse belongs to his grandparents. Mr. Montgomery has a construction business. I guess the business was struggling in Oroville and that's why they moved here."

"Let me guess. You met the son?"

I smiled. "You promise not to utter a word of this to anyone?" "You have my word."

"His name is Christopher and he is wonderful. He's a complete gentleman; and well, let's just say this summer is going to be interesting."

"Tell me more!" she exclaimed.

"I took a welcoming gift basket to his house and there was a conversation. It was short. I told him if he needed anything, he shouldn't hesitate to ask, and the next thing I knew I was taking him on a tour of the yacht club; and before he left, we made plans to go to the summer bash, but he wouldn't agree to it unless I went as his date!"

"Damn girl. He's not messing around," she sing-songed.

I sunk downward into the tub. "Oh my god, stop!"

She giggled. "Keep talking! Did you end up going?"

"Of course, I did, but then Armani and Santino had it out on the yacht."

"Oh god. Santino's still after you?"

I rolled my eyes. "Unfortunately."

"Did you get stuck in the middle?"

"Well, Santino kind of had me pinned to the rail. That's when Armani came diving in from left field, and Chris pulled me out of the lion's den to make sure I was okay."

Her face lit up like a light bulb. "Wait, he pulled you away from the brawl between Santino and your brother?"

My facial expression softened and dropped as I nodded. "Yes…"

"So, he was protecting you?" She raised an eyebrow.

"Uh huh."

"Damn! Does your brother or Santino know about this kid?"

I sighed. "I'm getting to that."

"Maybe I should go make some popcorn."

I laughed and narrowed my eyes at her. "Marie! This is my life! Not your Entertainment Weekly!"

"Psh! I don't need Hollywood gossip mags when Lorelai Castillo is my BFF!" She sounded off and laughed. "So, what happened when he pulled you away?"

"We went to the back of the yacht and we just sat and talked." I paused. "Marie? Have you ever been drawn into a conversation with a surge of lightning?"

She shook her head no.

"That's what this felt like. Christopher Montgomery anchored me, and then my Papino walked by and caught us."

"Ugh! Uncle Armani always ruins the fun. Oh god. What happened?"

I groaned. "I know. He forced me to step off to the side… and while he was giving me the third degree and demanding me not to see Christopher anymore, Armani escorted him out of the party before I had a chance to stop him."

"Oh wow. Maybe Santino has something to do with that. When did this happen?"

"I do not know, but Santino did ask me if I was running off to see the new kid again. He's been lingering around."

"In other words, he's still after you and Armani swung in throwing punches first with a side of 'Oh, hell no.'?"

"Basically, and now my father is telling me I'm not allowed to date either. He thinks when the Almighty King speaks, I'm supposed to bow down to his every word and I'm not doing it."

She nodded. "I get it. Tell me more about Mr. Christopher!"

I giggled. "Well, I walked off the yacht shortly after he did and went down to Cakes and Pies. I spotted him walking and reeled him in."

She giggled. "Of course, you did."

"Yes and, when he joined me, it was one of those moments that I keep swooning over because it keeps playing through my mind on repeat. We went for a ride on Cakes and Pies, and landed up in an empty boat house rental, talking over a glass of wine; and then... well, a girl doesn't kiss and tell." I stared up at the ceiling waiting for an anticipated squeal.

She barely concealed a loud squeal of excitement. "Who kissed who first?"

I smiled. "He leaned into me first…"

"And? How was it?"

I stayed silent for a moment as my mind took me back to the moment when I stood staring at him looking at me as if I was the single most important woman in his life. "The kiss? It was the most passionate, charged kiss I've experienced in my entire life."

I sat in the hot sudsy water half expecting her to want me to dish more details and she didn't. I slowly turned my head and looked at her. "I know I just met him, but I can feel it in my bones, Marie. He might be the one that changes my life for the better."

She smiled. "I'm happy for you, but is this the point when you ask me to sneak in and become a lump under your blankets to cover for you to go see this magical lover boy?"

I giggled and shook my head at her. "I wasn't going to, but now that you mention it."

Leaning over, she planted her palm at the center of her forehead. "Why did you open your big mouth, Marie? Why?!" I giggled. "Hey. Don't worry about it. I'll figure it out."

"No. No! I offered and, as your best friend and blood sister, it is in the unwritten law that I cover for you."

I knew she wasn't going to take no for an answer now. "You can still cover for me and do it from home. I'll just tell my parents I'm staying with you."

Her eyes lit up and she stood on top of the chair. "That's genius… and I'll go to work on making up the craziest best friend sleepover stories; so that when they call and I start rambling on at a thousand miles a minute, they'll take the hint." She stepped down. "Better go get started, this could take more than one bowl of ice cream to think out carefully. Call me tomorrow. We can hash out code names and fake news on where in the world Lorelai Castillo might be tomorrow, next week, and beyond."

I giggled. "You're the best, Marie!"

"And don't you forget it!" she said before she skipped off out of the bathroom and disappeared leaving me in silence. Christopher entered my mind not long after that.

I slowly snapped out of my daydreams as I realized the water had grown cold; reaching for the drain and emptying the tub, I started the shower and stood under the hot water. The lingering feeling of Christopher's arms wrapping me in a cocoon escaped my daydream, becoming very real. I didn't want to let go of it and so I didn't. Shutting the water off, I stepped out and prepared for bed before I crawled under the covers and swaddled myself into the blankets to replace the void of wanting Christopher's arms around me instead. I curled up in a ball as my eyelids became heavy. I felt myself slipping into a peaceful sleep, hoping to dream of adventures with my new-found Prince Charming.

Christopher

The next morning, I woke, and dressed myself in windbreakers, setting a white V-neck t-shirt and my best running shoes to the side while I ran a brush through the wavy curls in my hair and shaved myself clean. Applying an aftershave to smooth the skin over, I looked myself in the mirror before placing the V-neck over my head and checking the time. I had a few minutes and thought about what she said the night before about writing letters to each other.

Sitting down at my desk, I grabbed a pen and decided I would deliver it to the mailbox before meeting up with her that day.

Dear Lorelai,

It's Saturday morning, and while the Summer Bash was eventful and cast a cold blast to continue seeing you, I can't accept giving you up. You've been the only subject on my mind since the moment you showed up at my front door last week. Your dark locks of hair and piercing blue eyes against that flawless porcelain skin make you the most beautiful woman in my eyes. I know it's still early; but this is my declaration to say, I really like you and all of your quirks. Do not everchange.

X's & O's,

Chris

A smile cracked through my lips as I thought about the smile my words could possibly bring to her face. I finished getting ready and left before my parents woke for the day.

I stopped at the mailboxes, finding the post number for Cakes and Pies, and slid it through the hole before proceeding to the boardwalk to buy two coffees on my way down. I stood at the front of the parking lot and watched as she came into view, her dark brunette hair pulled back in a ponytail wearing yoga pants and a Pennington Penguins hoodie.

A smile crossed her lips, her eyes widening and lighting up as I held out her coffee. She took it between her hands. Closing her eyes, she sipped it. "Mmm… Nothing better than hot caffeine first thing in the morning."

I chuckled, sipping my own coffee. "I couldn't agree more. Did you have a place in mind for this morning?"

She pulled her keys out, and nodded her head. "I do. Come on. It's a surprise." She winked.

I wrapped an arm around her lower back and let her take the lead toward the car. Waiting outside of the driver's side, I shut her door for her after she was secure before making my way to the passenger side.

"The Pennington Penguins? Is that where you go to school?"

She looked at me. "Yes. The Penguin is our mascot."

"That's where I'll be attending my last year of school."

Her eyes lit up. "Really? You're going to Pennington?"

"I believe so." I fastened my seatbelt as she started the car. I looked at her and smiled as she leaned in and pressed her lips against mine in a gentle kiss.

"That'll make seeing you much easier once school is back in session." She pecked my lips once more before she pulled away to look at me. Her lips were sweet as candy, and tasted of coffee and mint. I placed a hand on her cheek leaning in for another kiss before she broke the kiss and locked her eyes on mine.

I flashed a smile and winked at her before I sat back as she pulled away from the parking spot. This woman was a fresh breath of air, but to determine whether it was more last night or this morning? I couldn't decide that. Her beauty continued to strike me deeper every time I set eyes on her. Last night, she was dressed up from head to toe; and today, she looked like she was ready to challenge me to a race through the mountains. She still managed to take my breath away while we sat idle in the car.

Arriving to the Muir Woods, I stepped out and around to open her door with my coffee in hand. The sun had barely reached the horizon as we walked down toward the trails.

"My parents love it down here. They have a set of parking spaces reserved for any day of the week, at an unlimited amount of time. My siblings and I take advantage of it more than they do." She said as we walked over the wooden paneled path through the redwood trees that stood high above our heads.

"The power of money, huh?" I said.

She looked at me as we walked. "Or, just power in general."

I nodded. "I remember you saying your father is very well known around here."

She paused as we walked for a few minutes. "I may not agree with a lot of what my father stands for; but I do give him and my Mom credit for how they raised us. We've traveled far and wide in my seventeen years. We're well educated and disciplined. They trust me enough to come and go as I want, though I'm not sure how much of that trust is left after last night."

I nodded. "They raised you well. You seem to have your head on straight; and in my opinion, it's very attractive."

She smiled. "I also inherited my father's stubborn trait. I want what I want and never settle for less."

I snickered. "I can see that." I paused. "And I have to be honest. I didn't think about traits I would want in a potential girlfriend before, but now that I can see it's one of your strong suits? It's at the top of my list." I reached for her hand, sliding my fingers around hers gently.

She intertwined her fingers into mine. "A girl knowing what she wants, at seventeen?" She winked and laughed.

I chuckled. "I think it would be attractive at any age." "What traits would you not stand for?" She asked.

"Immaturity. Dishonesty. Betrayal. Those are probably the top three I wouldn't tolerate."

She nods. "Fair enough. You can't build a relationship on any of those."

"I've watched my parents and grandparents take care of each other. My grandparents set that example and my dad implemented it with my mom; and that's how I plan to treat my future soulmate."

When she turned to look at me this time, the rays of sun shone through the Redwoods and lit up her eyes. "I love that. As crazy as this is going to sound, the day I turn eighteen, I'll probably move out of my parents' house and live on the yacht until I find something more permanent. I hate living under my dad's thumb. He says he respects my decision not to join the family business, and I'll still have access to my trust fund to go out into the world and do what I want…but I feel like the rest of the family would disagree and not support it."

A pang of sadness coursed through me when she predicted what her life would be after she turned eighteen. Perhaps I could be the one to make her feel a little less lonely. Flashing her a warm smile, I stopped her and pulled her close. "Let them think what they want, gives me more of an opportunity to keep you company."

She smiled and looked away before she peeked back over at me. "You're adorable and I would never turn down your company."

I chuckled. "You're sure about that? I can be quite grumpy sometimes."

She smiled. "I'll kill that grumpiness with my world class wit." My eyes widened as a smile broke free. "Oh really? And just how do you plan to do that?" I said as I slipped my hand from hers and wrapped an arm around her lower back as we continued down the trail and descended some stairs.

"Easy, mister. I would kiss every inch of your pasty skin." She said sardonically as she raised an eyebrow toward me and then winked.

I chuckled, rubbing my thumb on the small of her back in a circular motion. "Let me see if I'm getting this right. You want to cure my grumpy moods by allowing me to kiss every inch of you." I would gladly give her porcelain skin all my attention no matter what my mood was that day.

"Sounds about right," she said, and giggled.

I chuckled and leaned down to her ear. "I don't need to be grumpy to pay attention to you, Miss Castillo."

I felt her shift slightly in my arms. "Then by all means, Mr. Montgomery. You don't need permission to pay attention to me."

I cocked an eyebrow at her and leaned in to place a gentle kiss against her jawline. "I'll keep that in mind." My voice was husky as I teased her.

She turned toward me, locking her eyes on mine before she inclined her head indicating that I should follow her and led me toward one of the giant Redwood trees and pulled me inside. I chuckled, wrapping her in my arms and inching my lips toward hers. Grasping a firm hold on her chin with my thumb and index finger, I grazed my lips against hers before pulling her in close for a tantalizing, passionate kiss. Her dainty fingers pressed against my chest as our lips danced against each other's. I backed her up against the surface of the tree pinning her back with my hands against hers. We were hidden, but there was still a possibility of being spotted. The risk of being caught heightened my senses and every risk we took to get caught drove me deeper, the passion and heavy breaths between us continued. As serious as Armani's warning was, I couldn't keep my hands off of her. She clearly needed me as much as I needed her. Perhaps this honeymoon stage was hot and heavy because it was strictly forbidden by her father. What was at risk if we were caught? It didn't matter because I would have pursued her with or without permission. Lorelai Castillo was mine, and this was only the beginning of a beautiful bond

we were forming.

She moaned softly against my lips and I took no time to move my hands down over her arms to her waist, grasping the material of her sweater. A low groan left my lips as her teeth nipped and pulled at my lower lip. I smoothed my hands up under her sweater without hesitation. Trailing my fingers over her waist, taking in the feeling over the silky skin, I cupped her breasts giving them a firm squeeze.

Her lips curved against mine in a smile as she parted from the kiss, breathing heavy against my mouth as I pushed my hands up under her bra. "Christopher…"

My lips scaled down her jawline to her neck, biting at the sensitive spots against her neck. Taking her nipples between my thumb and forefinger, I twisted them gently. She gasped softly in pleasure which only told me one thing, she didn't want me to stop.

As I continued to play with her nipples between my fingers, I moved one hand back down her waist and down over the side of her thigh. I trailed the tips of my fingers over the back of her thigh, grasping gently onto the voluptuous cheeks and pressed my body against hers. I groaned against her neck as she moaned against my ear. She arched her back, pressing her impressive figure against mine and I stopped to watch as she rubbed against my body in a slow tantalizing fashion. She was upping the ante, begging me to continue.

As much as I wanted to strip her of every piece of clothing right here, I knew I couldn't. It was too risky, but that didn't mean I couldn't pleasure her.

Pulling her sweatshirt off, I set it aside and moved my lips back to her neck, nipping at the skin gently. Her hands traveled up under my shirt to the bare skin of my back. I smiled as I moved slowly to her collarbone, pulling the straps of her bra down over her shoulders. My lips traveled down her neck, not skipping over one inch of her skin as I trailed down to her breasts. Breathing heavily against her skin, I pressed succulent kisses against her breasts, while I played with the elastic waistband on her yoga pants. Sliding my fingers past the top of her pants, my fingers grazed down her inner thigh.

She laid her head against my chest, peering up at me. I flashed a gentle smile at her, scraping my dull nails along the sensitive skin, cupping my hand between her legs, curling the tips of my fingers against the thin material of her panties. A smirk rose against my lips as she inhaled a sharp breath, exhaling in a soft moan.

I grunted, biting my lower lip as her face scrunched with pleasure. Her breathing picked up as I brushed four fingers across the material. The warm moisture soaking through her panties, leaving my fingers damp told me that she was prepared. Sliding the material to the side, I brushed the pad of my thumb down over her clit. A moan left her lips as she buried her face into the crook of my neck.

"Mm…how's that feel gorgeous?" I whispered.

She pressed her lips against my neck in retaliation, the softest of moans leaving her lips. I smirked. Did she think she was going to distract me? The thought made me chuckle.

Picking up the pace, I flickered my thumb back and forth against the sensitive button. Her body twitched as she moaned against me. "Fuck, Christopher," she whispered loudly through an unsteady moan.

I smirked and moved back, quickly planting a passionate kiss against her lips, as I slid my index and forefinger past her entrance. Her hot tight core enclosed my fingers in a snug fashion. The passion and depth of the kiss heightened as I pushed deeper inside of her, pivoting my wrist and circulating my fingers to feel every inch of her hot core. Moisture accumulated and built up, sending my mind into an oblivious world. Whether we were behind closed doors, or out in the wild of these redwood trees… all that mattered was pleasuring Lorelai until she reached a sweet climax.

Harmonious moans escaped her throat against my lips. I nipped, nibbled and pulled at her lips and pulled my lips away, watching as she leaned back into the bark, arching her back and pivoting her hips into the rhythm of my fingers. Her body language and movement screamed in volumes of how she was feeling. The further I pushed, the faster I moved. She reacted accordingly with panting, breathy moans. It was such a damn turn on and made me want to discover how I could push her further to experience more pleasure.

Using my free hand, I pushed her pants along with her panties halfway down her thighs: and backed her further into the side of the tree, where it would be hard for someone to spot us and moved to my knees. I paced the movement of my fingers inside, watching as she pivoted her hips against my fingers flawlessly. My eyes moved up and down her body, locking onto her eyes as a ray of light shone through against the inside of the tree trunk to take in the sight of her disheveled clothes hanging in disarray on her partially naked body. Every contour and slim curve became visible as I locked my eyes on hers. I leaned in and teased my tongue up and around her sensitive nub.

Gasped breaths and soft moans escaped her throat as she pushed her fingers through my hair, gripping it between her fingers. I wrapped my lips around her clit and sucked gently as my fingers continued pumping faster inside of her wet folds. Her breathy moans intensified as I picked up the pace, using the tip of my tongue to stimulate her clit. Pulling my mouth away for a moment to appreciate the view above me as she started coming undone, I quickly moved my mouth back to her clit as the hot liquid leaked against my fingers. The intense orgasm dripped over my hand and into my mouth. Parting ways with her writhing body, I watched as my name fell flawlessly from her lips, and I knew that I'd brought her into a place of serenity.

Breaking Forbidden Rules

Lorelai

PERSPIRATION COATED THE surface of my body, as I came down from the intense orgasm Christopher gave me.

Here we were inside of a redwood tree of all places as pleasure coursed through my veins. I arched my back as he placed his lips against every inch of my skin, making his way back to his feet. I ran my fingers through his hair, looking up at him as he brushed his thumbs against my waist.

"Chris…"

He leaned in and planted passionate kisses against my neck. Reaching around, I grasped his back.

"You're so damn beautiful, Lor…"

I smiled. "Mmm… you sure know how to keep a girl wanting more, Montgomery."

He chuckled. "Guess we'll just have to see each other later to continue, won't we?" He husked against my neck.

"Bet your ass," I whispered back.

He leaned in from the side, drinking me in as he moved in close and grazed his lips against my jawline and whispered, "Hm… You wanna tell me about what these future endeavors might entail?"

I giggled softly. "Well, I'll definitely be searching deep for something special to wear."

A low growl left his lips. "Mmm… and what would this special something look like?"

I bit my lower lip. "Wouldn't you like to know?"

"Keep it up, Castillo. I will tease you until you are shifting uncomfortably… and leave you hanging in ways you couldn't imagine."

A stifled moan left my lips. "Mmm. Please do, baby. Two can play that game." I reached down and grasped his hard cock through his pants, gasping in a soft moan and knowing how crazy it drove him.

He pulled away, smoothing his hands up my arms, his fingers sliding through the straps to my bra back to my shoulders. "As tempting as it is to strip you down right here and pleasure you even more out here in the wilderness, I think we should wait, beautiful." He re-clasped the brackets together, and slowly but surely redressed me.

I glared up at him playfully. "Have you practiced the art of leaving a girl hanging before? Cause, I'm starting to feel like you're doing this on purpose."

He chuckled. "I'm driving you crazy?" He paused. "The feeling is mutual."

I bit my lower lip, holding back a giggle. "Then you'll just have to come out and play later, won't you?"

"I guess I will." He spat in a snarky tone, his grey-blue hues grew a shade darker with his tone.

I smiled sweetly as I slid my arms around his waist. "I'll find us a spot to spend the night, and then I'll be yours."

He moved his lips toward my ear. "All night? Are you sure you could handle such circumstances?"

I smirked. "More than certain, Mr. Montgomery." His smartass remarks tickled me. How was it possible to grasp such an intense connection so quickly? His claims of being grumpy hardly phased me. He was actually rather adorable when he was grumpy and even more so when he scolded and scowled.

He smiled, leaning in to peck a kiss against my cheek and finished fixing my clothes before he took my hand and pressed a gentle kiss to each of my knuckles. "Where will we venture next, my lady?"

I smiled, leading him out of the redwood back down to the trail. "Do you have anywhere to be soon?"

"Nope. My day is free."

I smiled, leading him down the trail. "Perfect."

Adventures with Christopher had become a cherished need. I couldn't accept the forbidden rule of no dating. I needed a plan, and to make sure Chris was on board.

The beauty of the Muir Woods trails was that they led to more beautiful sceneries, and in my opinion the only reason I spent so much time down here. The trail led us down the mountain to Muir Beach, which had spectacular views of the Pacific Ocean and beyond.

I looked back to Chris as we made our way down the last hill to the beach and smiled as he stared off aimlessly, completely taken away with the views unveiled. We walked hand in hand down the beach, without another human soul in sight. It was the two of us and the wide-open Pacific Ocean gently crashing against the shore.

He slipped his hand out of mine, wrapping an arm around me from behind and pulling me close. I looked up at him and smiled as he inched closer and pressed a gentle kiss against my lips. I held on for a moment before I broke it and turned to face him placing both of my hands against his chest.

"So, do you show all the boys next door these secret hideaways?"

A soft giggle left my lips. "Nope. You're the first one. You should feel quite special, Montgomery."

He chuckled. "Oh, I most definitely do."

I rubbed my hands over his back gently. "I actually wanted to talk to you about that. As much as I don't want this to end, we need to talk about how we'll see each other without being caught by my parents or anyone that would talk and spread the word around."

He ran his hands over my back gently, then reached around and ran his fingers through the ends of my hair. "My schedule is pretty wide open right now. What were you thinking?"

"I have to check which of the boathouses is free, but I figured we could make them our meet up spots? Have our own little getaway out of sight and away from everyone?"

He smiled, and pecked my lips. "I love the sound of that. Being away from everyone and taking in the natural beauty of this town has been a treat, and even sweeter because it's with you."

A wide smile crossed my lips as I gazed up at him. "We can continue discovering the beauty together then. I promised I would break you in easy, and one of the Castillo family values is we don't break promises."

He smiled, grazing his lips against my cheek before he let go and unwrapped his arms from around me, and took my hand, leaning down to untie his shoes.

"What are you doing?"

He looked up from a bent over position. "You'll see."

I held his hand. "You're not thinking about going in that water, are you?"

He raised an eyebrow as he successfully kicked his shoes off and pulled his socks off. "Maybe?"

"Christopher! That water is freezing!" I exclaimed.

He let go of my hand and I fumbled to grasp a hold of his back. "You are not taking me in that water, Christopher!" I warned.

He stood back up after I reluctantly allowed him to remove my shoes and socks, sweeping me off of my feet. He threw me over his shoulder. "No? You're not going in? Really? Because I think you are."

Bouts of laughter left my lips as I struggled to move out of his grip and watched as he made footprints in the sand down toward the water. "Put me down! You… you… scallywag!"

Low chuckles could be heard as I set my eyes on the foaming water at the shore. "We don't even have bathing suits!" I pleaded, but there was no use. For a man with such charm, he was quick to open up to his adventurous side; and he might not have seen it right there in that moment, but I was loving it.

I looked up to see we were about twelve feet from the shore. Gentle hands grasped my waist as he held back a chuckle. "You were right about one thing; this water is kind of chilly."

I felt myself sliding down as he pulled me into the water. I inhaled a sharp breath through my lips, and squealed. "Dammit, Christopher! No!"

He chuckled and submerged us both into the chilling salt water. "Don't worry. I'll keep you warm, I'm a furnace."

"You won't be when you go into hypothermic shock, Montgomery!" I spat.

He smiled and looked at me as we were now eye level. "I thought I was supposed to be covering the grumpy moods."

This boy was driving me crazy in the best and worst possible way. A growl left my throat as I narrowed my eyes at him. "Guess you're not the only grumpy bear in all of Marin County, Montgomery!"

His smile widened, as he laughed. "You're adorable when you get mad, has anyone ever told you that?"

"No! Well, no one besides you because you're absolutely absurd!" I yelled. This kid was a loon, and I really didn't mind it.

My words only sent him further into laughter before he cupped my cheek and pulled me close. Suddenly, the water wasn't so cold and everything he'd done to get me into the water somehow floated away and I wasn't mad anymore. Our breathing synced as we leaned in until his lips grazed against mine in a smooth intimate kiss. I wrapped my arms around his neck, and allowed his lips to press against mine.

We stood there for what seemed like forever, in a hot and heavy make-out session that never went further than that. We were both so content, but the emotions of how he made me feel started racing through my head at a million miles a minute. Our personalities meshed as well as my grandparents' recipe for their homemade spaghetti. There were so many ingredients and each one had to have the perfect amount or it was 'no good' as my grandmother said. Christopher wasn't supposed to come around me; and yet here we were two days later and I couldn't seem to let him go or push him away like my Father wished. He was the perfect recipe for a man. He had a sense of humor, he was protective, passionate, and most of all, he could keep up with my banter. While he hesitated to take my afterparty Summer Bash invitation Friday night, once he caved, he was all in.

His strong arms enclosed me, and he began rubbing his large hands over my body. Goosebumps covered my skin; and even though he was doing his best to keep me warm, he brought us back to the shore. He broke the kiss as he lowered us into the sand and maneuvered us both until I was seated between his legs. Ocean water dripped from our fully clothed bodies as I laid my legs across one of his and gazed up at him adoringly.

He looked back down at me studiously. "What's that look for?"

I paused to think about how I wanted to word this, and hoped that he would reciprocate with how I felt. "I know we haven't known each other that long, but I'm really happy and content when I'm with you."

A smile spread across his face as he rubbed a hand up and down the side of my waist. "To be honest with you? I am too. I had no idea what would come of this move; but if I could spend the rest of the summer spending my time with you, and allowing whatever this is to grow, I think I'd be okay with that."

"You mean, sneaking off and being naughty teenagers in the woods and at the beach?"

He chuckled. "Not just that, but being around you. I did not like how the situation was handled on Friday night, and I was unhappy being told to stay away from you." He spoke just above a whisper as he pushed a piece of hair behind my ear.

I placed my hand against his arm gently. "I know exactly what you mean, but I'm happy that I caught you before you hid yourself away. I want to continue seeing you, no matter what my family said and I have just the way for us to do it."

"Yeah? What's that?"

"I'll show you when we head back," I said.

"Do you have to be back soon?"

"I should be okay for a little while longer."

He smiled. "Good, because I'm not ready to go back yet."

I smiled back at him, leaning up to kiss his lips before I sat up and leaned back into him. "We need to dry off before we head back anyway."

He chuckled. It was a sneaky little chuckle. Did he think this sneaky act of his was cute? He laid his head against my shoulder, pressing a gentle kiss against my soaking wet shirt.

Slowly turning my head, I met his eyes with a glare in my own. "You're so smug," I spoke above a whisper.

He chuckled once more. "Me? Chris Montgomery, smug? Only when it comes to pretty young ladies, such as yourself."

A smile cracked through my lips, and I shook my head at him. "I should be enraged with you right now for pulling me into that freezing cold water; and for the life of me, I can't be mad at you."

He raised both eyebrows, a small smile tugging at his lips. "Oh, I'm sure you could. Let me hear you growl. I'll bet it's ferocious."

I held in my laughter as I prepared my best growl for him. Turning my head away from him, I inhaled a breath and looked at him with the meanest of glares. "Grrr!" My mission failed. I sounded like a pathetic cub. My poor excuse at the attempt pushed us both into a bout of laughter.

I looked at him after a moment of staring out at the water. "I can't fake being mad! But I promise you don't want to see me mad with the thick Italian blood I am cut with."

He pulled me closer in his arms. "I think I could handle any version of you that you threw at me."

"Is that so?" I stared up at him, studying his facial features. His defined jawline, and big, easy to get lost in, grey-blue eyes stared back at me. I realized that I was putty in his hands and that I would go to extensive lengths to keep him close.

"I couldn't imagine anyone else showing me the ropes to life here in Sausalito."

I smiled and planted a gentle kiss on his scruffy cheek. "I wouldn't want anyone else trying to achieve such a task either. They could easily steer you in the wrong direction," I said, and stopped to think about just how easy it could've been for him to slip into the wrong crowd. Turning slightly, I wrapped my arms around his waist, holding him a little closer as we sat in silence listening to the waves gently crash against the shore.

When we got back to the car, I watched as Chris climbed in the passenger side while I went to the trunk. I retrieved a box and joined him in the front seat.

"So, I have a little something for you."

He looked over as he shut the door. "Yeah? What is it?"

"Another way to communicate. As you might've figured out, my Father likes to run a tight ship."

He nodded and groaned a bit. "I did. So, what have you come up with?"

"I found these in the storage closet while I was working." I said, and handed him the box.

He took one look in the box and laid his head back against the seat. "Walkie talkies? Really, Lorelai? How old are we?"

I giggled. "Six and three-quarters!" I nudged him playfully.

He picked his head up and slid the box's contents out to set them up. "You're killing me. You know that?"

I smiled. "I only kill in the best ways, Montgomery. The person lives to tell about all the agony I put them through."

He chuckled. "Alright, for you I'll give it a whirl."

I squealed in happiness, and watched as he outfitted the two black boxes with batteries, and set them both to the same channel. "They should be ready to go. We can test them when we get back."

I put on my seat belt and smiled. "Sounds perfect."

Upon arrival back at the yacht club, Chris leaned over to steal a quick kiss. "I'll talk to you soon, beautiful."

I smiled. "Okay. See you." I blew him a kiss once he was out of the car and he looked back at me as he was walking away.

Turning the volume up on the radio, I waited for the first test to come through. Butterflies fluttered in my stomach and around my heart. Perhaps I was crazy, jumping in with two feet when I was told not to; but the radiant charm that shined around Christopher's aura was brighter than ever, and I yearned for the next time I would see him.

A scratching noise came through the radio. "This is Montgomery, calling over to Princess Lorelai."

I laughed and pressed the button to talk. "Loud and clear, lad. What's your location?"

"I'm about half way down the boardwalk going toward my house."

I was pleasantly surprised at how handy these walkie-talkies were working to our advantage. "Okay. Let me know when you're at the house."

"Roger that."

I smiled and shook my head. Stepping out of the car, I made my way back to the yacht club; and instead of going home, I decided I would go hide on Cakes and Pies for the remainder of the day.

Stopping at the mailbox, I unlocked the small metal door and pulled out a small pile of envelopes, and shuffled through them. A letter with unfamiliar handwriting sat at the top. Quickly locking up the mailbox, I made a bee line down the docks toward Cakes and Pies.

Once inside the cabin, I kicked my shoes off and made myself comfortable on the couch; opening up the mystery letter, I smiled as I began to read it. I held the letter over my chest upon finishing, and a scratching scribble bleeped through the walkie. "Lor? Can you hear me?"

I leapt off the couch to grasp the walkie and came back to the couch and sat. "I can hear you loud and clear, Mr. Montgomery, which means… we have success!"

He came back and chuckled a moment later. "That we do. What are you up to?"

"Funny you should ask. I was on my way home, and decided to check my mail. Lo and behold, there was this sweet little love whisper inside."

"A love whisper, huh?" I could hear the smile in his tone of voice.

"Yes. That's what it came off as."

"Who was it from?" he asked nonchalantly.

I giggled. "Some creep named Christopher."

He chuckled. "A creep? What did this creep have to say?"

I smiled. "Oh, just that he can't get me off his mind, and my beauty is striking."

"He's not lying."

"Hmm… You think I should write him back?"

"Did he leave a return address?"

I looked at the letter, noticing the mailbox number was coincidentally written in the corner. "He did." I paused. "Maybe I should leave him hanging for a few days."

"I'll remember that when I'm peeling your clothes off later…" His tone came out low and husky. I squeezed my legs together, as I stood up off the couch to go look through the rental book to see what was vacant.

"On that note, are you open to meet up tonight?" I ignored his teasing on purpose.

He chuckled. "Maybe? What'd you have in mind, gorgeous?"

"Dock C - number 217. Does ten p.m. work for you?"

"Sure. I'll manage to find it. See you at ten."

I smiled. "See you then." Setting the walkie down, I read his letter once more; and I couldn't help but giggle. He drove me nuts!

Christopher

Later that night. I tiptoed through my house, gathering candles, a small assortment of fruit, and chocolate bars to melt down. I stopped at the florist to grab a bouquet of daisies and arrived to the vacant boathouse around 9:30 p.m. I typed the code into the lockbox and gained entry to the house. Looking around, I didn't see anyone. I turned the lights up and went to work on melting the chocolate, arranging the fruit on a plate, lit the candles, and found a vase in the kitchen to place the daisies in.

Setting my surprise items up across the coffee table between the candles, I opened the sliding door to the living room and stood back to look at it. When I was satisfied, I searched through the wine bottle selection in the kitchen. Once I found a wine we could share, I set two glasses out on each side and heard the front door open and close, quietly. "Christopher?"

"In the kitchen, babe." I replied finding a radio to turn on soft music.

She walked through the doorway as I popped the cork off the bottle. "Go have a seat and make yourself comfortable. I'll bring your glass over in a moment."

She pursed her lips and eyed me for a moment. "What are you up to, Montgomery?"

I smiled and came up behind her. "Go look."

She proceeded through the open concept kitchen to the living room and took in the surprise. Stopping behind her, I wrapped my arms around her. Leaning in, I placed a gentle kiss to her jawline. "What do you think?"

She turned halfway toward me, placed her hand against my cheek and planted a passionate kiss against my lips. Wrapping her in my arms, I pulled her close as I returned the kiss, moving my hand up through her hair gently.

She broke the kiss a moment later and smiled. "This is the most romantic thing anyone's ever done for me, Christopher, Thank you."

I smiled back at her before I pulled her close, rubbing my hands up and down her back, placing my chin against her shoulder. "I want to be your getaway, Lorelai. I'll take care of you."

She stayed quiet for a moment, before she returned my embrace and laid her head against my chest. I laid my head on top of hers and closed my eyes embracing this moment. It was sweet, romantic, and meaningful and I wanted it to be that way. I wanted to show her she could rely on me to come through for her every time. This was only the beginning.

"Really? Because, I think I would really enjoy that." She spoke barely above a whisper.

"Let's give it a whirl, Princess," I whispered back and she tightened her embrace and giggled.

I held her for a moment longer, enjoying her body pressed against mine. Her breathing was calm and, from her relaxed state of mind, I imagined her eyes were closed. She was completely comfortable with me and I could not help but feel our connection deepening in that moment.

Pulling away only slightly, I kept one arm wrapped around her waist and guided her to the couch. We each grabbed our glasses of wine and sat back. I wrapped my free arm around her and pulled her close. "How was the rest of your day?"

She looked up into my eyes. "It was good. I took Cakes and Pies out for a ride, and cleaned the cabin. It's sparkling clean now."

I chuckled. "That yacht is like your child, it seems."

She looked up at me slightly amused, as if I understood. "Oh, she is. There's something about having ownership of a vessel. Cruising out on the bay, feeling the breeze running through her sails and my hair. It's definitely a strong bond."

I chuckled. "Well, maybe sometime down the line, you can give me lessons. I wouldn't mind learning."

"I'd love to teach you."

We sat and sipped the rest of our wine, and chatted about adventures we could take on Cakes and Pies. I learned that Lorelai was very educated on the rules of access to Yacht Clubs, and that being a Castillo allowed her access to almost any club on the West Coast. All it took was one little phone call, and she would be granted access to a docking space. She had only gone as far as North Marin County and down into San Francisco, being a minor gave her limited roaming space. We talked of going to Washington, Oregon, and even down to Southern California as possibilities.

After finishing our second glass of wine, we were both a tad tipsy. I set our glasses down, and grabbed the fruit tray. "Come with me! I have a surprise."

She giggled and stood up. I brought her back to the bedroom, setting the tray on top of the dresser, and pulled her in for a passionate kiss as I walked her back to the bed. I removed her shirt and bra, laid her back at the top of the bed, crawling over her before I broke the kiss. "Stay put. I'll be right back."

She giggled, and whined. "Christopher! Hurry! I need you!"

I chuckled darkly, getting off the bed. I pulled the white V-neck over my head and tossed it to the floor while I went to retrieve the candles, and placed one on each of the nightstands by the bed.

"Mmm…so romantic, babe." She turned her head, following me as I walked around the bed.

I winked at her. "I try." Crawling back up on the bed, I pulled her back into my arms and attacked her lips with another passionate kiss. She returned the kiss, never shying away from the passion. We could've lit a fire on a thousand candles with the heat we produced. Clothes disappeared one piece at a time; and before I knew it, we were both naked.

Taking me by surprise, she rolled me over onto my back and broke the kiss. Her lips planted succulent kisses down my jawline to my neck and over my chest and abdomen. Moving down to my hips, I watched her enjoying every touch of her lips against my skin. Reaching down, I pushed my fingers through her hair. I knew what she was going for and, while I would've enjoyed every second, I had other plans.

"Mmm… Get your beautiful body back up here."

She giggled and moved back up. I let her take her time before I flipped her back on the bed and straddled her. "Arms above your head, Castillo."

She smirked and didn't question my demand. Standing up, I grabbed the tray of fruit and chocolate and came back. Picking up a strawberry, I dipped it in the chocolate. "Open up."

She smiled and I moved the fruit to her lips, watching as she bit into it seductively. Fuck! She was so damn gorgeous, I couldn't take it.

"Mmm…delicious," she said, after finishing.

I smiled at her and noted the drizzle of chocolate that fell against her breast.

She bit her lower lip watching as I picked up the bowl of warm chocolate sauce with another strawberry. That dribble of chocolate gave me an idea. I snickered, dipping the fruit once more. This time, I let the chocolate drip over her chest on purpose. Taking a bite, I admired her from the straddled position I had on her hips.

I silently noted her wandering eyes from below, giggling and groaning at me in pleasure. I loved how playful and sassy she could get, and the fact that she was allowing me to turn her into a dessert tray right now made my head spin with ideas of what else she would allow me to do.

"You've made a mess, Christopher," she pouted.

I chuckled and looked at the lines and droplets of chocolate splattered across her breasts and stomach. "No worries. Let me clean that up for you." Leaning down, I started at her breast, sucking the sweet chocolate off of her breasts. Opening my eyes, I watched as her head fell back, moans leaving her lips. I closed mine once more and moved my lips to the drizzle that landed against her nipple, sucking the tip gently. She arched her back as a loud cry of pleasure left her lips.

When I finished cleaning her up, I planted kisses up her to her clavicle, neck, and jawline to her ear. "Hmm… Did you enjoy that, Miss Castillo?"

She inhaled a deep breath. "Oh god, yes baby. I love it when you tease me."

I chuckled quietly, nipping at her earlobe, rubbing my hands over the sides of her waist to her breast. I massaged them gently, before pinching at her nipples. Her moans filled the room as I continued. Breaking away, I grabbed the chocolate sauce and trailed it from the top of her breasts to her hips. I thought, 'she's going to need a shower after this…', which made me snicker quietly. She was too distracted by my continuous licking and sucking to notice my soft laugh.

Reaching her hips, I trailed a line of succulent kisses down and stop as I reached the top of her clit. Prodding my tongue against her in a teasing way, she moaned my name and I pulled away and moved my lips to her inner thigh, kissing and nipping at the sensitive skin.

Her breathing picked up at a heavy pace when I kissed down her inner thigh. Spreading her legs, I reached up on the tray of goodies and grabbed a maraschino cherry and placed it to her lips. "Bite this off the stem… but don't eat it," I instructed her.

She looked down at me, inhaling a deep breath covering the cherry stem with her teeth before pulling the cherry off. Quickly moving to hover over her, I grasped the fruit from her lips and looked at her with a devious hint in my eyes. "I guess I should've mentioned I had a sweet tooth."

My bad.

Moving back between her legs, I dropped the cherry against her clit. "If it drops, I'll start the entire process over."

She inhaled a deep breath and exhaled a moan; my name left her lips in a plea which made me smile and snicker. "You don't play fair…," she whined.

I glared up at her playfully. "Maybe I should make you lay there so I can admire you instead."

"Please don't do that Mr. Montgomery. I'll stay still. I promise."

The stern glare kept shape as I lowered myself, pushing her legs up, I slid my tongue between her lips gaining that sweet taste of her in my mouth. Her panting moans filled the room; and when I knew she was at the edge of releasing, I swept my tongue over the sensitive button and bit into the cherry making sure to drip the juice, placing my lips over the mound and sucking softly before pushing a finger inside and then a second. Feeling her wet folds wrapping around my fingers, I moved in and out of her picking up the pace the longer this went on.

Looking up, I locked my eyes on hers as she moaned wrapping her legs around my lower back and moved her hips to meet each push of my fingers.

Quickening the pace, I didn't stop until she released a hot, intense orgasm. I groaned against her as her continuous moans became music to my ears. Without missing a beat, I moved up her body, planting sweet suckle kisses against her skin, pulling her legs up with my legs, dipping my hardened penis into her hot wet core and watching as her head fell back as she gasped out in a moan. Our hips danced together, as I picked up the pace. The pleasure coursed through my body as she pushed her fingers through my hair and pulled me in for a passionate kiss.

I smiled against her lips, grasping firmly onto her hips and sitting up to get a different angle. I felt driven by the need to give her the most intense orgasm of her life.

"Close your eyes," I huffed out, groaning as I grew closer.

She did as she was told without a question. Damn. She was so obedient and I was loving it. I ran a finger against her clit in quick motions to bring her closer to her climax. I bit my lip at the sight before me.

"Mm, come for me princess."

She gasped out and her wave of moans aligned with the orgasm releasing against my cock. In the midst of a groaning moan, I reached to retrieve a candle and blew it out. A smirk rose over my lips before I tilted the jar, dripping the hot wax over her breasts and stomach which made her scream. Exploding inside of her, I slowed the pace to ride out the rest of our orgasms. Setting the candle aside, I laid against her and pressed gentle kisses to her shoulder as we both attempted to catch our breath.

Laying my head in the crook of her neck, I smiled and thought, 'how did I get so damn lucky?'

Nine

Emotional Distractions

THE FOLLOWING WEEK, each morning and night revolved around carefully planning times and days to meet with Lorelai. My parents trusted me; but I didn't want to break their trust or cause them to ask questions, so I told them little white lies in order to get away and see Lorelai. We had been here less than two weeks and I already felt change taking over my life, but only for the better.

After the weekend was over, I received a letter from her. It read:

Dear Grumpy Bear,

I promised to keep you waiting on your toes, but I thought I'd be sincere and write back. From the moment you opened your front door almost a week ago and I set eyes on your brilliant grey-blue eyes, and listened to your parents bickering in the background, I couldn't help but feel like I'd fit into your life like a missing puzzle piece. Lo and behold, coming to welcome you to the community turned out to be my best decision this summer! This past weekend was amazing. Let's meet in the parking lot tomorrow. There's another place I'd like to show you; and as usual, it's a surprise.

XX,

Lorelai

P.S. I really like you and how caring you are, despite your recent grumpy moods in the morning. I will break you of that habit… and that's a threat, not a promise.

I chuckled, and went to look for something to keep the letter in. Opening the closet door, I pulled out a wooden box. My father gifted it to me on my thirteenth birthday. Inside were letters he and my mother sent to each other in the beginning stages of their relationship. Sending handwritten letters was how they fell in love. Of course, they weren't forbidden to see the other. My mother's family lived across the street from Dad, Nana, and Papa. Her father received some big promotion as a pilot to go live overseas and work as an international pilot, and Mom refused to leave my Dad. Nana and Papa set her up a private room, and the rest was history.

Picking up the letters, I lifted the top tray from the box, setting the letters inside. I placed Lorelai's first letter into the top of the box, shut it and placed it back in the closet. I sat at my desk and grabbed the communication radio and pressed the button.

"Lor?" I asked simply, waiting to see if she was around.

A few minutes passed before she came through. "Christopher?"

"Hi, beautiful. Just confirming plans for tomorrow morning?"

"Can you meet me tonight?"

I paused for a moment thinking about how I wanted to respond.

"Sure. Is everything okay?"

"Not really. I mean, physically yes. I can explain better in person."

I stood up going to listen at the door. My parents were still awake and if I told them I wanted to go see Lorelai, they would ask questions that I didn't feel like answering.

I grabbed the walkie. "What's your location?"

"Meet me at C-217?"

"I'll be there soon, sweetheart," I spoke quietly.

Placing the radio on my belt, I slipped into my flip flops, and grabbed a jacket before I headed downstairs to find my parents each sitting in their chairs with a book in their hands. "I'm going out for a walk. I can't sleep."

"Christopher, what's wrong?" Mom asked.

She didn't believe me. Shit.

"I think I'm still getting used to a new space."

"Let 'im go," Dad said. "This place is quiet and calm. He'll be fine."

I looked back and forth to each of them going back to their books and didn't wait a second longer before I walked out the door and headed down to dock C. Approaching the door, I put the code into the lock box to take the keys out and grant myself access. Walking in, it was quiet. She hadn't arrived yet.

I walked through the house, finding a chilled bottle of wine and some candles and decided to light a few, placing them on the table in front of the couch before I went to sit out on the patio and stare into the dark starry skies while I waited for her to arrive.

A few minutes later, I heard the door shut quietly and stood in the doorway of the sliding door waiting for her to come into view. When she walked into the living room, she looked around in complete silence. I noticed that her cheeks were wet. Why was she crying?

Panic filled me and I walked to her, embracing her and placing gentle pecks against her cheeks. "Lorelai?" I whispered as she dug her face into the crook of my neck. I rubbed her back with both hands. "What on Earth is wrong, baby girl?"

She sniffled softly. "It's nothing. I just really needed to see you."

She was lying. She wouldn't have been so upset over nothing. I wanted to question her, but I didn't want to push the envelope too hard. "Okay. Well, I'm right here baby. Come sit down."

Keeping one arm wrapped around her snugly, I walked her to the couch and sat down, gently pulling her into my lap before embracing her petite body against mine once more. I began to rub her back up and down.

We sat in the candlelit room and she finally calmed down and picked up her head. "You know how you were telling me about your visits to Napa to visit your Nana and Papa?" "Yes?" I whispered.

"Did your parents ever leave and go off without you?" she asked.

"Not that I can recall," I said honestly.

She remained silent for a moment. "My family does it all the time. They leave and never say a word to me. There's been times where they would leave me and my siblings for days or weeks at a time. We have a private driver if we need one, and a cook that is also a maid; but we were on our own to get up for school on time. We were on our own for a lot. They think it's okay to just throw money at us to make sure we're fed and dressed well. There's nothing I didn't want that I couldn't have except for the love of my parents."

I continued to rub her back with one hand, and pressed my lips against her forehead for a moment. "I'm so sorry, Lorelai,"

My heart hurt for her. How could any parent think it was okay to leave their children to fend for themselves?

She shook her head. "It's okay, you have nothing to be sorry for. You've shown more care for me in the last week than my own parents have in years." She paused, nuzzling her head into the crook of my neck. "If I ever start a family, I swear I will never be like them. I will show my husband and children unconditional love."

I sighed softly. "You have every right to feel the way you do, Lor. You're not wrong, sweetheart."

She looked up at me. "Stay with me tonight?"

I smiled at her and leaned my head down to press my lips against hers in a slow sweeping kiss. Pulling her close, I picked her up, walked back out to the deck and laid her out on the lawn chair. I hovered over her, slowly breaking the kiss. "Stay here. I'm going to grab us a blanket and candles. Do you want a glass of wine to take the edge off?"

She smiled up at me. "That would be wonderful, babe." She paused. "Thank you…"

Leaning in, I pecked her lips gently holding onto it for a moment before I let go and walked inside. I retrieved a folded-up blanket and the candles first and brought them out.

Covering her up, I tucked the blanket in gently. "Are you warm enough?"

She nodded. "Yes. I'll be much warmer once you come join me."

I smiled at her. "I'll be right back with your wine."

"'Kay," She spoke above a whisper returning a warm smile.

I winked at her playfully before I retrieved our drinks and returned a few minutes later. Handing her the glasses, I climbed in behind her and placed my legs at her sides. I grabbed my drink before placing my free arm around her waist. "Mmm… Better?"

She turned on her side and looked up at me. "Much. Thank you."

"Anytime, sweetheart. You know, I was thinking about what you said earlier. If you ever feel alone, don't ever hesitate to reach out to me. I know this whole thing between us is new, but I want to be there for you if you'll let me."

She sipped her wine and smiled. "I'd like that." She leaned up and planted a kiss against my lips. I closed my eyes, returning the kiss slowly, rubbing my hand up and down the side of her waist.

As we lay there under the stars and I kissed her lips gently, the passion entered without effort. She opened up to me about such a personal and deep issue in her life. I understood her more. I understood why she was so independent, but the cause of it shattered my heart into a thousand pieces. She deserved love, attention, and care in all areas of her life, and I wanted to give her all of it. For now, we had the night, lying under the dark skies, and millions of stars to gaze at.

She broke the kiss slowly and looked up at me. I flashed a gentle smile at her and we sat in silence drinking our wine. I didn't care if this was all we did for the rest of the evening. If lying here, holding her in my arms sipping wine was her idea of not being alone, then dammit, that's what we would do.

Lorelai

Sometime later in the night, I opened my eyes to realize I had fallen asleep without meaning too. I looked up to Chris who was also sound asleep and smiled. He looked so peaceful. I laid my head in the crook of his neck, planting a gentle kiss against his neck moving up to his jawline. I turned slightly and laid my forehead to his, brushing my lips against his in a feather-like touch. I pulled away far enough to watch his chest rise and fall steadily. I placed both hands against his cheeks and leaned in, slowly pressing my lips to his in a full kiss. Pressing slow, but firmly over and over again. He stirred as he puckered his lips back against mine, his arms pulling me closer as he deepened the kiss with a longing to hold on.

I smiled against his lips. "Mmm…do you have to go home?"

He groaned quietly. "I should, but I'm not going to if you don't want me too."

I giggled softly. "Am I turning you into a rebel, Montgomery?"

He chuckled. "Maybe a little. But, in all fairness, you're not handcuffing or holding me hostage. I chose to be here," he whispered, brushing his lips into mine. I returned the favor, moving in for a full kiss as I wrapped my arms around his neck pulling myself up. I sat against his leg as his hands played with the bottom seam of my shirt sliding my hands up under my shirt as the kiss continued to deepen with passion. The innocence quickly turned into a heated moment as we breathed heavily against each other's lips.

He broke the kiss and moved his lips down my jawline, "Lor?"

A soft sigh left my lips. "Yeah, babe?"

He moved his lips against my ear. "I want to make love to you." His voice was smooth and sweet as his hands moved up and down my back.

I bit my lower lip, smiling a moment later. "Mmm…I want you to make love to me…"

He smiled and brought me down to the chair, hovering over me after removing my shirt. Clothes fell flawlessly to the wooden surface below us. Making sure to keep the blanket close, he draped it over his back before he knelt between my legs and tackled my lips in a slow, sweeping kiss. I placed my hands against his cheeks, slid them down to his neck and finally settled them against his chest while he played with the settings on the back of the sunchair and laid me back.

Large warm hands smoothed up my calves to the top of my knees before slowly spreading my legs. I watched as he hovered over me, using one hand to steady himself. His biceps flexed as he took a proper position above me. My heart raced, the crisp air in the night not affecting me one bit as heat radiated from his body and the blanket.

I smiled softly, placing a hand against his cheek.

"What is it?" he whispered, planting his lips against my jawline. I didn't have to say a word, he knew I had something on my mind.

"Mm…" I arched my back pressing my body against his. "You're… you're the best part of my world, Chris."

He continued to plant more soft gentle pecks down my jawline toward my neck. "You've turned my world upside down, Lorelai," he whispered against my ear. "I'm falling in love with you…"

When he spoke those words, heart palpitations thumped through my chest, as I pushed my fingers through the back of his wavy curls, a soft hum left my throat and I watched as he pulled back to look me in the eyes.

I locked my eyes on his which were glowing from the faint candlelight surrounding us, wrapping an arm around his neck before attacking his lips in a sweet, passionate kiss. No more words needed to be spoken. I needed to be one with him again, and maybe as much as we could from here on out. The timing and place couldn't have been more perfect.

The passionate kiss caused heavy breaths against each other's lips. A light coat of sweat covered my body as I became enamored with his sweet lips pressed against mine. His large hand covered and massaged my breast with the utmost skill. I tugged and nipped against his lip as he used his forefinger and thumb to twist gently at my now hard nipples. Breaking the kiss, a moan escaped my lips as he moved down my neck.

He was going take his sweet time buttering me up; and I didn't mind one bit as his mouth found my other breast, continuing to press sweet gentle pecks. I felt an arousing sucking sensation around my nipple. Leaning my head back into the cushion, my breath caught in my throat. My fingers found their way through his hair as a soft moan left my lips. He switched sides, kissing, nipping around every inch. Soft, suckling kisses were planted down my stomach and around my hips.

He placed his hands at the sides of my waist, holding me delicately and caressing his long thick digits up over my waist, grasping at the natural curves of my slim figure. I inhaled a deep breath through my nose, and exhaled through my mouth as I watched his head move down between my legs. His lips grazed over the folds practically passing them all together. Fucking tease. I arched my back, breathing out a soft moan. Soft kisses continued over my inner thighs and I felt my insides warming, pleasure circulating through my veins.

He made his way back up over my body with a needy urgency and held himself over me with one arm, cupping my face before he planted a gentle kiss to my lips once more. Our lips danced against each other's in a sweet synchrony as he positioned himself over me. His penis pressed past my entrance, his hips pivoting against mine until I felt him deep inside of me. I gasped out in soft moans, his motions slow, sweet, and satisfyingly hard.

He wrapped me in his arms. He was not only protecting me physically, he was doing it emotionally as he made love to me. Something shifted from past intimate encounters. I felt like I was the most important person in his life and I had inevitably begun to fall for him. These sacred acts of lovemaking only intensified my feelings toward him. He broke down walls I placed up when Santino intruded.

My problems fell away flawlessly at the seams. I let him in because his entire aura felt different from anyone else I had met in my short seventeen years. His avid emotions surged against my lips and soared down into my soul. He made the worries of my home life and the decisions I'd made feel justified, and if I was wrong for feeling that way… I didn't want to be right.

Christopher

The following morning, I fluttered my eyes open to the beautiful Lorelai curled up against my chest, sleeping peacefully. The first thought that entered my mind was the night before. We spent hours outside on the deck making sweet love to each other. My want to protect her from the life she lived at home grew tenfold in such a short time. Finding out the reason behind why sweet Lorelai was so independent didn't settle right with me; and while I couldn't legally do a damn thing about it now, I would be there for her however she needed me, day or night. I was going to make sure she knew just how serious I was before we parted ways this morning.

She stirred and snuggled closer to me, pressing her pink lips against my chest. "Mmm…you awake, handsome?"

I smiled. "Yes." I spoke quietly, running my fingers through her hair. "How'd you sleep?"

"Good. I don't think I moved all night." She looked up at me with sleepy eyes.

I smiled at her, sweeping part of her hair behind her ear. "Happy to hear it, beautiful."

She smiled and leaned up pressing her lips against mine in a sweet kiss. I ran my fingers through her hair and returned the gentle kiss, pulling her in close and wrapping my arm around her slim figure, placing a hand at the small of her back.

She smiled against my lips. "Mmm…" She broke the kiss, leaning her forehead against mine. "As much as I want to lie here and kiss those perfect lips. Time is of the essence."

I groaned. "Baby. Do we have to?"

She looked up at me, her facial features remaining gentle. "I want to take you somewhere before you have to go home, babe."

I groaned. The idea of leaving this warm bed was less than thrilling. "But it's warm here."

She rolled her eyes. "Would it help if I made you a coffee to go, Mr. Grumpy Pants?"

"I'm not grumpy." I scowled and furrowed my eyebrows.

She pecked my lips. "What if I promised it will be more than worth all your whining?"

I gasped quietly. "I'm not whining." I sat up with her and placed a hand on her cheek. "But staying here with this view sounds a lot more appealing," I said, looking her naked body up and down.

She smiled. "Yeah? Well, that just guarantees me more time with you later, right?" She winked and grabbed the sheet and escaped off the bed before I could object.

I left first, and walked down to the parking lot with her car keys. Pulling out of the parking spot, I stopped at the curb and took my place in the passenger seat while I waited.

She came down the walkway, stepping into the car. "Before we go. I need you to shut your eyes."

I glared at her playfully and did as she asked. A moment later, I felt a cloth being wrapped around my eyes. "What on Earth are you doing?" I said, and made sure she knew I was less than thrilled when I crossed my arms.

"Don't worry about it, babe. Just, don't take that off. 'Kay?" She was way too chipper for her own damn good.

I grumbled and sat with my arms crossed as she took off. The drive was shorter than I expected through the quiet roads. The quaint calmness north of the big city was a change of atmosphere; but I was adjusting without complaint, regardless of the dark mystery of what lay behind the Black Diamond Club archways, and the same group of men I saw walking in suits several times in the days we had been here.

My thoughts were broken up when the car stopped, and she turned the engine off. She opened her door and exited the car without a word before coming around and opening the passenger side door.

She reached for my hand, guiding me out of the car before we walked a short distance. The wind was cold and had picked up a little as she guided me down the path and up some stairs.

We stopped and she took both my hands in hers. "Are you ready to see where we are?" She spoke against my ear.

"Yes. Would you take the bandanna off already?"

"You really need a coffee IV in the morning…" she grumbled, taking her sweet time untying the cloth material.

She pulled it away, leaned into my ear and whispered, "Open your eyes."

I took a moment before opening my eyes, and took in the view of the bright pink and orange colors coming up in the sky behind the mountains reflecting on the bay, and then my eyes focused on the bright golden light shimmering off the infamous Golden Gate Bridge. We stood on the side of a mountain taking in the beauty laid out before us as the day started. When the beauty of it all set in, I looked beside me and saw who stood beside me as I linked my fingers through hers and flashed a gentle smile, pulling her into my arms. We stood facing each other for a frozen moment in time. Keeping my hand in hers, she turned around, pulling my arms around her one at a time. We stood looking out at the view before us in silence and it was perfect.

The bright rays from the sun reflected against her face. A smile curved over my lips as I laid my head against hers. Every emotion fell away as we fell further into this serene moment. I hadn't had the chance to set my eyes on the Golden Gate from this kind of view yet. Pondering over the time I'd been here, I realized that she jumped in with two feet right beside me from the beginning.

Caressing a hand up over her waist to her arm, I placed a hand against her cheek, moved her head gently to look her in the eyes. "This is incredible." I paused. "Thank you for bringing me here…"

She smiled softly. "I thought you might enjoy it. It's one of my favorite places in Marin County. I do some of my best thinking up here."

I smiled back at her. "You have a strong head on your shoulders, Lor. You're smart, kind, beautiful, compassionate, and mature. Most importantly, you may not know what you want, but you know what you don't want."

I felt courageous, bold, like no one or nothing would stop us from here on out, no matter what. "Would you…be my girlfriend?"

Her smile widened up to her eyes. "I would be honored to be your girlfriend, Mr. Montgomery."

I chuckled and leaned in slowly as the sun peeked further over the horizon; and my lips clashed against hers in a deep, slow passionate kiss.

Shine in My World, Montgomery!

Lorelai

WHEN THE KISS broke, we stood holding one another until the sun began to warm the air. I looked up at him. "Your parents… they're probably wondering where you're at."

He sighed. "That should be fun to explain… staying out all night. Maybe I'll get lucky and they'll be asleep."

"Maybe?" I turned to take my camera out and quickly set up the pod stand. "Let's get some pictures and then we can head back?"

He looked at the hefty DSLR camera equipment. "You like photography?"

I smiled at him. "It's one reason why I prefer that my parents don't keep track of me all the time. I'm able to get out and around to take photographs of the area. When I have a collection, I take them up to the boardwalk and set up shop to make my own money."

He smiled. "You should show me your work sometime. Maybe I'll buy a photo off of you…" He paused. "What else do you like to do for fun?"

"Hmmm…I've gotten really good at applying makeup and styling hair from all the black-tie events my family hosts."

He smiled. "You're just a jack of all trades, aren't you?"

I giggled softly. "Uh huh. I know how to cook, too. I learned from Armani and Luci over the years. Then they realized I was better than they were and would take advantage of it." She shook her head before focusing on the camera. "Okay, we're all set. Ready?" I walked toward him with the remote and smiled as he pulled me into his arms closely before the camera flashed.

We continued to take a few more shots for good measure. I snapped one of just him in front of the bridge for the first time. I snickered as he stuck his hands in his pockets trying to be the cool man on campus.

"Any other requests, Montgomery?"

"As a matter of fact, yes. Can you set up the timer again?"

I looked at him, refocusing the lens and stepped over to him. Without saying a word, he brought me in slowly with both arms, pressing his lips to mine in a slow sensual kiss. He smiled against my lips after the first couple of shots went off and broke the kiss, looking up. When I looked back into his eyes, his astoundingly handsome features struck me a bit deeper and all I could think was how my luck had changed so drastically since summer arrived, and I suddenly questioned when it would run out.

Arriving back to the club, I dreaded saying goodbye to him. I leaned against his arm lying across the front seat, placing a hand on his chest. "Let's not say goodbye."

He looked back at me, "What would you suggest then? Adios? Or… what's goodbye in Italian?"

"Goodbye in Italian is Addio." I pushed my fingers through the back of his hair, a smirk rising over my lips. "I was going to suggest 'see you later.'"

He tilted his head, studying my face before he spoke. "I think I could get on board with that. Could get creative with it, too. Speaking of which, are you free tonight?"

"For you? Always. Why?"

"I was thinking we could have a picnic on the beach for dinner."

"Just let me know what time. I'll be there."

"How about seven?"

I smiled. This boy. He really knew how to keep me on my toes. I watched as he left the car and walked around to my side. I rolled the window down and met him for a quick, gentle kiss. He pulled away and smiled as he walked backwards. "I'll be seeing you."

I waited until he was out of sight and laid my head on the back of the seat. Really? Where had he come from and why had he taken such a deep interest in me? I was the yacht club owner's daughter, a mob boss's daughter. The itch of the healing burn and tattoo were ever present reminders. Of course, he didn't know that, but it was only a matter of time.

Hitting the cool air of the early morning, I walked briskly back toward home. Walking out of the elevator on the top floor, I looked out the window taking in the view of the mountains beyond the Bay, a million-dollar view to match my million-watt smile and feels. I was a taken woman.

Chris Montgomery had my entire heart and I wished I could shout it to the rooftops and let all of Sausalito and San Francisco hear it!

Walking through the dark penthouse, the Castillo house was calm and quiet, just the way I liked it, especially for all the sneaking out we would have to do soon.

"Marie!" I whisper-yelled. "Marie! Wake up!"

She grunted, opening one eye to look at me. "What time is it, you bloody fool?"

"It's time to wake up and smell the coffee grounds! Let's go!" I pulled her out of bed in her pajamas, and we disappeared into the early morning cool air.

I stood behind her and helped guide her down the boardwalk to Cakes and Pies. "This better be important, L. Castillo!"

"Oh, trust me, it is!"

She grumbled all the way down the docks until we arrived to Cakes and Pies. I sat her down in the kitchen area and brought her a cup of coffee and a gallon of ice cream with a spoon. "Sip the hot deliciousness!"

She glared at me. "You are way too chipper. What did Montgomery do to make you swoon this time?" She opened the carton of ice cream and stuck the spoon in.

I giggled. "Marie." I paused. "I…I think I'm in love."

"It's only been a week! Don't get ahead of yourself! What if this move doesn't work out for his family?"

I grabbed the pile of love letters Christopher sent me multiple times on a daily basis. Allowing her to read them was a sacred act.

She picked them up one at a time and started reading through them, tears flowing down her cheeks, a sob left her lips. "You think? You think you're in love?" She grasped the tissue box and blew her nose, her eyes red and puffy. "Is this a man or a boy? Are you sure he's not lying about his age? He sounds like he's a geriatric in love with his wife of fifty years!"

I giggled. "He's very mature for his age, but doesn't act as old as you think. He has his moments, though. He's a hopeless romantic. He can be very dirty and a huge tease when he wants to be; but at the end of the day, what matters is that he cares about me and takes care of me. We have a mutual understanding of what a relationship should and shouldn't be. He gets me, Marie."

"Wait! Slow down. Let me ask you this. Have the 'I'm going to hang out with Marie on Cakes and Pies' excuses worked?"

All of my facial features dropped, and I sipped my own coffee. "They haven't suspected a thing. I gave him a walkie talkie from the club, and that's how we've been communicating."

She crossed her arms. "How long do you think you can go on sneaking around?"

"We don't turn eighteen until after school lets out next year. We're literally one day apart. His birthday is on June 25th."

She rose an eyebrow and sat back in the booth. "Seriously? Maybe you two are meant to be."

"Speaking of which, we went down to Battery Spencer this morning to watch the sunrise."

"Yeah, how'd that go?"

"Really good. He…um, he asked me to be his girlfriend."

Digging her spoon into the ice cream, she pushed a mouthful in and pulled the spoon out. "Shut up! What did you say?"

"I said yes. We took pictures with the camera my parents bought me for Christmas last year. Marie, the time we've spent together compares to lying naked on silk sheets. It's always guaranteed to feel refreshing and intimate with that man."

Marie giggled. "Sounds kinky, Lor."

I bit my lower lip in a moment of weakness. "You have no idea. He wants to go down to the beach tonight for a picnic."

"Daw! Lor, he's really into you. You better keep him on a short leash and not let him stray."

"We've been spending our nights at vacant boat houses. Even though he has no issues in the pleasuring department, these last couple of nights he's been making me swoon with his romantic tactics. Candles, music, lying out on lawn chairs staring up at the stars. He's been pushing for more time to see me, wanting to watch sunsets together. It's moving so fast, and I can't say no to him even if it is a risk. I've never felt this way about anyone, Marie."

She smiled brightly, moving her spoon into the ice cream. "I don't see this as your average high school sweetheart relationship. One, school isn't even in session. Two, this is a hot summer romance; but if you think it's going beyond that, you go for it."

I sighed and shook my head. "It's not like that. It's so easy with him. His playful moodiness fits my quirky personality, and he's even taken a liking to how fast I talk. Did you know wit is contagious?"

She laughed. "Yeah? I would've never thought Lorelai Castillo could pass on her wit."

I laughed. "Yeah, who would've thunk?"

"So what time is this hot date?"

"Seven p.m. sharp."

"Do you have something to wear?"

"Yeah, I brought it down here yesterday and stashed it away just in case we ended up crashing here."

"Looks like we have a girls date planned. You think we can get last minute spots up at the spa?"

I pursed my lips and stole her spoon, helping myself to a heaping scoop of ice cream and slipped it into my mouth. "Mmm…Mhm!" She laughed, which caused me to giggle uncontrollably.

"Definitely!" I said with a mouth full of the melted creamy goodness. She shook her head at me. "Swallow!"

I covered my mouth staring at her with narrowed eyes, before I managed to save myself from spewing the sweet cream everywhere. "I hate you with a burning passion."

She laughed. "I love you too! Next time, I'll groan. Come on! Let's go indulge in some luxury relaxation time! Since you two are official, does that mean I get to finally meet this sweet Prince Charming?"

I sighed. "I'm not sure it's safe, at least not right now."

She nodded. "Right, I understand."

"But, I have something for you in case one of our parents decides to question my excuses."

"What is it?"

I pulled a radio box out and set it down in front of her. "The best kept secret on how to keep in touch."

I knew when Marie gave me her word that she would keep my secret safe. I stood up and snatched the ice cream and placed it back in its proper place. Grabbing my keys before we made our way out and back down to the boardwalk toward the spa, we joked the entire way.

Christopher

Walking into the house late Saturday afternoon, I was hot, sweaty, and full of saw dust after preparing for Dad's first big job for the re-launch of Montgomery Construction.

"Chris? Your mom and I are going to go up to Napa and visit with Nana and Papa and stay the night. Are you coming with us?" I heard him say as I tried to escape to go shower.

I sighed. "Do I have a choice?"

"Do you really feel comfortable staying the night on your own?" he asked.

I turned around to look at him. "Yeah, Dad. I'll be fine."

"Okay, well. Your mom has the final say. Go shower."

I groaned and continued upstairs to go clean up. I needed to convince them that I would be fine on my own.

Walking downstairs in khaki shorts and a tank top, I went to sit on the couch where my parents resided.

Mom looked at me staying quiet for a moment. "Your father tells me you want to stay home overnight while we go to Napa?"

"Is that okay?" I decided not to beat around the bush. She was going to agree, or there would be an argument.

She sighed. "I don't know, Chris. Why don't you want to come along?"

My parents and I were too close for me to lie, and besides that, I didn't want to lie. I knew if I told them the real reason that staying home wouldn't be an option. "I'm tired. I would rather cook something quick here at home and go to bed early."

She looked to my dad, and he nodded. "We trust you, Christopher. I'll leave my cell phone here for you to utilize and keep in touch."

I nodded. "Okay. Thank you." I played the tired act, when really my stomach was jumping into my throat for plans with Lorelai to pan out perfectly for tonight. I stood up and walked back up the stairs to my bedroom, quietly shutting the door to go prepare my clothes for the evening.

Within the hour my parents had left, the picnic basket was packed up, and I wore black slacks and a white button up collared shirt keeping the first couple of buttons undone.

Grabbing the two-way radio, I turned the volume up. "Hey sweetheart. Are you about ready to go?"

Silence took over for a moment. "Hey babe. Yeah, I'm all ready to go. Where do you want to meet?"

"Kirby Cove. Should we go ahead and drive separate?"

"Probably a smart idea. I may have Marie drop me off."

Sneaking around to see each other was easier than we thought it would be with all the warnings Lorelai had given about her family, and the men and women hiding in plain sight throughout the club. We left in early morning or late-night hours and we were never stopped or followed to my knowledge. "Sounds good. I'll have my radio so just let me know when you're close."

"Okay baby. I'll see you soon."

"Hey wait. Don't leave yet. Give it about an hour, and then leave. Okay?"

She came back over the radio, sobbing playfully. "Christopher! I've been waiting all day!"

I chuckled. "I know. It'll be worth it. Promise. Bring your walkie and let me know when you've arrived."

An hour later, a blanket lay on the sand with the picnic basket and a bouquet of red and white roses sitting next to it. Four tiki torches were dug deep into the sand and the fire blew lightly with the breeze coming off the bay. I turned on the radio and found soft tunes. Standing barefoot with my black slacks rolled up, I waited for my love to arrive with the radio in my pocket.

The scratching static sounded off. "The Princess has landed. I'm heading down."

I smiled at the sound of her voice, pulling the radio toward my mouth. "Okay. I'm waiting, beautiful."

A few moments later, I saw her come down the hill. Her hair was in wavy curls, and she wore a black, knee length dress. God damn. She looked more beautiful with every day that passed, I couldn't get enough.

She walked down to where I stood on the shore with her roses in hand. I pulled her into my arms as soon as she was close enough, cupping her cheeks as I planted a gentle kiss to her lips.

She wrapped her arms around my neck as I lifted her off her feet and twirled her around, a soft giggle leaving her lips as I carried her back to the blanket and set her down.

Breaking the kiss, I locked my eyes on hers. "I missed you."

"Mm…I missed you, boyfriend." She placed her hand on my freshly shaven cheeks. "You shaved…"

I chuckled. "I thought I'd clean up for our date."

She smiled as I held up the roses. "What's this?"

"These are for you. A beautiful arrangement of roses, for an even more beautiful princess."

She looked around at the set up and leaned in to smell the roses before she locked her eyes on mine. "This is so romantic, Christopher. I love it."

I pecked her lips. "I did all of this with your reaction in mind. Let's sit down and eat, yeah?"

She smiled from ear to ear and planted a deep passionate kiss against my lips. Returning the kiss, I pulled her close, running each of my hands through her hair.

Pulling away from the kiss slowly, I kissed her nose before we sat. I pulled her between my legs. I watched as she admired her roses, becoming entranced in the view. She didn't just look exquisitely beautiful tonight. Her kind heart and passionate, loving soul shined through, and I paused just to watch her for a moment.

The sandwiches and Mom's homemade egg salad I packed were satisfying. When we finished, I wrapped my arms around her. "Are you full?"

"Yes, thank you. That was really good."

I smiled, kissed her cheek and placed the leftovers in the basket watching her for a few minutes as she relaxed back. I wrapped an arm around her and pulled her in close.

As the sun began to set sometime later, I kissed her shoulder and moved my lips to her ear. I whispered, "Miss Castillo, you look beautiful tonight."

She smiled and turned to look back toward me. "Thank you. You clean up very nice yourself, Mr. Montgomery."

I winked at her. "Hmmm… Would you like to dance with me?"

She bit her lower lip. "Right now?"

"Yes," I whispered back.

She turned to look back at me, a smitten smile crossing her lips. "I'd be honored to."

Helping her to her feet, I wrapped an arm around her back, took her hand and began to sway. She wrapped an arm around my waist and moved naturally to the slow motion, closing her eyes and laying her head against my chest. I smiled, pressing a kiss to her forehead, and left my lips there for a moment. Opening my eyes, I lifted my head, rubbing my hand up and down her back as her hair blew in the light breeze. I would forever remember this moment as a time I slipped further into love with this young woman. Her beauty was beyond words, her soul passionate, and so bright that it blocked out the darkness. She allowed me to take care of her, she opened her world to me and I promised myself right then and there that I wouldn't let go without one hell of a fight.

Eleven

Reality Check

Lorelai

Fall

MY EYES FLUTTERED open as I laid snuggled into Christopher after we stashed ourselves away in the cabin on Cakes and Pies, our naked bodies entangled in a sheet. I sat up on my elbow and looked down at the newcomer that had become my boyfriend, and I couldn't stop myself from smiling. He looked so damn peaceful when he was sleeping. I leaned down and pressed my lips to his forehead, moving loose strands of my hair behind my ear as I laid my head against his chest and listened to the steady beat of his heart against my ear. I inhaled a deep breath of his natural cedar-wood scent and smiled.

My eyes diverted to the pictures we took over the summer from hikes in the Muir Woods to walks down to the beach. While most of our time was spent together at night, I managed to sneak away from the yacht club for a few more daytime adventures. The picture of us under the Redwood tree, taken during one of our first official dates, brought back memories of time well spent. We went running in the woods and over the mountain before we raced into the water on the beach and got into a playful water fight, where we shared another perfect kiss. The third picture I managed to print was one of us in front of the Golden Gate around the time Mr. Montgomery re-launched the Montgomery Construction company with the help of Hodgins Incorporated, an up and coming marketing firm. Billboards rose in the city, radio ads ran, and I even saw advertisements and promotional offers in the Gold Clipper. The jobs were rolling in; and from what Christopher had told me over the last few weeks, they were swamped the entire summer. Jobs were being booked a year in advance with no space in-between.

My eyes diverted to the second shelf down that was eye-level with the bed. We were silhouettes in the sunset on Cakes and Pies locking lips as the sun set from behind. From the first time Christopher pressed his lips to mine in that sweet kiss after the ride on Cakes and Pies, I was 'Hooked on Montgomery'.

I heard a low grunt and looked up at him and smiled. "Well, good morning there, sleepyhead."

He looked at me with one eye open and stretched before his other sleepy eye opened. "Good morning, beautiful. What are you doing awake?"

"The sun woke me… and I was admiring our pictures."

"I suppose it pays off that you are a woman of many talents."

I smiled. "I will admit that the cooking, cleaning, beauty obsession, and photography hobbies do have their perks. Would you like some coffee?"

"You should add sailor onto that list, captain." He chuckled. "When do I say no to coffee, love?"

I giggled and leaned up pressing my lips to his gently. He returned the kiss more than willingly. "This is true. I'm lucky if I get a grumbled good morning out of you if the coffee isn't made," I said as I broke away and hovered over him and took the sheet with me to go make our coffee.

Before I could get away, a strong tug pulled me back, and two strong arms wrapped around my waist. "If you take the sheet, I'll be cold," he whined.

I laughed and leaned against him. "You poor thing. What would you like me to do?"

He groaned. "Don't move."

"If you want your coffee, I have too." Reaching I grabbed the blanket that was kicked to the bottom of the bed and pulled it over him. "Here…" I attempted to slip from his arms only to find myself stuck once more. "Christopher!"

He laughed. "Fine, fine. Go. But, you're mine later."

Looking down at him, I bit my lower lip. "Is that a threat?"

"Indeed, it is. The biggest threat. Now go, before I throw you back down on the bed and take what's rightfully mine."

I rolled my eyes, trying to hide a smirk. "You're insane, you know this right?"

He pulled the blanket over and buried himself into it. "Insane? No... No, I'm just cold and my girlfriend won't cuddle with me."

"I'll make it up to you later…" I said as I stood and made my way out while he grunted and grumbled in anger.

A few minutes later, I was dressed and sat out on the deck sipping the hot caffeine waiting for grumpy pants to join me. I found a dock far enough out of sight where I knew my family wouldn't come looking for me. As I brought the coffee cup to my lips, a fishing charter passed by on the bay making its way up to the marina at the club before I saw Chris stepping out of the cabin.

He grumbled as the sun hit his eyes and pulled his sunglasses on. "So, what's the plan for today?"

"Well, it's Saturday. I'm not working, but I should probably go check in with the family. I should be free after that."

He sipped his coffee. "I think we're supposed to be going to Napa for the weekend."

I lowered my bottom lip. "Really? That's so far away, babe."

"I know. I might opt out and stay home."

I rose an eyebrow at him. "You think they would allow it?"

"It wouldn't be the first time they've allowed it. Besides, I'm not even sure we're going."

I nodded and sipped my coffee as we sat in a comfortable silence watching the boats float out into the bay. I was ready to accept the possibility of his absence when I heard an earth-shattering scream come from the main boardwalk. I stood and peaked around the cabin into the distance and a crowd of people gathered around the fishing charter that just pulled in.

"Uh-oh. I smell trouble. I should go see what's going on."

He furrowed his eyebrows. "Lor…" I looked at him with gentle eyes. "Be careful."

I made my way toward him and sat on his lap, placing both hands on his cheeks and brushing my thumb against the stubble on his cheeks. "I will." I pecked his lips and held onto the gentle kiss he returned.

He broke it, enclosing his arms around me. "Are you coming back?"

"I-I'm not sure; but if I'm not back in an hour, I'll have my walkie."

I pecked his lips, while holding onto hope that my promise would be enough to keep his worried nature at bay before taking off toward the mainland. Walking down the docks, I saw the people of my community emerging from the cabins of their homes looking to one another and around their surroundings trying to figure out what was going on.

My heart raced, feeling as though it would burst through my chest as I neared the crowds of people on the boardwalk.

"Lorelai?" Our former housekeeper, Amanda Jo, emerged from the crowd and grabbed onto my arm. "What is going on?"

I swallowed a hard lump as I looked to her. "I'm not sure. I'm on my way to find out."

"I'm coming with you." The look on her face told me not to question her.

I turned back to face the crowd, squeezing and pushing my way through, trying not to let go of Amanda Jo's hand on my way through.

Everyone in the community knew that my family operated a commercial fishing business. We were the largest in the area and the reason San Francisco and its surrounding areas still had successful Fish Markets.

As we cleared the crowd, I ducked under the yellow caution tape. Flashing lights from police cruisers and an ambulance shone across the boardwalk. Papino did not handle law enforcement he didn't know well. What the hell was going on? I looked around for familiar faces and saw Marie run between my parents and Luciana towards me. I wrapped my arms around her and pulled her close as I stared at my parents and Luci who were in obvious distress.

"Marie?" My voice trailed off. "What's going on?"

She wrapped her arms around me tight before she stepped back and looked at me. She opened her mouth as if to speak, but heart wrenching sobs left her lips instead.

I gathered her in my arms and looked around desperately trying to determine the cause of her anguish. Everyone seemed to be staring at a net of fish anchored in the air. Squinting my eyes, I struggled to understand what I was seeing. I gasped loudly and looked at Marie and back to the net of fish.

Armani… it was my brother! Oh god! H-how?

Tears welled in my eyes as I took in the condition my brother was in. He was covered in blood. His clothes ripped and soaking wet. Without thinking, I let go of Marie and walked to the edge of the boardwalk to get a better look. Son of a bitch! Some coward murdered my brother and then put him in a net full of fish.

A hand touched my shoulder and I turned around to meet eyes with Luciana. "Don't fucking touch me!" I snapped.

"Luci…what's…" I looked up at the net of fish that was being held by the anchor and inside was a lifeless bloody body.

I clasped my hands over my mouth, while tears sprung to my eyes and I looked at Luci and then my mother. I felt an arm wrap around me leading me to the family yacht, speculative whispers surrounded me as we made our way through the crowd of people.

I clasped my hands over my mouth as tears clouded my vision and fell freely down my cheeks. I felt an arm wrap around me and someone led me toward the family yacht while speculative whispers surrounded us.

My father passed by on a mission to go investigate, and I stopped, watching until he disappeared into the crowd of gawking strangers.

"Don't stop or say a word. Just keep walking," Luci snapped quietly as she pushed me along.

Turning around, I saw Marie in tow as Mother stepped in on the other side of me to guide us away from the scene. As we made it onto the yacht, I pulled away from them. "What the hell is going on?"

Luci couldn't make eye contact and mother's eyes were filled with tears as she stared off aimlessly. "We don't know for sure, but your brother has been missing for a week now. We think he crossed into enemy lines."

I furrowed my brows. "W-why would he do that?" I trembled as I felt my heart beating in my ears.

"From what we know? Santino had plans for you, Lorelai. Your brother was trying to chase him off and deter him from getting near the yacht club."

I swallowed the lump in my throat. I couldn't believe what I was hearing. "What kind of plans?" I sobbed.

"The kind of plans that may not give you a choice but to step up and take a role in the family business, Lorelai!" Luci snapped. "You need to learn to defend yourself."

I felt empty and helpless. "Who the hell are you to tell me what to do, Luciana? I can make my own damn decisions on what I want to do in my life. Mama knows! Tell her, Mama." The thick inherited Italian accent climbed its way through the anger.

"Running to Mommy isn't going to bring our damn brother back, Lorelai. Don't you get it? You're a Castillo, fear doesn't exist in our blood. Start acting like you belong!" She paced the room and eyed me with red fury as if I was the reason that Armani crossed into enemy lines.

"Fuck you, Luciana!" I crossed my arms and turned to walk out when my father stepped through the door with his undercover security guards.

Footsteps clicked toward me. I turned when my father stepped in and grabbed Luci by the arm as she ran toward me. "Enough!" He raised his voice. "We have bigger issues on our hands. Amelia, perhaps we should have a word in private."

I sat down in a chair in the corner of the room and stared off out the window as the coroner moved in to remove the body from the scene. Tears filled my eyes as I realized that my brother died not only at the hands of our family business, but at the hands of the enemy. My parents may not have approved or liked the choices I was about to make, but they wouldn't be the only ones spreading truth today.

Papino returned a moment later. "Lorelai..?" He waited for me to control myself. I wiped my tears away on the sleeve of my shirt and sniffled. In his eyes, crying was a weakness.

When I had my emotions under control, he continued. "After we give your brother a proper service, your mother and I have decided that we may not have a choice but to pack up and move the Black Diamond Club out of Sausalito, for good." I furrowed my brows and stood up. "I'm not leaving."

"Excuse me, young lady?" Papino snapped.

Tears welled in my eyes as I tried as hard as I could to swallow them. "I said I'm not leaving. I'll file for emancipation if I have to."

The vein in his forehead popped. Shit. He was not happy. "What is this about? Are you seeing that boy again, Lorelai?"

I stood and spoke firmly. "His name is Christopher, and I love him, Daddy!" Spilling the beans about my relationship with Christopher could've been my biggest mistake; but in that moment, I didn't give a damn.

"You are a child! You don't even know what love is!" he yelled.

I shook my head and stood up to leave. Stopping just before exit, I looked over my shoulder at the furrowed eyebrows in my parents faces. "Luci was right about one thing. Fear doesn't exist in Castillo blood, and I won't allow you to tell me who I can and cannot love." Turning around, I stormed out from their line of sight without giving it a second thought.

Twelve

Darkened Pathways

AFTER LORELAI HOPPED off the vessel and took off, my mental state collapsed in silence. The earth-shattering scream echoed around the bay; and while we couldn't see anything, a voice in the back of my head told me it couldn't have been anything good. I finished the coffee in my cup and disappeared back into the cabin, where I cleaned myself up before I locked up and took my set of keys to the boat and left.

As I made a close descent to home, I stopped short as I saw my parents out on their routine morning walk.

"Christopher, thank God," Mom said. "We were just out looking for you."

"Sorry, Mom. I was out for an early morning walk," I lied.

Without another word spoken, Mother came to my side and placed a hand on my back and silently led the way back home.

As we entered our home and the door shut, Dad spoke as I went to make my way upstairs. "Christopher? Just a minute, your mother and I need to talk to you."

The voice in my head disappeared and reappeared as a sinking feeling in my stomach and a lump in my throat. I didn't like the sound of this one bit.

"Okay…" I turned and came back to the kitchen and sat on a chair by the island. "What is it?"

"Christopher, people talk around here. We know you've been seeing the Castillo girl and we thought we were okay with it, but red flags from the family that own this place have been going up all over this place for weeks now!"

I sighed in distress and crossed my arms. Panic rose as I realized that they had more of a clue on the suspicious activity that took place around here.

"Did you happen to pass by the boardwalk on your walk this morning?"

"No, I didn't. I stayed around the docks," I spoke quietly.

"Armani Castillo Jr. is dead, Christopher. His body was found in a net full of fish."

I swallowed hard and stared off as the shocking disbelief started to settle in. This was going to destroy Lorelai. "I…I…I don't know what to say, but I need to go to her."

Mom stepped up next to my father and grabbed my shoulders giving me a hard shake. "She's dangerous, Christopher! Being involved with her could have you killed!" She was nearly hysterical.

I shook my head. I was angry with both of my parents at this point. "You can't tell me who I can or cannot love!" I snapped.

"Christopher!" Mom scolded.

"No, Mom! I don't need your reasons or your rules. I love Lorelai. If her brother was murdered, she's going to need me! I will take care of her and myself without your help or approval!" I stormed off and slammed the door once I reached my room. Retrieving a suitcase from my closet, I threw it on the bed and started packing my clothes and belongings. I would leave the house and run away while they were sleeping. She'd be at Cakes and Pies when I went there tonight. She had to be.

Later that night, I paced the floor in my room quietly waiting for my parents to go to bed. It was after midnight before I grabbed my suitcase from the closet and tiptoed down the stairs and slipped out the front door after making sure it was locked. I carried the suitcase until I knew I was far enough away to roll it against the wooden docks.

I hated going against my parents' rules, but this was one area in my life that I wouldn't budge against. I loved Lorelai, and I needed to see her now more than ever. As I approached the main boardwalk, I looked around and the club was quiet. Almost too quiet. I made my way down to the dock where I last left Cakes and Pies hoping that I would find her where I left her.

Upon my arrival, I placed my suitcase down on the vessel and stepped on. There was no sign of Lorelai, and I could only hope she was inside the cabin. Unlocking the door, I walked in and set my bag to the side.

"Lorelai?" I called out.

No response came, but there was a long light slivered against the floor from the back of the vessel. Taking a deep breath, I moved through the main living space and the kitchen toward the bedroom and bathroom.

I walked in silence and saw no one in sight. Opening the bathroom door, I walked in. There was a box sitting on the counter. I came to discover that it was an at home pregnancy test. My hand fell against the cold surface as I looked around to see if the test was anywhere in sight, but there was no such luck. Was I going to be a father? Did she dispose of the test and run away? Or worse? Had her family found out and decided to take care of it their way?

I closed my eyes and inhaled a deep breath and exhaled a moment later.

"Lorelai? Are you here?" I called out once more to make sure. Setting the box down, I searched the vessel and she was nowhere to be found.

"Son of a bitch!" I yelled, grabbing the radio off of my belt. "Lorelai? Lorelai, if you can hear me, please respond with your location."

I paced the living room area of the cabin, a million other scenarios running through my mind. She normally didn't leave the area without Cakes and Pies. Where could she be? At home? It was a possibility if her brother was murdered, maybe she was on lock down and she couldn't escape. Or maybe her parents confiscated the radio and forced her to tell them why she had it.

Making an exit, I jumped back to the dock and made my way back up to the boardwalk. My eyes scanned for her in the dark night. I was more than halfway down the boardwalk minutes later and she was nowhere to be found.

Standing in the middle of the boardwalk under a street lamp, darkness clouded my sight when a cloth bag fell over my head and I felt two large hands grip each of my wrists forcing me to walk. From the feel of their hands, I was sure it was two burly men.

"Don't say a fucking word, Montgomery, and we might consider not killing you." This had to be the work of her father. I was given one warning, and one warning only.

A few minutes later, a firm hand grasped the back of my neck and I was thrown down to the ground of wooden panels.

"On your knees, bitch." Another man yelled before fingers grasped at the back of my hair and pulled me into a kneeling position. Tight ropes were wrapped around my wrists. The men pulled me to my feet and forced me to continue walking.

We walked so far that I lost track of the direction we were headed. We only stopped upon entering a cold room, and I was shoved roughly into a chair where they tied my wrists and ankles to the arms and legs to a chair. This was it, I thought. I would leave here a dead man; they were going to wrap me up, tape my mouth shut and tie bricks to my ankles. I would sink to the bottom of the bay of Fog City, never to be seen again. If this was for pursuing my relationship with Lorelai, I wouldn't have one regret.

A pinching needle pierced my bicep, and I could not contain the low groan that left my throat as I slowly fell back into the chair. My eyelids became heavy. Did they sedate me? I felt myself slipping into an unconscious state and realized that I did have one regret; I shouldn't have allowed Lorelai to leave on her own earlier that morning. Now I would disappear into thin air, and I couldn't make the call on whether I would see her again or not. My heart broke, not just over Lorelai, but for her. If I made it out of this, there would be no questions. I would protect her at all costs.

I heard footsteps disappearing off into the distance. Was I alone? Would I live to see the woman I'd fallen head over heels with that could be carrying my child? I couldn't be certain of anything at this point.

"Mr. Castillo, we did as you asked. How would you like to proceed?" I heard a voice say sometime later.

I couldn't be sure how much time had passed by, but the ropes felt like they were cutting off circulation to my blood supply in my wrists and ankles.

Footsteps came closer and I felt eyes zooming in on me. The material over my head slid off and I locked eyes with Mr. Castillo. He leaned down to eye level and narrowed his dark, beady eyes. "I'm not certain yet. Maybe if we keep him here, he'll get it embedded into his head to stay away from my daughter. What do you think, Mr. Montgomery?" His voice was as smooth as it was cunning. He stood back up and circled around me. When I didn't answer, he proceeded to walk to a red toolbox and pulled out a knife. "Maybe you need a proper lesson on what it means to stay away from my daughter."

It was a risk to talk, let alone speak my truth; but if he wanted me dead, there was not a damn thing I could do or say to change his mind. "With all due respect, sir. I would never hurt your daughter. I...I love her and all I want is to take care of her."

He stayed silent and looked toward the doorway. "Santino, give us a moment. Would you?"

The young man disappeared and Mr. Castillo circled around the chair he sat me in, placed the blade under my chin tipping my head back. He wore a pristine suit, his arms covered. Closing my eyes, my mind flashed back to the bandages around Lorelai's forearms. Thinking back on what was under them, the vision of the flocking birds came to mind. I spent so many mornings watching her sleep, studying how peaceful she looked. What were the birds a sign of?

Come on, Chris, think. The marks looked like fresh scars on her arm, but they were in the same exact spot on the opposite arm. She fled her father's flock. She was a free bird. This was why she was isolated. This is why she needed me. She wanted more in life than what her family could offer.

"You were warned, Montgomery." His tone came out in a harsh whisper before he drew the blade down the front of my cheek. The sharpest point of the knife sliced through the skin causing a warm drip of liquid to trickle down like a teardrop.

Squeezing my eyes shut, a dull pain from my fingernails dug into the bottom of the wooden arm rests. Inhaling a sharp breath, I squeezed my eyes shut doing my best not to scream through the excruciating pain. Screaming would show weakness, and that was the last thing I needed.

"Do you know why you're here?" he asked a moment later, flipping the knife in the air, catching the weapon by the handle before he looked in my direction.

Looking away, I stared off and took in my surroundings. This looked like the bottom of an industrial vessel. The temperature as cold as a refrigerator… perhaps this is where he kept his victims that were no longer breathing. The walls were painted white, and the only visible pass through to leave was up a ladder and through a circular hole in the ceiling.

A firm hand grabbed my chin and pulled it up. I looked into the black beady eyes. His hair gray, a shaven-down beard on his face, and black suit sat fitted to his form. He looked like a professional business man, working in an organized crime syndicate. Thinking back to the freedom I had before I landed here, I remembered the mysterious men and women walking through the club in suits. They were a part of his cult. A homicidal smirk fell over his face; and while I should have been scared of this man, I rolled my eyes. Nothing or no one would steer me away from the love I had for Lorelai, not even the fear of death.

"Answer me, dammit!" he growled.

I snapped out of my thoughts. "Yeah, I do and you're not going to like what I have to say. You want me to stay away from Lorelai, and

I'm not afraid to let you know that it's never going to happen."

The grip on my chin tightened as he clicked his tongue. "Do you realize how easy it would be for me to snap your neck and make you disappear before the sun comes up?"

"With all due respect, sir? I do, but you wouldn't do that."

He leaned down and narrowed his beady eyes on me. "How can you be so sure?" he spat.

"Because, Lorelai is your little girl. You would never do anything to hurt her." I paused. "We have that in common," I said in a dark husky tone.

The grip of his hand tightened once more as he chuckled darkly. "You think you have it all figured out, kid? Let me tell you something. You don't! You have no idea what I'm capable of, but I'm not going to go there. I'm going to give you an offer, whether you take it or not determines how this ends." He narrowed his eyes down at me before he continued. "Ten thousand dollars, cold hard cash can be yours if you agree to never see my daughter again."

I shook my head in disbelief, the anger building up inside of me. Perhaps I had no idea who or what I was dealing with; and that was why Lorelai kept me a secret from her family.

Gritting my teeth together, I rose my brow and subtly began playing with the knots in the ropes. "Sorry. That's not going to work for me."

"I see...then I'm afraid you've left me without another choice." Taking a towel from the shelf, he wiped the small streak of blood away from the blade, towering over me the blade sliced through the skin under the first slice he made a few minutes prior.

I stared off gripping the arms of the chair, attempting to turn my damn emotions off.

Squeezing my eyes shut, I desperately tried to escape the physical place I was in.

I pictured Lorelai's stature standing in front of me, placing her hands on my face like the way she had right before she kissed me. Slow and then all at once like a rain shower turning into a torrential downpour. She stood smiling from ear to ear, walking backwards through the downpour, soaked and said, "You have to catch me if you want more… Come on, Montgomery. Come get me."

A warm substance dripping against the thin material of the V-neck t-shirt I wore intercepted my thoughts. I opened my eyes back to the reality of Mr. Castillo's fun chamber.

"Santino! You're just on time. I need you to sit with Mr. Montgomery here while I run a quick errand."

A crooked smirk rose on the young man's lips. "No problem, Armani. I'm sure I could paint him a clearer picture on what Lorelai's future looks like."

"Ah…don't take it that far. I'm not sure that's a done deal quite yet. Just… keep him in line."

"You got it, boss." He took the knife from Armani before they walked out of sight. I heard beeps that sounded like buttons on a keypad, narrowing my eyes. There was another entrance and exit? Or, was the one in plain sight just an illusion?

I stared down at the floor feeling the blood trickle down my neck and onto my chest as Santino walked back in and paced back and forth in front of me. He grunted, inhaling and exhaling heavily. "Did you really think you would get away with Lorelai wrapped around your fingers and not pay a price, Montgomery?"

I sighed quietly. "She made her choice, Santino," I spoke quietly.

He jumped at me, gripping his hand around my neck and hovered over me. "Shut…your…fucking mouth. No one asked you to speak!" he yelled through gritted teeth.

I rolled my eyes, and eased my head to look away from him. There was nothing more to say, but Santino should be counting the blessings on all ten of his fingers and toes; because if I wasn't locked down, he would be the next guy that came up missing. I'd kill him with my damn bare hands and throw him into the bay and being tied to this chair wouldn't stop me.

He stepped off slowly, and before I knew it his hand gripped a tight hold against my chin. "You will only speak when you're asked to." He spoke into my ear before he stepped away and began pacing slowly back and forth.

A smug smirk tugged at his lips. "You know, I had plans for Lorelai. She just had to go and mess them all up, but she could've had the life. She wouldn't have to work and when Armani finally gets rid of you, I have a new plan for her."

My eyes followed his every footstep, fury building within me with every word he spoke. Had I not been tied down with the ropes, I would've taken him down to the ground and beat the ever-loving shit out of this man without thinking twice.

"What's this plan? Oh, I'm glad you asked." A crooked smile crossed his lips. "You see, my family works very closely with the Castillo's. The Castillo's saved our casinos by buying them out and turning them into the Black Diamond brand name in Sin City. I'll whisk Lorelai back to the city that made me a man. We'll get married by one of those Elvis impersonators and I'll give her a lush honeymoon in Italy, and then when we return, she can go to work managing an escort business. The broad running it now clearly has no idea what she's doing." He paused, pressing his lips together firmly. The more he talked, the angrier I grew. Being as subtle as possible, I started pulling at the knots in the rope once more. Fuck, they were tight.

To my disgust, he continued, "I know that Lorelai could manage matching these little sluts that work for us with the wealthy men that desire them with the cash to pay properly. She has it all between the beauty and the brains."

That did it. I pulled, tugged and struggled on the ropes trying to break myself free. "You are so goddamn lucky I can't move or you'd be a dead man!" I gritted the words through my teeth.

His head fell back in laughter. "Real funny, Montgomery. The only way you're leaving here will be under a white sheet."

I continued to pull on the ropes, I became determined to free myself. How dare he belittle the love of my life down to the leader of those prostitutes! She deserved so much better. Closing my eyes, I inhaled a deep breath, making a silent vow that I would stop at nothing to make sure she didn't end up in that situation and went back to working on the knots while Santino was too distracted silently plotting my death.

Getting lost in my thoughts, the fist coming into contact with the side of my face caught me off-guard. That brought my attempt to free myself to a halt for a moment before I struggled and used every muscle to break through the ropes. Standing up, I pulled my fist back and swung hitting the target of Santino's face with one strong hit, watching as he fell to the ground in slow motion. When I tried to make a run for it, I was pulled back with a strong hand, and felt a piece of cold metal against my head.

"Where do you think you're going?" The cold voice came from Mr. Castillo.

I stilled, and decided not to respond. I needed to be smart about my next move.

A low chuckle left his lips. "Have a seat, Montgomery! We're going to talk about the stunt you just pulled."

I fell back into the wooden chair at full force as he tied me back up twice as tight. A sharp pain traveled up my spine and into my neck.

Inhaling a sharp breath, I tried to calm myself with the gun pointed at my head. I would do as he said or die at his hand and Lorelai would be left with Santino. I dug my nails into the palm of my hand as I shook with anger from head to toe thinking about that scenario.

"Sir? With all due respect, I did defend your daughter's honor."

He walked around slowly, pulling the barrel of the gun away from my head slowly. "I can see how you might think that Mr. Montgomery, but I'm not here to listen to reason. In fact, I'm ready to double what I was offering. Twenty thousand dollars, you take yourself and your parents away from here and don't look back."

I shook my head without a second thought. "Your money won't drive me away, Mr. Castillo."

He was silent as he paced back and forth slowly. Placing the safety on the gun, he sighed and disappeared for a moment.

I stared off, and swallowed silently as he came back into view with the knife in his hand once more, hovering over me from the side. The prickled pain from the knife being drawn across my cheeks hit once more.

"Do you know what happens when I get to your carotid artery?" he barked. "You bleed out. You have one hour before I make the next cut. I'll be marking twice an hour, the decision is yours, Montgomery." With that, he was gone and I was left to feel the blood trickle down my face while I stared at an unconscious Santino at my feet, dreading the moment he woke up.

Thirteen

The Time for Self-Preservation is Now!

Lorelai

"LORELAI?"

I sighed silently at the sound of my sister's voice, but didn't respond. I sat against the back of the bathroom door staring at the sink and the porcelain throne that I had met several times since I made it home a few hours ago.

"Lor…" She stood at the back of the door this time. "Please let me in?"

She had been crying, I could hear it in her voice and feel it deep within my soul. I sniffled softly, the bathroom vanity and other surroundings blurred in my vision. I couldn't talk about this. I didn't want, nor need, to talk about the fact that I was a second- or third-party reason for my brother's unforeseeable death.

I laid my head against my knees as I felt a warm streak of moisture trickling down my cheek and a soft sob fell through my lips. Trembles shook through my body limb by limb as the emotions became too damn much to hold inside. My heart had been ripped out of my chest and crushed with a sledgehammer. I swore I'd seen the blood splattered on the walls through a blurred peripheral vision.

I was cold. Freezing, actually. I looked up and saw Luci standing across from me, her curls in perfect shape, eye make-up smeared from the tears she cried, her red lipstick still perfected. Her face was paler than usual and she looked down at me before she crossed the room and sat on the floor next to me.

I felt her arms swaddle around me in a tight embrace. "Lorelai…" She barely spoke above a whisper. "You…you have to know that this is not your fault."

I shook my head. "Don't say that," I snapped quietly.

"No…Lorelai. Look at me, dammit." She pulled out of her hold on me and placed both hands on each side of my face. "You didn't force Armani to step into territories he didn't belong in. He went in at his own risk." She paused.

Staring off, I inhaled a few deep breaths. "Luci. I… I need you to do me a big sister favor." I sounded desperate, because I was.

She was silent for a moment. "Okay. What is it?"

I knew Marie had my back, but my parents would expect me to stay close to home after my brother was brutally murdered. What a fucking mess all of this was! I wanted to scream in frustration.

"I need you to cover for me. I can't stay here. I know Mama and Papino. The family will be flying in from everywhere, and I can't be around people right now. I need to find Chris. I need time away."

She eyed me carefully. I knew she didn't agree with this plan, I could hear her inner thoughts screaming silently through the furrowed eyebrows. How could I be thinking of Christopher when our brother was just murdered? The long silence present in the room filled with tension could be cut with a butter knife and it would still explode.

She took my hand holding it with both of hers. "I will cover for you under two conditions."

I straightened up my posture sitting on my knees. "Name them."

"You have to show up at Armani's funeral; and you have to promise me wherever you plan to go, that you'll stay safe."

I gave her a gentle smile and nodded. "That I can promise," I spoke above a whisper.

Her lips pressed to my temple before she looked at me. "Are you feeling okay? Your face is flushed."

I bit my lower lip. "Not really, but I'll survive." I could see the concern in her eyes.

She nodded and stood up. "I should go check in."

I stared off, quietly taking in the reality of life and death that surrounded me on this daunting late fall day. I knew what I had to do, and that my family would not approve of it; but it wasn't just about my parent's values and opinions anymore. This was my life, and I'd be damned if it ended like my brother's had.

Standing quickly, I went to my room and started packing as many clothes as I could possibly fit into my suitcase. Going back into the closet, I stood in front of the safe, turning the combination numbers until the door popped open and I grabbed the stacks of cash sitting in paper band holds. I didn't need the family business, nor to wait around here until I graduated. Hell would freeze over before I allowed them to dictate my life choices.

Once the essentials were packed, I zipped the bag closed and placed it on the floor, picked my keys and purse up off the bed, and grabbed a few coats and blankets, placing them into a trash bag for easy transfer.

Stopping at Luci's room, the door was cracked open. My sister had a niche for style and chic design. I realized then that when I agreed to walk away from the family business, it meant that I would also be leaving my family behind; and that Christopher was meant to come into my life so that I wouldn't be left alone when this time came. Walking out the front door to the building, I knew there was no turning back.

Arriving inside the cabin on Cakes and Pies, I made my way to the bedroom and threw my bag and the blankets in the closet. I grabbed the stashed pregnancy test, and decided to take one more for good measure.

Setting the test on the sink, I went to hide the money away in a safe spot and came back. Two bright pink lines were painted over the window. I knew what I had to do now.

Arriving to Planned Parenthood, I signed in and took a seat looking around at the variety of men and women sitting in the waiting room. Is this where the helpless came to find answers to the questions they feared the answer too?

Signing in, I looked at the woman behind the counter. "Hi. I um, I need to confirm a pregnancy."

She slapped a board against the counter. "Fill that out, I'll need your state ID or driver's license when you bring that back up."

I flashed a gentle smile, taking the clipboard to go sit down and start filling out the paperwork. I tried to focus on filling out the general information and found myself getting distracted by intimidating eyes staring toward me.

Ignore them. Get this taken care of.

Sitting down after turning in the paperwork, I pulled a Walkman from my purse, covered my ears with the headphones, grabbed one of the many parenting magazines sitting on the table and sat back to start reading. My mind raced at the thought of bringing a child into this world to raise on a yacht. Would Christopher still be there once he found out I was due to have his child in nine months? How could I break this news to him when it had barely been six months since we met? Perhaps I had just answered my own question. Even if he wasn't there, I'd emancipate myself and raise this child where he or she wouldn't be exposed to the danger of the Castillo family. I was raised in and around parents, a brother, sister and many extended cousins, aunts and uncles that ran an organized crime business. They hurt people and got paid to do it! How could my parents think it was smart to raise their children around such an atmosphere? The stacks of cash I took came to mind as well. Was it earned blood money? No, I refused to believe that! They owned many yacht clubs and casinos out in Vegas. This wasn't blood money.

I never understood why they had to hurt people and orchestrate crime to make a better living, and I never would. Perhaps, the voice in my head telling me to ignore these people in the waiting room spoke beyond that. I needed to ignore anyone standing in the way of my visions and dreams.

"Lorelai Castillo?"

I turned my head toward the nurse holding the door open sometime after all these thoughts marinated into my head. "Yes?"

"Come on back. We're ready for you, dear."

The universe had spoken, and it was calling my name. I stood and walked toward the nurse ignoring the narrowed eyes, staring at me as I approached the door.

"Right this way. How are you today, Miss Castillo?"

"I'm good. Just in a little bit of a hurry, to be honest."

"We'll do our best to get you in and out of here."

She stopped at the exam room. "We'll be right in here, but first we'll need a urine sample. There's a bathroom right across the hall with a cup all ready for you."

Following the instructions from the nurse, I did as I was told and returned to the exam room.

A few minutes later, the doctor walked in. "Good morning, Miss Castillo."

I smiled nervously. "Good morning."

He set down a folder on the counter and took a seat. "I just had a look over the pregnancy test. Congratulations, you had a positive result."

I nodded, before I looked down.

"Was this unexpected?"

I nodded. "Very unexpected and not planned for."

"Hm. I understand. The good news is, you've come to the right place to get all the information you need to make a decision in what route you'd like to go. Is the father in the picture?"

I inhaled a deep breath. "Yes, he is, but he doesn't know yet. I'm unsure how he will react."

The doctor nodded and proceeded to stand and gather a number of pamphlets. "Do you know what you want regardless of his position?"

"Yes. I will have this child with or without him, doctor."

He looked back at me and walked over. "Can I answer any questions for you right now?"

"Can I make an appointment for a follow-up on further prenatal care?"

"Of course. Stop at the desk and let them know and the girls up front will take care of you. I would strongly recommend you make time to read through these materials." The elderly gentleman placed the pamphlets of all shapes and sizes in a bag and handed them to me.

"Good luck, Miss Castillo. I hope to see you again soon."

"Can I get a letter of confirmation on the pregnancy?"

"Of course, they can provide that at the front for you as well."

I jumped down off the table. "Thank you."

The doctor opened the door, and I took my bag of information overload and walked through. Stopping up at the front desk, I made my next appointment, and made sure not to forget the letter of confirmation before I headed out to the car. Tossing my bag and purse on the passenger seat, I dug into the center console and hooked up the car phone, dialing in a familiar number.

The phone rang in my ear, and I sat back praying silently for an answer.

"This is Matteo Castillo. How can I help you?"

"Matteo? This is Lorelai. I need a favor."

Uncle Matteo came up from Vegas after completing his law degree under Uncle Thad's orders.

"Lorelai?" The husky voice replied. "Lorelai! Oh my… What's the favor?"

"Is your firm in Sausalito still open?"

"Yes, it is. I'm actually in town right now."

"Okay, good. I'll be down there in a few minutes."

"Hey wait!"

"What! I said I was on my way, damn it!"

"I know, I know. But answer me this. Is everything okay with you? I heard about Armani."

"No! Nothing is okay. As far as Armani goes, I can't talk about it right now."

"Fine! Fine! I'll see you when you get here."

I heard a click on the other end indicating that he hung up and slowly pulled the phone away from my ear. Once put away, I drove back toward Downtown Sausalito.

Fourteen

Discovering Betrayal

Lorelai

UPON ARRIVAL AT the Castillo Law Firm, I walked through the door and sat down. A window slid open and a blonde bombshell stuck her head out the window pulling her pencil skirt down. "Hey, Lor. What brings you here?"

"Can you please let Matteo know that I'm here? I called to let him know I was on my way"

She nodded. "Sure thing."

I furrowed my eyebrows and shook my head. It's just like Matteo to fuck his secretary at the office. Now wasn't the time.

The door opened a moment later and she stood in front of the door tucking her shirt into her pencil skirt. "Matteo is ready for you now, Lorelai."

I chuckled as I stood and walked toward the open door. "You might want to check yourself in the mirror… I think you misaligned the buttons on your shirt." I mumbled and moved swiftly past her. I heard a scoff from behind me as I approached his office, and pressed my lips together to hold back a bout of laughter before I entered my dearest Uncle's office. "Are you fucking your secretary?"

He narrowed his eyes at me. "It's nice to see you too, little niece."

I sat down, pulling out the confirmation letter from Planned Parenthood. "I'm not here to play catch up Matteo. I just happened to notice the lack of customer service skills the front office had, and put two and two together when her clothes were in disarray."

A smug smirk rose on his lips. "Okay then. I guess I won't fuck and tell. How can I help you?"

I opened the letter. "I would like to file for emancipation."

His face fell, and the tension in the room rose off the charts.

"You're divorcing your parents?"

"Maybe you would understand if you opened that letter."

He pressed his hand over the letter, sliding it across the desk before he opened and studied the words. "And the plot thickens. You're… pregnant?"

I nodded. "Your dad would blow a gasket, or… turn into the Incredible Hulk-King Kong hybrid and destroy everything in his path, if he knew." He widened his eyes. "And not stop until whoever did this to you was dead." He paused and turned to his file cabinet, pulling out a stack of paperwork and setting it down with a pen. "Fill out the first page, and we'll go over the rest. I can have this filed by the end of the day, and mail the certified letters tomorrow morning." I nodded and did as I was told.

One hour later, I finished with the paperwork, and looked up at him. "Thank you."

"You got it. Lor, before you go…" "What is it?" I spoke above a whisper.

"Was Armani in trouble?"

I swallowed hard. "I… I don't know. All my Dad said was that he crossed into enemy territory, or that's what they think."

He pursed his lips and stared blankly as the mystery was unsolved.

"Do you remember Santino?" I said in a matter of fact tone.

"Too well," he mumbled.

"He had a thing for me, and Armani warned him to stay away; but Santino refused and I think Armani had enough. They got into a fight at the Summer Bash. Whether Santino was behind it or not. I can't be sure."

He shook his head. "Fucking bastard. He will be next, I have no doubt. Armani won't let him live."

Lifting my arm, I flashed the tattoo on my arm.

He gasped. "You opted out, huh?"

"There's more than one reason I need out."

He nods. "I get it, but you know we'll always have your back if you need us."

I stood up. "I know." I paused. "I have to go now, Matteo. Keep in touch about the filing."

He stood up and walked me out in silence. We exchanged glances before I walked back to the car and took off. I needed to drive and clear my head before I went back to seek Christopher and give him the news.

Driving up to the Muir Woods, I found a parking spot, and decided I needed time. I walked the trails and found myself up at the Muir Beach lookout, taking in the endless views of the Pacific Ocean. Sitting down on the bench, I pulled my knees up to my chest as tears filled my eyes.

I was going to be a mother whether Christopher stood by my side or not. This was a turning point, and only one struggle I would remember as long as I lived. I would get through this.

I sat at the lookout letting time pass by me. Memories of Armani filled me. Holidays, birthdays, the Castillo Yacht Club parties our parents threw. The years we spent walking to and from the school bus stop with Luciana. He always had mine and Luci's back. Closing my eyes, I buried my face into my hands, sobbing out the emotions. Tears dripped over my cheeks like a leaking faucet, only the leak was petrifying. A leaking sink should not have been this devastating!

"God damnit Armani, why couldn't you just leave it alone? Who's going to protect us now that you're gone?" I spoke between sobs.

My vision blurred as I curled into a ball and lay on the bench and buried my face into my arm as I wept. My cries echoed through the mountains. I cried until I couldn't cry any more. When I opened my eyes, the sky was bright pink, and the sun reflected off the ocean water.

It was eerily quiet, no one in sight; yet I felt his presence like he was sitting next to me. The wind blew gently.

"Find him."

I looked around. “Is someone there?” I swallowed the lump in my throat. I was hearing voices, and now I was sure that I had lost it. “Get it together, Lorelai. You’re not hearing voices.” I whispered. Standing up, I wiped the tears away and took a deep breath.

“Find Christopher.” The male voice was clear and dominant this time, as if there was a physical human being speaking. Looking around once more, the entire area was clear and panic filled me. Was Christopher in trouble?

“Oh god… Christopher.” I took off running back toward the car. The distance to the parking lot left me breathless by the time I found myself in the driver’s seat scrambling to push the key into the ignition. Peeling out of the parking lot, I made my way back through the city traffic toward Sausalito. Nightfall was near, which is when we normally met up. I would find him, and it wouldn’t be an obstacle. He was safe. Santino wouldn’t be dumb enough to strike twice in one day, would he? Gripping the steering wheel tight, another question came to mind. Was Santino really the homicidal psycho that went after Armani? Or was there a huge piece to my puzzle missing? I couldn’t be sure, but I couldn’t focus on that. I would find him at all costs. If someone laid as much of a finger on my Christopher, let alone hurt him, there would be a price to pay.

Walking into the Castillo Yacht Club, I went into mission ‘Find Christopher’. I walked down the ramp onto the boardwalk and my first approach was going directly to his house.

I took a deep breath and knocked.

His father answered the door in his pajamas and stood there staring in silence as his eyes narrowed.

I took a deep breath before. “Hello, Mr. Montgomery. Is Chris home by chance?”

“He’s not. I haven’t seen him since last night. But you listen to me, young lady.” He stepped out and shut the door. “I know my son is quite fond of you, but I don’t want you anywhere near him. You stay away from him! Do you hear me?”

I shied my eyes away from him for a moment before I met his glare. “I’m not sure why you’re so angry, but you have to know that I love your son, Mr. Montgomery. Regardless of what my family's reputation is or what you think my family's reputation is." I paused as emotions choked me from continuing. "I'm sorry for bothering you."

"I meant what I said...you leave Christopher alone." He slammed the door and left me standing there by myself with wide eyes for a moment. I swallowed hard and turned to walk away from the house, heading down toward Cakes and Pies.

I couldn't be sure if he had a fight with his parents, but something had understandably changed. People in this place talked; and if they hadn't heard it through word of mouth, there had been an explicit murder delivered to the yacht club this morning and it just so happened to be one of my family members. I couldn't blame Mr. or Mrs. Montgomery for having a change of heart, but that was the least of my problems. I needed to find their son before it was too late.

Making it to the end of the docks, I jumped aboard the vessel and made my way into the cabin. "Chris?"

No answer. I did a quick walk through; and when I found the cabin empty, panic struck. My chest tightened. "God damn it!" I yelled, making a mad dash out of the cabin, and onto the dock grabbing my walkie. "Christopher? If you can hear me, please respond. I need to know your location." I checked the unoccupied houseboats failing to find my beloved boyfriend at every last one. Throwing my hair back in a ponytail as sweat dripped down my forehead, I found myself back at the boardwalk, keeping my eyes peeled.

"Where are you, Christopher?" I spoke just above a whisper as I stopped and closed my eyes, trying to clear my head.

He was close. I could feel it. I opened my eyes and a blurry vision of Luci came into my line of sight. She stood outside of the Black Diamond Club. Bile rose to my mouth as I slowly made my way down, and approached her standing in a black hoodie and yoga pants. "Luci?"

She turned slowly and her eyes widened. She stayed silent for a moment. "It's about time you showed up."

I studied the stern look on her face. Something was wrong, or something had happened.

"W-what are you talking about?"

"This is normally about the time you meet up with Christopher, right?"

"You've been spying on me?"

"That's not important. We have bigger problems on our hands."

I narrowed my eyes at her. "Go on."

"I think someone on our father's team swiped your boyfriend into the Black Diamond Club. I've been watching foot traffic, but no one has come in or left in over an hour, Lor."

"Then we need to go in and look ourselves." I started past her only to have my arm caught by her hand pulling me back to look at me face to face. "You know you're not allowed back there, Lorelai."

I snapped my wrist out of her grasp, narrowing my eyes at her. "Doesn't look like I have a choice, do I?" I crossed my arms, pacing the pathway in front of her and stopped after a few minutes. "Are you coming with me or not?"

She sighed. "Yeah. You leading the way, Catwoman?"

I rolled my eyes, continued under the arch and made my way down the walkway. There were at least a dozen yachts anchored. Turning to Luci, I bit my lower lip. "Where do you think he's being kept?"

She stayed quiet for a moment. "Keep going, to the end of the dock."

I nodded and continued down the docks, being sure to be light on my feet. When we walked close to the end, she spoke once more. "Turn to your right. It's the yacht parked in the middle."

I followed instructions and walked to the entrance only to be stopped by a key code. Luciana gently moved me aside to enter the code, I could hear the gears turning to unlock the door before the door slid open on its own.

Luci led us onto the yacht, only this yacht appeared to be used for industrial reasons. The floor was concrete and filled with giant yellow and black canisters. There were boxes that could fit bodies into them and an eight-foot-tall refrigerator and freezer doors on each side of the narrowed walk way. We came to another door, where Luci placed another code; and this time, the wall slid open to reveal two stainless steel double doors.

Pressing my lips together, I inclined my head giving her the signal to lead the way; and I followed her across a bridge that overlooked a lower level lounge. This must be where our father went whenever he disappeared for work.

Just as I reached the other end of the tunnel, I peeked out and saw Papino pacing with his cell phone to his ear. "Amelia, I'm sure whatever you decide to do for the funeral will be fine." He paused.

"I'm not being insensitive. Okay, okay. Look, I'll finish up and be home just as soon as I can. Please stop crying, sweetheart." He hung up promptly and started down to a door. I silently followed behind him staying out of his direct line of sight against a wall as he made his way into one of the interrogation rooms.

"Mr. Montgomery, we meet again," Papino spoke first.

I darted around the corner, waiting impatiently as Luci punched the code into the keypad and opened the door. Walking through, I spotted Santino on the floor passed out, and my father standing in front of Christopher. Blood streaking down his cheeks and on his neck. I gasped out in a horrified sob. "You let him go this instant!"

"Lorelai, get out of here," Papino yelled.

I ignored his command, setting my eyes on the dried-up blood, the swelling, and bruised eyes on my love's face as I fell to my knees next to the chair he was tied to, looking to my father holding a hot clothing steamer in his hands.

I looked from Santino with a glare to Papino as anger hit a top tier. "You let him go this instant!"

My father sighed and shook his head. "You know you're not supposed to be back here, Lorelai. What the hell were you thinking?"

"Let…him…go," I yelled in a stern voice.

I looked up at Chris's swollen face, refusing to move until he untied him. Hearing the quiet footsteps, I watched as Papino cut through the ropes restraining him. Looking up at him with furrowed eyebrows, my jaw and teeth clenched together.

"Get him the fuck out of here," he growled.

I stood up and wrapped my arm around his back and helped him up. "Can you walk?" I whispered.

He nodded, and I eyed Luci as she stepped in to help me walk Chris out of the interrogation room, moving out on a journey to safety.

Fifteen

An Undeniable Truth

I PLACED AS much weight on myself as I could bare, relying on Lorelai and Luci as they led me off the yacht and under the Black Diamond Club arch. Stopping once we were out, Lorelai turned toward me as we reached the closest bench on the boardwalk.

"Oh my god, Christopher." She pulled me down gently.

I shook my head and grabbed her wrists. "Let's just get somewhere safe, okay?"

She trembled and shook her head as tears welled in her eyes. "Are you sure? We can sit, and you can rest if you need to."

"It's better that we don't right now." I swallowed hard through heavy breaths.

She stared at me as she sucked in a breath and held it. Her face fell and she locked her concerned eyes on me, wrapping an arm around my lower back. I returned her embrace as she helped me stand before she led us back to safety. Luci stepped back in on the other side to help. I turned to look at her and the look she returned was one of reassurance. I couldn't help but feel that she was only helping because of Lorelai.

Feeling concerned eyes locked from the other side, I turned to Lorelai as she stared at me breathless. All of her facial features fell into a frown.

Luci leaned forward to catch Lorelai's attention. "He's right. We should take him somewhere safe. He needs to be cleaned up, Lor."

I returned the girls embrace as they helped me stand and led the way back.

Settling into the bathroom on Cakes and Pies, I watched as Lorelai turned toward Luci. "Thanks for helping. Are you staying?"

Luci shook her head. "I should probably go keep look out."

Lorelai nodded slowly, pausing before she spoke. "Luci?"

"Yeah, Lor?"

"Thank you for helping me tonight."

Luci flashed a small smile. "You're welcome, little sister."

Settling into the bathroom on Cakes and Pies, she sat me down on top of the toilet, kneeling on the floor next to me.

"Luci? Before you go, can you grab hydrogen peroxide and cotton balls?"

Luci disappeared; and when she returned, I turned my focus on Lorelai in silence as she cleaned the cuts with hydrogen peroxide. She inhaled a deep breath once she finished and broke the emergency ice pack apart. "Here, put this over your eye. It's swollen." She paused for a long moment.

Luci cleared her throat loudly. "Lorelai. Can you step out now that we know he's stable?"

She stood up and narrowed her eyes at her sister before she looked down at me. "I'll be right back." She kissed the top of my head and disappeared.

Lorelai

I followed Luci down the hall, and watched as she exited the cabin. I followed behind and shut the door.

She began to pace back and forth. "Do you realize how bad this is?"

I scoffed. "Yeah I do."

"You violated the rules. Chris will now have a target on his back, Lorelai. You're both in danger. I'm not sure you realize how much damage has been done here."

"He had no right to do this to Christopher! None. I will stand by his side and defend him until I know he's safe."

She shook her head and crossed her arms, "And, if he starts asking questions?"

My anger and panic rose. "I'll tell him the truth!"

"That's the last thing you should do!" Luci yelled. "He was exposed, Lor. He's a target. Don't you get that?"

"Papino will keep his grimy hands away, if he knows what's good for him."

Luci walked to the edge of the vessel and stepped off. "Good luck with all that, Lorelai. I hope everything works out the way you want it to."

I glared at her. She looked back toward me and the daggers in her eyes were red with rage. She wasn't being reasonable; how could I not tell Chris the truth? He lived through it! I didn't have time to argue with her. I needed to get back to Christopher. I pushed back the thoughts and possibilities of what would happen in the aftermath of Christopher's abduction by my family. His state of mind must've been going at a thousand miles a second, and I needed to reassure him that this mishap would never happen again.

When Luci was completely out of sight, I walked back inside, locked the door and made my way back to him.

Sixteen

Protection Orders

WHEN SHE LEFT, the cabin went radio silent. I stared off at the wall, replaying everything through my head, trying to figure out where I went wrong. I didn't stay away, but I couldn't. Now, her brother was dead and her father wanted to burn me alive in a chemical tank or murder me in the most torturous of ways. Maybe he'd make it quick and fast, as long as I was gone. Nothing else mattered.

I heard yelling, which interrupted my thoughts. I tried to comprehend what was being said, but they were too far away.

I sighed as I heard the door open then shut, and waited.

She appeared in the doorway and walked in, kneeling down in front of me. She looked at me with concerned eyes. "Do you want to talk about what happened?"

I sighed. "I'd rather not." She had enough to deal with. I couldn't place my burdens on her.

"Christopher, don't hold back on my account. I can handle it." She spoke in a stern voice and I knew she meant business.

I hesitated for a moment. "Our parents have a lot in common, but your father is a lot more persistent to prove his point." I paused and thought about telling her that her father tried to offer me a large sum of money to stay away from her; but she already had enough heartbreak caused by her own flesh and blood. I had to protect her, and not telling her was the only way I knew how.

She covered her mouth with her hand as tears welled in her eyes. "I'm so sorry that you were caught up in this."

Lifting my free hand, I gently wiped her tears away with the pad of my thumb. "Your tears aren't worth his spiteful ways, Lor."

She locked her eyes in on mine and I leaned down and pressed my lips to her forehead. Dainty fingers caressed the skin against my scruffy cheeks.

"I won't let him come between us, Christopher." She stood up from a kneeling position and gently sat in my lap, pushing her fingers up through my hair at the side of my head. I wrapped her in my arms and laid my head against hers. "I couldn't stay at my house a moment longer. I had to find you. I came here first."

"None of it matters now, okay? We're here and together. That's all that matters." She spoke above a whisper against my ear.

"Actually, I have one question."

She pulled away to look me in the eyes. "What is it?"

"Your tattoo, some of your family members have one in the same spot. I feel like it's a significant symbol that means something."

She sighed. "It is significant. Every Castillo family member has a choice to make. They either want in on the family business, or they want to go in a different direction,"

"You mean, the yachting business?"

She shook her head. "Not exactly. My father is the leader of an Italian Syndicate."

I furrowed my brows, it hadn't made a lick of sense until now. The boating business, the rich family, the fancy black tie events that took place year-round, the Black Diamond Club, the location of the club being on the water? I was dating the mob boss's daughter. "Syndicate? Is that another word for mafia or mob?"

She nodded slowly. "Yeah." She spoke barely above a whisper. "If you feel the need to walk away, I would understand completely."

I ignored her statement for the time being. "Can I see your arms?" I asked after a moment.

She inhaled a deep breath and showed me. "The tattoo was a
Sausalito Nights – Stephanie Salvatore
symbol of me fleeing; but in order to complete the ritual to not join the family business, my father burnt the fleeing birds into my other arm with a black iron stencil. That's how we're identified."

I wasn't sure how to react. I was horrified for her. I couldn't imagine agreeing to go through something like that; but I lived through the syndicate's wrath, I could only imagine what else went on in the Black Diamond Club. One thing was for sure. I now understood Lorelai's warning about staying away from that place.

"What are you thinking about, Chris?"

He shook his head. "I would never walk away from you, not in a million years."

She laid her head against mine where it wouldn't hurt too much. Her warm breath tickled the hairs inside of my ear. Silence filled the space between us as we allowed each other's presence to sink in. I couldn't have been more grateful to be back here with her. She didn't have to speak words to let me know she felt the same way.

Pulling away, she stared into my eyes for another long pause.

Perhaps she was trying to identify me through my cut-up face.
"Chris?"

"Yeah?"

"I'm pregnant," she whispered.

My lips fell open as I turned to look up at her. "Y-you're pregnant?"

She smiled. "Yeah. We weren't all that careful." Her tone was nonchalant which caused a smile to curve up on my lips.

She was right, we weren't. "So, we're going to be parents?"

"That is correct, Captain."

I stayed silent for a moment before I did my best to look at her and flash my best smile at her. "We're going to be parents?" I sounded spaced out, which made her giggle.

"Yes! Christopher, snap out of the fake stoner act and tell me how you feel."

I chuckled softly. "A baby…a little human child? A little bit of you and a little bit of me? Hmm…" I waggled my eyebrows at her.

"Yes, stop goofing around and tell me how you feel!"

I chuckled and flashed her a smile. "Baby girl, I think it's great. I love you and I know us. We will make it work no matter what."

Her hand moved under my chin and rose my head, her lips pressing into mine. I returned the kiss and smiled after I broke it. "How are you feeling about it?"

"Well, I'm not sure. I'm afraid of what happens if or when my parents find out. Neither of my parents would approve, and my father acts out on zero remorse, Christopher."

She was afraid for me, and showed it well. "Then we can't let them know. We'll live here on Cakes and Pies, use Planned Parenthood for all of its glory, and in the meantime, I'll continue working with my dad. We'll just have to keep our relationship and our little bean a secret until we turn eighteen. We can make it work."

She looked at me with that same loving look, and smiled from ear to ear. "How are you staying so calm through all of this? You have every right to hate me and want nothing to do with me; and yet, you're sitting here with an ice pack on your eye looking at me like Blackbeard the Pirate telling me everything is going to be okay."

I laughed softly. "I love you, Lorelai. No one on this Earth could keep me away from you."

Her soft hands cupped my cheeks where the cuts ended and her lips pressed against mine in a deep, passionate kiss. I did not hesitate to return her kiss, regardless of the fact that we still hadn't touched on one other important piece of information that probably had her heart shattered.

"I love you too, Christopher." Her facial expressions softened as I placed both of my hands around her waist and brushed my thumbs against her stomach.

She smiled down at me and embraced my neck with gentle ease. Even under the circumstances of only having one good eye to look at her, I saw the loving expression; and in that moment, I realized I was head over heels in love with her. I could feel it in the silence, the depth and passion of our love was mutual.

Her words sunk in with our new reality. She smiled down at me and embraced my neck with gentle ease. Inching in closer, I gently attacked her lips with my own in a wistful kiss. Lorelai Castillo placed me under her love spell and I had no qualms admitting it.

She returned the kiss, cupping my cheeks where it wouldn't hurt.

Heavy breaths surrounded us as the moment of passion drove us deep.

Breaking the breathy kiss, she whispered. "As much as I would love to stay in this cocoon with you. It's not safe for us to stay docked here, Chris." She spoke above a whisper.

I stayed silent taking in this realization.

"I have a safe spot where no one would find us."

I leaned in and pecked her lips softly. "Then, we should go."

Later that night, we docked at the Golden Gate Yacht Club. Lorelai turned on the generator to heat the cabin, and I watched as she crawled into bed before I laid behind her. We watched out the window, taking in the lights on the Golden Gate Bridge.

The night grew cold and I attempted to warm her up with my body heat and the thin quilt. "You should sleep." I spoke above a whisper.

"I couldn't even if I wanted to." She turned to lay on her back and looked up at me.

I propped myself up on an elbow and circled my hand over her hip and stomach.

"What about for our little bean?"

She smiled up at me. "There's too much on my mind."

I stayed silent for a moment. "Well, I'm here."

"It's everything. My dad trying to make you a victim under his rule of thumb was unforgivable. I'll always love my family, but I can't stand back and watch them act selfishly on their pedestals anymore." She paused. "That's why Armani is dead, and why you were hurt. The Syndicate has hurt me for the last time, Chris." She choked her words out in a soft sob. A sharp pain shot through my chest as my heart shattered for her.

We only had each other and I would be damned if I let her down. "Do you have a plan?"

She nodded. "I've filed for emancipation. My parents won't dare to fight it. I know too much. There's an account with my name on it at the bank. I'll have access to it once I turn eighteen, hopefully sooner if I play my cards right."

I pressed my lips to her forehead taking in her words. Lorelai Castillo was the strongest young woman I ever had the pleasure to meet. She was my partner in crime, my hero, the absolute love of my life. She was giving up her family so we could be together and, more importantly, so we could start our own family.

Pulling away, I laid my forehead against hers. "I'll do my best to support you however you need me to."

She looked me directly in the eyes, a smile tugging at her lips. "I appreciate that, love." She snuggled against my chest and I pulled her close as she entangled her legs between mine.

We were finally warm when a loud popping noise came from behind.

"What was that?" I asked.

"The heater kicked off, it's an energy saver my father set up. It's designed to rise up to a certain temperature. I think he did it on purpose, so I couldn't run away and survive the cold nights."

Except she did run away. We ran together. I would now be responsible for taking care of the essentials for her and our little one to be. Even though her father wanted to disintegrate me in the bay and fought with all of his might to push me away, he did not win. Lorelai saved me and we came out stronger on the other side. As long as we had each other, I knew we would be okay.

Seventeen

The Castillo Arrow Strikes Again

Lorelai

THE NEXT MORNING, I woke before Christopher and I was freezing cold, so I got up to check the thermostat on the heating and cooling system. There was an error up on the system. Was it

broken? Or did my father have something to do with this?

I knew nothing about fixing heating and cooling systems. Returning to the bedroom, I hated to wake Chris; but I couldn't sleep even with his furnace heated blood, it wasn't enough.

Sitting on the bed on his side, I leaned down and kissed his forehead. "Babe?"

He grunted and reached a hand out blindly wrapping an arm around my waist. "What is it?"

"Something is wrong with the heater. There's an error up on the thermostat, and it's freezing cold in here."

He rubbed a hand on my back before he sat up and pushed the blanket around the back of my shoulders. "Come show me. Bring the blanket, so you're not so cold baby."

I led him to the thermostat to show him, and he finagled with it. "Where's the heater located?"

I showed him to the utility closet.

He stepped in and looked around, taking the cover off the front and pulled the filter out. "When's the last time you changed this out?"

I looked at it and pursed my lips. "No idea. But there should be an extra one around here. I'll get it."

Walking away, I retrieved the new filter and handed it to him. He installed it, replaced the cover and walked back to the thermostat and finagled with it for a few more minutes, before I heard a click.

"Did it just turn on?" he called out.

I went to a vent, feeling the warm air come out. "Affirmative. We have heat!"

He chuckled. "You're welcome."

"Thank you, babe. Do you want coffee?"

"That would be fantastic, babe. I'll cook breakfast."

I turned and smiled back at him. "Shouldn't you be resting?"

He walked out to the kitchen, waving me off. "I'm fine. A few cuts and a couple of black eyes won't put me down." He went to the fridge and brought out a bowl of fruit, and two yogurt cups.

Exiting the cabin, we sat out on the deck and ate breakfast, watching the birds fly over the bay as the sun rose from behind the San Francisco skyline, filling the sky with colors of pink, orange and yellow. It was a perfect sight for a beautiful day. Christopher was alive. We had much planning to do with the baby on the way; but first, I had to deal with my family.

Pulling my radio out from my lap, I turned to Marie's channel. "Marie?"

A few seconds later, I heard a grunt come through and smiled.

"Does that mean you're awake?"

"Maybe? I'm still deciding. Are you and Montgomery okay?"

"Define okay."

"Alive and breathing?"

"Yeah, we're okay. A load of shit went down yesterday, but I don't want to talk about it now. Long story short, I'm hiding at the Golden Gate yacht club for now."

"Oh shit. Where at the Golden Gate?"

"Dock B."

"I can come to you. Plans for Armani's memorial have been made."

"Come over whenever. We'll be here."

"Roger that." She giggled. "I've always wanted to say that."

I shook my head and smiled. "I'll see you soon." I set the radio on the table and looked at Chris. "So, you get to meet Marie today. She's my cousin, but you have nothing to worry about with her. She's also a free bird."

He smiled. "You two sound close."

"We are. She's more like a sister than a cousin. To be honest, I've always been closer to her than my siblings. She is also the one that's been covering for me when my parents ask where I am."

He chuckled. "You have a little wingman?"

I laughed. "Damn straight. She's my ride or die."

A little while later, Christopher and I sat outside at the table set for three, and Marie came aboard to join us, sat down and looked from me to Chris. "You must be the infamous Christopher Montgomery. I'm Marie."

He smiled. "I am. It's nice to meet you."

She shook his hand and looked at me. "Do I want to know what happened yesterday, and if Chris's cut up face has anything to do with it?"

I sighed. "Well, after everything with Armani went down, shit just kind of went haywire." I said and continued to explain everything from the pregnancy tests to the rescue I had to make when I trespassed into the Black Diamond Club and finally finished with the argument I had with Luciana.

Marie crossed her arms. "Holy shit. Well first of all, I'm glad both of you are okay. Second of all, I'm going to be a fucking aunt! I'm so happy for you, but what are you going to do about attending Armani's memorial?"

I sighed. "If I don't show up, someone's going to come looking for me and that's the last thing I want."

She nodded. "True. Well, they're cremating him, and your parents want to spread his ashes throughout the bay."

"That'll be nice." I sipped my coffee. "When is it happening?"

"Thursday at 10 a.m."

I nodded. “I’ll be there, but don’t tell anyone where I am, please.”

“I promise I won’t. You focus on you and Chris, and I’ll deal with the family. Worry about nothing.”

I smiled and stood up to hug her. “Thanks Marie. You’re the best.”

She hugged me back, holding me for a moment. “No, you’re the best. I love you. I’ll see you soon, Lor. Okay?”

I let go of her slowly. “Okay. Thank you for everything.”

She stepped away and went to climb off on the dock. “That’s what family does for each other. We have each other’s back.”

I smiled and waved her off and returned to Chris, sliding into his lap gently, kissing his temple as he wrapped me in his arms. I didn’t know what would come after all this chaos, but I knew that Chris had my back, and whatever happened next, we would get through it together.

Thursday morning, Christopher was insistent to take a run down in the Muir Woods. Two black eyes and taking a knife to his face would not stop him from his everyday routines. He was stubborn like that, but it was also why I admired him.

After running through the Redwood Trees, we made it to our final destination which was the Muir Beach Outlook on a circular platform. We had some of our most meaningful conversations here.

Leaning against the railing arm to arm, the sunlight hitting our faces, I looked at him after pulling sunglasses over my eyes.

“How are you feeling about today?” He asked.

I groaned quietly, and turned to look out over the water.

“That bad, huh? Do you want me to come with you?” he asked in a singsong tone.

I lowered my sunglasses as I turned to look at him. “Are you crazy? My father almost killed you. Absolutely not. You stay where you are safe on Cakes and Pies, rest, read a book, eat yourself into the deepest of food comas; but you will not come near that funeral. Got it?”

He saluted me quickly and laughed. “Fine. But you best be careful.”

"I am not afraid of the Castillos. I might not be a part of their "Family Business", but I know how to kick ass when I need to."

He snickered. "That's really hot, Lor."

I flashed him a smile placing a hand on his cheek, planting a gentle kiss to his lips as he turned his head toward me. He held onto the kiss for a moment as I caressed the pad of my thumb against his cheek. Slowly breaking the kiss, I pressed my forehead against his. "In all seriousness, we'll have a quiet night to ourselves tonight when I get back."

His warm hands cupped over my cheeks. "I'm looking forward to it, beautiful."

I nuzzled my nose into his, as he pulled me close to plant a passionate kiss against my lips. Returning his kiss, I wrapped my arms around his neck; and he pulled my legs up around his waist as he walked back toward the parking lot in a lip lock. I giggled profusely as he managed to get us back to the car with little to no sight on where he was going. Looking up at him with admirable eyes as he set me down and opened the car door, I took his hand as he helped me in. He planted another gentle kiss against my lips and I couldn't find it in me to push him away.

The fresh thoughts of mingling with family members I hadn't seen nor spoken to in months had my head spinning and stayed with me as we returned to Cakes and Pies. I disappeared into the bathroom to start the shower.

One hour later, I exited the cabin to find Christopher on the deck with his laptop set up on his lap. A whistle left his lips and I flashed a smile as I approached him and pecked his lips. "I gotta go. I'm running late. I'll see you in a few hours, handsome. Don't work too hard, okay?"

"No promises, beautiful. Be careful driving and I'll see you soon." Planting one last peck to his lips, I left.

Upon arrival to the yacht, I went straight to the top of the vessel, and sat on one of the couches staring off into the bay and the San Francisco city skyline. Family members began to gather around, and quiet whispers were exchanged as an eerie feeling of sadness took over.

There was more to what Armani went through. Had he really protected me? Did he put a stop to the advances Santino wanted to make on me? Was I actually in the clear of Santino trying to force me into a life I didn't want? Would I ever get an answer?

I pushed my thoughts away as I spotted the poster boards filled with photos. The first one held pictures of Armani from infancy to becoming a big brother. He was only human. No matter what he did, he did not deserve this. I moved from one poster board to the next, taking in the memories of our childhood to becoming teenagers and beyond. We were far from normal, the Castillo name said it all. We came from money, there was no denial in that; but one trait we all had in common was that we were adamant about supporting each other. Sometimes, I felt that the support came with a price.

I felt a gentle hand lay against my back and turned to see my mother. She gave me a gentle push and we walked to the front. Papino grabbed a microphone from Luciana, "If everyone could find a seat, we're going to get started."

Taking a seat next to Luciana, I stared off as Papino took center stage and began the service. "Good afternoon. Today, we are gathered to remember the life of the beloved Armani Castillo Jr., son to Amelia and myself, a loving brother to our girls Luciana and Lorelai. What I learned raising Armani is that he was a passionate and protective young man to his sisters. He adored his mother, looked up to me and followed instructions like a true soldier. He loved the outdoors and taking adventures with his sisters whether they rode their bikes through Sausalito or ventured out to the Muir Woods. He was always looking out for them. As a parent to Armani, I admired his strength and admiration to walk in my footsteps." He paused as tears filled his eyes. "While I live to regret not being more on top of his actions, his passing came out at the protection of family." He stopped there and dropped his head slightly, looking down he inhaled a shaky breath before he spoke, "Rest easy, Son."

Mother rubbed her hand over his arm as she took the mic from his hand and settled it into the stand. The wind blew through her dark locks gently as she looked around at the family surrounding us. "As our first child, Armani was a very special young man. His passion for life in all aspects, including success, was always over the top. He was loved by many for his sense of adventure and overall caring and protective instincts he inherited from his father. Armani and I did our best to raise our children to be noble, respectful, kind-hearted human beings. Armani always exceeded my expectations from the time he was just a baby." She looked toward the urn and shook her head as she sobbed.

Papino stepped in when he noticed that Mother had become overwhelmed and looked toward me. "Lorelai? Do you mind?"

I read between the lines. He didn't want her to say anything more. God forbid she revealed how she really felt. Swallowing my own tears behind my sunglasses, I stood front and center, taking the mic.

Mother's wails of sobs and cries grew louder before she screamed. "Get your hands off of me, you bastard! He shouldn't be dead!"

Heads turned and the whispers began. I pushed past the drama and tried to focus back on what I wanted to say. "Armani…" I smiled. "When our father said Armani loved the outdoors, he wasn't exaggerating. From the time that I was just a young girl looking up to my siblings, Armani was there to do what big brothers did best. He showed me the world and how I could keep it at my fingertips through the world of sailing, which he learned from our father and his passion for being on the water. Armani would take me down to the docks, or down to Muir Beach on Saturday mornings where we would paddle board or jet ski depending on his mood. He gave unsolicited advice; and while I never seemed to appreciate it in the moment, I always looked back and realized how important it was." I inhaled a sharp wayward breath. "Armani was not just a son to our father and mother, he was a brother admired by many, a man of his word, a protector… and most importantly, a hero." My voice trailed off through the tears that choked me up. I paused and stilled before I found a seat and stared off into the distance as tears fell from beneath my sunglasses frame.

As the shock value wore off from my mother's dramatic exit, the emotions kicked in and sobs left me as Luciana took the front of the room. Mother returned with red puffy cheeks and daggers in her eyes as she stood between Luci and I. We walked down the center aisle to the port of the vessel. Reaching in to gather a handful of ashes one at a time, we held onto it until each of us had the grainy textures in our hands. Watching the ashes slip through the cracks of my fingers, I swiped my hands together to rub the residue away and turned to Luci, who had put on a brave face until now. I embraced her in my arms as we walked back to the front and took our seats. I knew that today of all days, we had to come together for Armani's sake.

The reception took place immediately after the memorial. I sat alone at the front of the yacht in the outdoor seating area, which happened to be the same spot Christopher and I had our first date. My sobs dwindled down as the cool air dried the tears against my face. The air felt so much colder outside of Sausalito. I was ready to leave this yacht and get the hell away from these people. I wanted to be alone with Christopher to mourn Armani's loss. He was the only one I needed right now besides our little peanut.

Footsteps against the wooden panels interrupted the massive amount of thoughts running through my head. "Lorelai? May I have a word?"

I jumped slightly at the sound of Papino's tone. "Of course."

He walked over and Uncle Thaddeus and Matteo followed as they all took a seat. I was ready to make a mad dash overboard and into the bay. Why were all three of them moving in to surround me?

"You wanna tell me what this is all about?" Papino snapped and slapped the golden yellow envelope on the table with "Emancipation Notification" stamped in red capital letters across the front.

I clenched my teeth and pressed my lips together, narrowing my eyes toward him and then Matteo. "You had to do this today?"

Matteo shrugged as he walked from behind the couch. "You said you needed it taken care of, Lorelai."

Uncle Thad followed him and made himself comfortable. "What I want to know is why you think it's okay at all to divorce your parents after they've done everything for you."

I shook my head. "It's none of your business, Uncle Thad. Stay out of it!"

My father filed in and sat on the other side of me, making me feel trapped.

"No! You will give us an explanation, Lorelai!" Papino yelled.

"You're leaving Sausalito with Mama and I told you I wouldn't leave Christopher behind! I love him and I will go to any length to make sure you don't get another chance to hurt him!"

He furrowed his eyebrows and snatched the letter up looking down at me after looking it over. "Is this what you really want, Lorelai?"

I stayed quiet and avoided all eye contact. "Yes, Papino."

"This kid really means that much to you?" He continued with vivid intimidation. "Yes."

The hesitation from my end was zero, but the fact that Uncle Thad tagged along made me nervous. I pushed the thought away as Papino leaned down to sign the paperwork and set it down. "I hope you're happy then." He said and leaned over, pressing his lips against my cheek before he stood up and walked off without another word.

I sighed as Matteo took the paperwork and followed after him.

Uncle Thad remained on the couch, his ankle against the top of his leg, looking me over. "You'll regret this someday, Lorelai."

I crossed my arms and narrowed my eyes toward him. "Is that a threat?"

"A Castillo never turns his or her back on family." His tone was dark and cold.

I narrowed my eyes at him before I stood up and walked away, shivering as I felt the hair on the back of my neck standing straight. I needed to get the hell out of here and back to Christopher. Without blinking an eye in the direction of my family, I isolated myself inside of the cabin of the yacht until we were docked. I stood in the distance watching the dock workers drop the bridge walkway; and the second the coast was clear, I fled the scene.

Eighteen

The Human Furnace is a Security Blanket

Lorelai

RETURNING TO CAKES and Pies, I found Christopher lying in bed sleeping. Climbing into bed behind him, I tucked myself against the back of his body and pressed my lips against the bare skin between his shoulder blades. I smiled as the comforting smell of his body wash wafted through my sinuses. The mixture of cedar wood and his signature musk cologne was comforting. The reality of his presence made me feel a hell of a lot safer than being around my own family which confirmed that I had made the right decision.

He lay still before he rolled over slowly, wrapping his arms around me. "How'd the memorial go?" he mumbled quietly.

"It went. How are you feeling?"

He groaned, "I'm okay."

His pressed his lips to the top of my head as I returned his embrace and looked up at him.

"What do you mean, 'it went'?" he asked.

"My father and uncles basically cornered me on the couch to confront me about the emancipation. My uncle, Thad, acted as if I was betraying the entire family. I left as soon as I could to avoid it all."

He sighed. "This wouldn't even be an issue if they all had nine to five jobs."

I snuggled further into him. "Oh, I know baby. It's done. I'm sure Matteo will let me know when everything is finalized." I paused. "Let's not talk about it, okay?"

He planted a kiss against my head once more as he ran his fingers through my hair. "What do you want to talk about, Princess?"

I smiled as I scooted up to his eye level, pressing my nose to the tip of his. "Us. Our lives. Where do you see us in ten years?"

He smiled, pushing his fingers through my hair slowly. "Well, by then I'll have gotten down on one knee, given you a wedding of your dreams, and bought you a house. Our little nugget will be…nine…"

He gasped playfully. "And probably eating us out of house and home."

I giggled, leaning in to peck his lips. "And, we will make him or her our entire world. Hopefully, we'll have a few more adorable Montgomery babies to spoil too. You'll either have taken over Montgomery Construction, or have a really high paying position and we'll have our very own house and we won't have to live on a boat. Who knows? Maybe I'll be helping your parents run the winery by then."

He pressed a gentle kiss into my lips. "I am sure that you will be, but you honestly don't have too. If you want to be a stay at home mom, then I will support that. What else fills your Mrs. Montgomery dreams?"

I giggled. "Well, I know Sausalito is great and everything, but I want to make sure our children know and love wine country as much as we do."

"Hmm…I actually love that idea. We'll make Sausalito our home town and travel on the weekends. I think letting our children see the beauty this state has to offer is a must." He smiled as he brushed his fingers lightly under my hair.

I smiled big. "We'll have to get them well acquainted with our favorite places in the bay area first. We could wake them up before the sun rises and take them up the mountain to watch the sunrise. We'll show them love and support first. I don't want them to turn on us."

He shook his head. "That would never happen, it's not possible with Montgomery blood." He paused. "Waking them up before sunrise? That's a good way to make them hate us." He groaned.

I gasped. "They will not hate it…you want to know why?"

He cocked an eyebrow. "Why?"

"Because by that time, we'll have their trust and they'll want in on our crazy shenanigans as much as we do!"

He chuckled. "I could see that." He paused. "Wait. Are you calling me crazy?"

I giggled. "Damn straight I am."

He smiled. "I like our crazy, though. We'll be the fun, trusting parents. Maybe our kids won't rebel as hard as we have."

"I love the way you think, Mr. Montgomery; but our children won't have to worry about the stress of living up to the expectations of a family that commits crime to make a living either." I said as I snuggled my head into the crook of his neck.

He wrapped me in his arms, laying his head against mine. "That is very true, my love. You're going to make a great mother and wife someday Miss Castillo." He whispered.

"You really think so, Mr. Montgomery?"

"I know so." He paused, sat up and crawled out of bed. "Close your eyes. I'll be right back."

Confusion struck me, but I sat up and did as I was told. I heard the soft shuffle of his feet against the wooden floors. I heard a rustling near the closet before his feet shuffled once more and the bed lowered as he sat next to me. He placed what felt like a gift bag between my hands. "Okay. Open your eyes."

I fluttered my eyes open and looked down at the gift bag. Stripes of pink, blue, yellow and green were printed down the bag with a giant green square and a yellow duck in the middle. A giant smile crossed my lips as I looked at him and reached into the bag, pulling out a set of green and yellow sleepers. I set them beside me before I reached back in the bag and pulled out a small yellow duck plush. Tears filled my eyes and threatened to spill down my cheeks. "Awe, Christopher! It's our baby's first stuffed animal! This is precious. Thank you." Picking up the sleepers, I looked them over and looked at him with gentle eyes as overjoyed tears fell down my cheeks. I placed a hand against his cheek, kissing him deeply and passionately. He was so damn thoughtful, loving, supportive and personable. How I managed to get so lucky just when I needed him was only a question the universe could answer.

He pulled away just enough to look me in the eyes. "You're welcome, sweet girl." He paused, placing a hand against the side of my waist, brushing his thumb over my stomach. "I love you and our little bean."

"We love you too, Christopher." I whispered and closed my eyes taking in his words.

Vivid images of Christopher and I becoming husband and wife and raising our children how we wanted took me to a land of bliss. I imagined mini Christopher's and Lorelai's running around in Napa through the vineyards while Chris and I trailed behind them with a glass of wine. This daydream was so vividly clear, it felt real. I wanted to cling to it until it was our actual reality; but for now, our present reality was good enough to hold onto. I couldn't rush the time I had with him. I wanted the rest of forever to pass by as slowly as possible because as long as I had Christopher Montgomery at my side, life was imperfectly perfect.

Winter

The holidays had come and gone. The spirit of Christmas and plans for the future of my life with Christopher and our little bean were talked about mostly during the cold nights we endured sleeping in the cabin of Cakes and Pies. We had gone to my first official appointment for an eight-week checkup a few days before and I woke up to the sonogram sitting in the corner of a picture frame. A sigh left my lips as I realized that my human furnace had already woken and had gone to grab breakfast for us somewhere. A feeling of fatigue came over me as I lay there which made me want to fall back to sleep. The aches and pains this morning were worse than normal. I curled up into a ball trying to warm myself up until I heard yelling from the familiar voices of Christopher's parents. Sitting up, I ignored my screaming bladder while I rushed to the door and stepped out silently to listen in on the conversation.

"This is ridiculous, Christopher. You are almost eighteen years old. You know what's right and wrong, and continuing this affair with that girl is wrong." A female voice said. "That entire family is nothing but trouble."

"Your mother is right. We've been out looking for houses, and we'll be moving out of here soon."

Chris sighed. "You're right. I am old enough to know right from wrong, and I'm sorry that you can't see what I see in Lorelai." He paused. "She's not like the rest of her family. She's been betrayed by them on more than one occasion."

Distressed sighs could be heard; and I knew if I didn't interrupt to back him up, they would just continue giving him a hard time. I stepped out to where they were sitting over coffee and stood behind Christopher. "What he said, it's not a lie," I spoke softly.

His parents eyed me carefully. "Without going into detail, I haven't been home in weeks and I don't plan to go back. To say that my family has their issues is an understatement, but not what's important here. I am in love with your son, and I would never let anything happen to him. He's… he's all I have."

They eyed Christopher with a twitch of their lips. I could tell they were looking for a reason to dismiss me as I placed my hands on Chris's shoulders.

I smiled down as I felt Christopher's broad, rough hand being placed over one of mine. "You two are a prime example of knowing what true love feels like. You know what it was like to be on your own and rely on each other to get through the hard times, and Nana and Papa supported you."

His parents looked at each other, and his mother spoke first. "He's right, Nathan."

"Grace…" His tone filled with annoyance.

"Don't you, Grace me! He's right and clearly head over heels for this young woman!"

I breathed a sigh of relief.

His father looked to me. "Perhaps." He paused. "I suppose if Christopher is that adamant about this relationship, then we can look past the connection to your name."

I smiled. "Mr. Montgomery, I promise I'm nothing like them. My cousin Marie and I, we grew up being the odd balls in the family. We never cared to stay and listen to their updates even when my Father said we should, because we needed to learn it sooner rather than later. I've always been the odd ball, or the black sheep if you will."

Grace turned to Nathan and they both looked to Christopher.

Grace moved her chair to take my hand. "My parents didn't like Nathan. They stuck their noses in the air when I told them I was in love… and coincidentally enough, my father was offered a job across the country. I cried to Nathan, and he bravely talked to his parents who took me in without a question. It would be wrong for us to not give you a chance, Lorelai."

A lump formed in my throat, and I fought back the emotions and lost as the tears filled my eyes and fell down my cheeks. "Thank you, Mrs. Montgomery."

She leaned in and gave me a hug and I accepted it. To be accepted by not only Christopher, but his loving parents touched me on a deep personal level. I never received that from my parents. It was business first, always.

Letting go of Grace, Nathan stood and came to give me a hug. "If Chris says you are what he needs in his life, I suppose it's time we trust our boy's instincts; and trust me, you won't be the oddball out with the Montgomerys. We're all a little strange."

His parents laughed, and Chris looked up at me. "Why don't you go clean up, love? We have an appointment today."

I nodded, "Okay." I leaned down to kiss his cheek and looked at the Montgomerys once more. "It was nice to see you again, Mr. and Mrs. Montgomery."

"You too, Lorelai." They spoke in unison before I left to go inside the cabin.

I ignored the pain I'd been experiencing from the time I woke up. I narrowed it down to being tired from work, school and growing a human body inside of me. Stepping into the shower, the warm water fell over me as I prepared for our first couples' therapy appointment. The tension of how we were going to get through our predicament of our parents trying to pry us away, being out on our own, Armani's sudden death, becoming young parents before we had a chance to attend college or get married hung over our heads; and instead of allowing it to push us further apart, Christopher had suggested we take on counseling.

A few minutes later, I saw the door open and Chris came in.

"Baby?"

"Yeah?"

"Why is there blood on the floor?"

I looked out at him as he peeked into the shower. "Lor, you're bleeding everywhere!"

I inhaled a sharp breath as I spotted the droplets of blood on the floor and looked down at the pool of blood mixing into the water. My hands clasped over my mouth. "Chris…. Wha-what's happening?" Tears sprang to my eyes, and I felt a tightness in my chest and sharp painful cramps shot across my abdomen. The overwhelming fatigue feeling intensified. I found myself bent over and grasped a hold of my stomach crying out in pain.

The glass door to the shower swung open, and Chris turned the water off, wrapping me in a towel. helping me get dressed. "I'm not sure Lor, but I think we need to take you to the emergency room." A million concerns and thoughts raced through my mind. I was scared. The fear and anxiety that took over paralyzed my mental state of mind. Laying my head against his shoulder, my lips opened but I couldn't speak. I didn't know what was wrong, but I had a gut feeling this wasn't a good sign for our little bean. He looked at me with reassurance as he helped to dress me before he pulled me into his arms and carried me out of the cabin and down the docks toward the car.

The ride to the hospital was silent. I cried until we arrived and Chris brought me to the counter and signed me in.

"Who's being seen?" The young female asked.

"My girlfriend. Her name is Lorelai Castillo. She's pregnant and bleeding."

"Did she fall or experience any other immediate trauma?"

I shook my head. "No."

"Okay, it'll just be a few minutes. Have a seat, we'll call you into triage shortly."

Chris led us toward the seating area and we sat down. I laid against him and tried to breathe as I placed a hand against my abdomen. "It hurts, Christopher."

"I know, baby girl. The doctor's going to help, okay? Just try to hang in there, okay?" He brushed his fingers through the long locks of hair lying against the front of my shoulder.

A few minutes later, the door opened. "Lorelai Castillo?"

I opened my eyes, lifting my head from Christopher's shoulder and looked at him before I made eye contact with the nurse. I followed her back to triage where she asked me a slew of questions before she called over her walkie to make sure there was a bed available.

"Okay, Miss Castillo, you can follow me." She led us back to a room where Christopher helped me undress and put on a dreadful gown.

The doctor arrived a few minutes later. "Miss Castillo? Hi. My name is Dr. Harris, I'm going to be taking care of you today." I turned my attention to the young woman in a lab coat.

"Can you tell me why you came in today?"

Tears threatened my eyes. "I'm pregnant, but I started bleeding while I was in the shower today."

"Is that the first time you noticed the bleeding?" I nodded slowly.

"Okay. We'll take a look and see what's going on." She washed her hands and turned to Christopher. "I'm going to ask that you step out for now. I'll come get you when I'm finished with the exam."

I looked from the doctor to Christopher with pleading eyes. He took both of my hands into his, leaning down to press a kiss against my forehead. "It's okay. I'll come back in as soon as I can."

Searching his eyes with sadness in my own, I bit my lower lip. I preferred that he not leave at all, but clearly, I would not get my way about this one. Tears trickled down my cheeks as he slowly left the room and the doctor went to grab a nurse to assist.

Lying there through the examination while the doctor did a full pelvic exam and sonogram, she stayed quiet until she was finished and spoke in whispers to the nurse outside of the room when they finished. Why was I being left in the dark about my damn child? I needed answers. I needed to know that my child, my little bean, was okay. I opened my mouth to speak words and nothing came out.

The nurse came back with supplies and looked at me. "Dr. Harris left to go get Christopher. For now, I'm going to have you place your underwear back on, and I'll give you a more absorbent pad that will help soak up the blood."

I thought for sure I would go bat shit crazy if someone didn't tell me what the hell was going on. The blood should have been the biggest clue as to what was happening, but I refused to believe my little bean was not okay.

The nurse left me with a gown, instructing me to place my underwear back on so I wouldn't bleed on the bed and left me to get dressed. I did as she said before I laid back on the bed staring off at the supply cabinet.

A knock on the wall turned my attention to Christopher standing in the doorway. His tall, slim stature leaned against the wall as he stared at me with those big grey-blue hues filled with sadness and I couldn't stand it. Did he know something I didn't?

"How are you feeling, Lor?" He spoke quietly as he moved the chair next to the bed.

"Mostly tired, but the pain is still pretty bad. This…this can't be normal for a pregnancy," I said.

He reached his hand to take mine into his. "The nurse said the doctor would be in soon."

I took his hand between both my hands as tears clouded my vision. "I'm scared, Christopher."

He wrapped his fingers around mine, while his eyes settled on me. "I know, but you're strong Lorelai. We'll get through this together." He spoke above a whisper.

I closed my eyes and tried to hold onto his words for everything they were because I knew something was not right. I was sure that I was not as strong as he thought I was.

Dr. Harris returned, peeking her head into the curtain. "Lorelai?"

I turned my attention toward her as she walked in to take a seat with a chart. "I apologize for the wait. I'm very sorry to tell you this, but the bleeding you're experiencing is your body miscarrying the fetus."

Bean? My little bean was no longer? I was sure I heard her wrong. Tears filled my eyes and threatened to spill down my cheeks as I turned my head away from her. Christopher stood quietly next to the bed and pulled me into his arms. Sobs left me quietly as I grasped a hold on his shirt. Dr. Harris let the words sink in before she continued talking. "I know this is hard to swallow, and no one expects either one of you to take it lightly; but I want to make sure you receive the proper care."

Her voice echoed off in the distance as she continued talking. Her voice eventually stopped, and I stared off. I was no longer in the hospital. I didn't know where I was. I was in a land of nowhere. I felt Chris holding me, but I wasn't there. I shook from the inside out as the tears fell down my cheeks and I began to sob. The sobs grew louder. I pulled away from him and curled up into the fetal position as I felt the remains of our bean seep out between my legs.

Darkness closed in around me. This wasn't happening. No harm or heartbreak could touch us. We were Lorelai and Christopher. The most uncomplicated pair of love birds. Nothing or no one would come between us because our love would conquer all; but something did and now, I felt numb of every emotion and I wasn't confident in anything including myself or my relationship. Maybe Uncle Thad was right. A Castillo should never turn his or her back on family. It would bring traumatizing heartbreak into your life.

Hours passed before I was signing discharge papers from the emergency room. Handing the papers back to the nurse, Chris stood with a wheelchair in front of him and came around with the nurse to help me stand from the hospital bed and sit down in the chair.

I sat silently and looked up at the nurse that held out the aftercare paperwork. Slipping it out of her fingers, I folded it in half and shoved it in my purse.

Chris knelt down and moved my feet into the footrests on the chair before he looked up to me with concerned eyes. "Let's get you home."

I nodded in silence and looked on as he backed me up out of the room and wheeled me toward the exit. Locking the wheels, I felt his breath against my ear. "I'm gonna go get the car, okay?"

"Yeah. I'll be fine waiting here," I said, feeling detached. There were no emotions left in me. I felt blank.

He left and came around with the car a few minutes later. He stepped out and carefully helped me into the car before he returned the wheelchair to the lobby. We took off back toward the Golden Gate yacht club. Upon arrival, we walked back toward home and headed down into the cabin. I went straight to the bedroom, kicked off my shoes and climbed into bed.

Christopher stood in the doorway and we stared at each other in silence. I didn't know what to say to him. I wanted to be left alone, but I knew he wouldn't go for it.

"Do you want me to make you something to eat?" he finally asked.

I turned over, my back now facing him. "No."

He sighed softly. "You should eat something, Lor."

"I'm not hungry, Christopher."

"Okay. Fine. Do you need anything else?"

I remained silent. "I…no. I just want to be left alone right now."

"You shouldn't be alone," he pleaded.

Tears filled my eyes and spilled down my cheeks. "I don't care right now. Please, just leave me alone. I'll fend for myself. Okay?"

He inhaled a deep frustrated breath. Perhaps he felt as helpless as I did? "I'll come check on you in a little while then."

Stubborn man. That's all he was. What didn't he understand? "Fine." I left it at that because I didn't want to say something I would regret.

I fell asleep as soon as he left and slept until the next morning. Opening my eyes, I looked around and saw Christopher passed out in the recliner in our bedroom. I had a million thoughts going through my mind as I placed a hand over my stomach and sat up. Going into the kitchen, I pulled out the eggs and bacon and placed them in a skillet. Once the heat on the stove had started cooking the protein for a hearty breakfast, I cut up some fruit and poured two large glasses of milk. After setting the table out on the deck, I returned to retrieve Christopher. Leaning down, I pressed a gentle kiss against his lips.

I smiled as he began to kiss me back, the gentle touch of his fingers smoothing against my waist as he pulled me into his arms down onto the bed gently. I wrapped my arms around his neck and held onto the passionate kiss. "Mmm… breakfast is hot and ready on deck, handsome."

He pulled back and looked up at me. "Mmm… you're feeling better today."

I smiled at him. "I feel amazing. Little bean needs nutrition to grow big and strong."

He looked up at me with furrowed brows before his facial expression dropped and he sighed. "You should go keep an eye on it before the seagulls steal it and fly away."

Giggles left my lips. "I covered it, silly. Come on. Get dressed." I pecked his lips once more. He agreed with my statement. Perhaps yesterday was a nightmare and I wouldn't have to accept anything more of it. Leaving the bedroom and heading up on deck holding his hand, I decided I would go with the positivity despite the empty feeling; the lack of flutters replaced by painful cramps.

He pulled a chair out for me and pushed me in. We sat down to eat and watch the boats float by and the birds fly over the water as they too were looking for breakfast.

Silence remained between us as we ate, and I noticed him watching me closely. "We should talk about the elephant in the room, Lorelai."

And now it was ruined. "We don't have to." I said simply.

"We do though. This is a big deal, and it's okay to grieve or be angry and disappointed."

I shook my head. "I'm fine, Christopher. We're going to be parents to a little bean. My brother will protect him or her from the other side and my parents are leaving Sausalito. Everything is more than okay."

He sighed deeply and I looked at him and then past him. Why was he doing this?

"Lorelai, I know what you're trying to do here and I understand that it hurts in more than one way." He trailed off. I knew he wanted to continue and say more.

I shook my head. "I don't think you do understand. I know you think we can get through this together, but there is no getting through this. A life was lost, hell, lives have been lost and…and I can't help but feel at fault. There was something I could do. I know there was and whatever it was, cutting stress out, eating healthier, cutting ties off with my family sooner. Exposing Santino for what he was trying, could've saved my brother! I could've prevented this entire mess."

He stood up and walked toward me. I stood up before he reached me. "Don't, Christopher. Look. I know you want to help but you can't help me. I'm not able to be helped."

Tears filled his eyes as he stared at me before I turned away from him. I couldn't face him. I couldn't face any of this. It was too hard. Too much. I accepted that I was just a stupid girl that could not do anything right. I fucked up being a daughter, a sister, a mother; and because I didn't do everything exactly perfectly right, I fucked up being a lovable woman.

I heard footsteps come up behind me, and his long arms wrapped around me from behind. "Please, Lorelai," he pleaded. "These terrible things that keep happening are not your fault. I promise they're not."

Pushing his arms away, I stepped back. "I know what I've done and I know the burdens I've caused you and everyone else around me." I turned around to face him because he deserved eye contact while he heard these words so he knew they were true. "I fucked up, Chris; and I know that I've hurt you. You don't deserve this and I'm so sorry."

Tears fell down his tanned skin. "The miscarriage was not your fault. Neither was the fact that your parents tried to keep us apart, or the fact that Armani is dead. None of it is your fault, baby."

I shook my head. "Yes, it is, and that's why…." I choked on the tears rising in my throat. "That is why we can't be together."

He looked at me with those lost puppy eyes. "What? Lorelai, no! I love you…I'm head over heels in love with you."

"I don't deserve your love, Christopher! You may not be able to see it now, but you will!"

I didn't know what came over me. I felt angry and shattered, and I didn't want to tear him down with me.

Tears filled my eyes and fell down my cheeks. I spoke barely above a whisper, "I think you should leave now."

His eyes flared as a multitude of emotions crossed his face. I caused so much turmoil everywhere in the people's lives that meant the most to me. I turned away from him as I imagined myself tearing the heart out of his chest, watching it turn to glass and shattering right before me. I could almost feel the shards of glass causing blood to drip slowly down my hands and arms.

"Y-you're breaking up with me?"

I snapped out of the dark images haunting every corner of my brain. "It's for the best, Christopher." I trembled. "Don't make this harder than it already is. Please." I sobbed through my words.

He turned me around, and placed both his hands against my cheeks. "For whom exactly?" His voice cracked. God. What was I doing? Forcing him away from me would break both of us, yet I was so goddamn insistent that this is what we needed.

"For both of us," I lied. I was lying both to him and myself. We wouldn't be better off apart, but I couldn't admit that to him.

He shook his head. "No. I know this isn't what you want. If you need time and space, fine. But I won't let you push me away for good."

I paused for a long moment as I sank my teeth into my lower lip. "Chris…don't make this harder than it already is." My voice cracked as a sob found its way through.

He brushed his thumbs against my cheeks, leaned in and planted his soft lips against my forehead. He inhaled a shaky breath, and I could tell he was fighting back his own emotions. "Okay, if this is what you want. I'll pack my stuff and go."

His fingers slowly fell away from my cheeks before he took a step back and disappeared into the cabin. More tears fell freely, soaking my cheeks. My knees wobbled as I turned to look and see if he would come back and fight me on this. When he didn't, I sobbed quietly and fell to my knees against the wooden boards beneath me. He couldn't know that I felt any different. I wanted him to be free of the dreaded Castillo Curse that I was. I brought nothing but angst, drama, and heartbreak into his life. He deserved more, and I was sure he would find it without a problem. Any woman would be lucky to have him. I would have to accept that I could no longer fill those shoes.

Quickly moving to my feet, I realized I couldn't stay here once he left. I would disappear into the Pacific Ocean, maybe permanently.

A few minutes later, Christopher emerged from the cabin with his bag over his shoulder as I prepared to set sail. "If you need anything, you know where I'll be."

I turned to look at him. "Thanks, but I think we both need to keep our distance." I wore a brave face so he wouldn't change his mind, but I could feel the shattered pieces of my own heart breaking further. He bit his lower lip. "Right. Well, you take care of yourself then, Lorelai."

I stared at him for a moment. Part of me… my whole heart, wanted him to stop and fight for us. Instead, I said, "You too, Christopher." I stood frozen watching him step off the vessel. The further he walked away, the urge to scream for him to come back became stronger; and yet, I continued to resist.

Nineteen

Shattered Glass

LEAVING LORELAI BEHIND on Cakes and Pies paralyzed my state of mind. My heart beat loudly in my ears while memories of the time we had raced through my mind. My own voice multiplied yelling and screaming, telling me to fight. This was not how it was supposed to play out. We were stronger than this, we were supposed to be stronger than this. I know that our parents didn't want us together, but we jumped those hurdles. We were Montastillo strong. She represented beauty in all forms. She proclaimed me to be the perfect man for her, her prince charming, her hero, the human furnace that kept her warm through the cold Sausalito nights. What she didn't see was that she was my hero, too. She saved me from her father when I believe he would have murdered me out of spite after I refused to take his money.

Placing the car in park as I arrived back to the Castillo Yacht Club, I rubbed my hands over my face. Stepping from the car, I paced back and forth. I left because she wanted me to. I followed through because that was her wish. Had I really made the right decision? Was she testing me? Should I have refused to leave and stuck by her side? Was she lying about how she felt? There were so many questions that I couldn't decide whether I made the right move. Moving my hands behind my head, I began to pace once more. I shouldn't be here. I should be there making sure she was okay. That's what any man would do after his girlfriend miscarried his child. Did I dare go back? Or, did I respect her decision and give her the space she asked for? I bit my lower lip as tears filled my eyes and threatened to spill over. Swallowing the godforsaken tears back, I grabbed my bag from the backseat and made my way back toward my parents' house. My parents sat out on the patio with their morning coffee; and from their raised eyebrows, I could see that they weren't expecting me.

I avoided them and went straight toward the staircase.

"Christopher? Are you okay?" My mother called from the bottom of the staircase.

I stopped in my footsteps. "Yeah. I'll be fine, Mom. What time is Dad leaving for work?"

"In a little while. Should I let him know you're going to ride with him?"

I paused for a long moment and sighed. "No. I'm going to take a shower and work on homework."

"Are you sure?"

"Yes, Mother." I tried not to give away my shattered heart and soul.

"Okay sweetie."

Heart palpitations coursed through the left side of my chest after I made it to my room. Leaning against the door, I closed my eyes, taking myself back to our first touch, kiss, the first time I saw her with, and without, clothes on. I thought about the way she looked at me with her brilliant blue eyes that showed every emotion she felt. I was madly in love with every part of Lorelai Castillo. She had a heart of gold and she gave it to me. Oh god. What had I done by leaving her? Did I break her? The answer was yes. I might not have been able to protect her from Armani's murder, but there had to be something I could've done to comfort her through the aftermath of the miscarriage. My head spun with memories and possibilities of how this break up would pan out. Would she show up to my house with a box to give me back everything that I left on the boat? Would some of those items be the framed photos she took of us and decorated the inside of Cakes and Pies with? Would she want her radio and the key to Cakes and Pies back?

Hours passed and my head was in an awful place. The reality of the breakup and our future as parents, or lack thereof, set in. I locked myself in my bedroom, refusing to eat or socialize with my parents who had both come up to check on me in the last several hours. I tossed and turned throughout the night, fighting my thoughts and hoping for sleep, but failing at the task.

The following morning, I managed to convince my mother that I wasn't feeling well and she called me out of school. Going back to my room, I stripped my clothes off and decided to take a warm bath thinking that the warm water would relax my mind enough to sleep. Slipping into the tub, the attempt to take Lorelai off of my mind proved to be impossible. I started the water and plugged the drain, allowing the water to fill the tub. Submerging under the hot water, images of the last thirty-six hours ran through my head in slow motion. Discovering the blood in the shower under Lorelai's feet blasted an arrow through my heart. The course of the weeks that passed us by since we'd found out she was pregnant were busy, but they were some of the best days we spent together. Outside of school, we spent the days decorating for the holidays, lounging around in our pajamas while she read from a parenting magazine. She would tease about our child naturally giving me a hard time, she thought it was the funniest scenario in the world. When she wasn't teasing me, we were plotting out the sailing adventures we would take our child on. Places we could drive on land were pinpointed on a map, with red dots; and Lorelai managed to find little sail stickers to stick on ports we could venture to up and down the West Coast, from Seattle down to San Diego. The memories of Lorelai continued right up to the present day. What was she doing now? Was she resting or getting enough to eat and drinking water to keep herself hydrated? All of these key components to living a solid healthy life circled through my mind. I wasn't only head over heels in love with her, I cared about her well-being like any damn good boyfriend should. Here I was at home when she needed me there most. Unplugging the tub after the water grew cold, I showered and dressed myself. I sat down and attempted to work on my homework, another task Lorelai and I tackled together.

Sighing, I gave up. There was no focusing in the moment. I crawled into bed, burying myself under the covers. Perhaps if I went to sleep, I would wake up and this nightmare would be over. Closing my eyes, I drifted off to sleep. The image of waking up to Lorelai watching me sleep when I woke up came to mind; and if she wasn't, I would go to her.

Hours later, I blinked my eyes open and it was pitch black in my room aside from the alarm clock that sat on my night stand that read 10:00 p.m. Silence filled the house. Leaning on my elbow, I reached to turn the lamp on and stepped out of bed. I couldn't accept the reality of this break up. Using the bathroom, I came back to my room, sliding a baseball cap over my messy hair, and slid my flip flops on before I tiptoed down the steps with my car keys and wallet in hand.

Arriving to the parking lot, memories of meeting Lorelai here ran through my mind. Sadness grew through my mind as I spotted her car, but she was nowhere in sight. Getting in my car, I drove to the Golden Gate Yacht Club, parked and made my way inside to where I left her earlier.

Stepping over the threshold to the yacht, I saw lights on through the curtained windows and knocked.

A moment later, the door opened and Lorelai stood there in her robe. She looked drained, her hair back in a messy ponytail. "Christopher? What are you doing here?"

"I needed to see you, Lorelai. I don't think this… this breakup is right. I love you. I'm in love with you, and we… we should be dealing with this together."

She bit her lower lip. "Chris…I-I can't be with you."

The broken shards of my heart shattered into tinier pieces hearing her speak those words as I pressed my lips together. "That can't be true. I know you're hurting, I know this is hard, but I want to be there to help put the broken pieces back together. Let me help you."

She looked away from me. "You should go home. I've caused enough damage in your life, Chris. You deserve someone that will bring you joy and happiness and a lot less drama. I mean, look at me. I'm a damsel in distress ninety-nine percent of the time. I've caused you grief and heartbreak…" She trailed off as her voice cracked with emotion and dug her teeth into her lower lip. "I'm sorry, Christopher… but I can't."

"Give me one good reason. Has your love for me faded?

Everything we had? Was it a lie?"

She was fighting back tears with every last ounce of strength she had; maybe I was getting somewhere. "My love for you was never a lie, Christopher! My father tried to kill you. Can't you see how bad I am for you?"

I shook my head. "No, I can't. Cause I would stand by your side until I took my last breath if it meant you were mine."

"It's late. You should get home before your parents wake up and realize you're gone."

"Lor…" I took her hands in mine squeezing them gently. "Never mind my parents. I need you in my life. I love you so much, and it hurts that I can't be here to take care of you."

"I need to take of myself now, okay? I'm sorry for pulling you into my messy life, but you're free now."

I sighed. "I can't accept that. Look, maybe we need time and space to ourselves. I'll come back in a few days, we can talk then." I wouldn't take no for an answer.

She finally looked at me and nodded. "Maybe, you're right. Let's take a few days."

Relieved that I got through to her, I inhaled a deep breath. I brought her hands up to my lips and kissed them gently, keeping my eyes on hers the entire time.

"Go home and get some sleep," she whispered.

I let go of her hands. "You too." Stepping back, I watched as she shut the door.

Heading home, I knew I wouldn't be able to sleep and decided I would write her a letter, maybe reaching out instead of bombarding her would allow her to come around.

Dear Lorelai,

I'm not sure where to start, but I can't seem to get you off of my mind. I've sat here trying to distract myself in every way I know how and still our memories, and your well-being through these hard times, run through me at a million miles a second.

I know I'm the last person you want to hear from, but I can't let time slip away without getting some things off of my chest. You are the love of my life; and as

I sit here thinking about it, we spent months planning our futures. The traveling we wanted to do, buying a house, and creating mini Lorelai and Christopher monsters. I feel the loss of our child and it tears me to pieces that all the plans we had were ripped out from under us. The miscarriage was neither of our faults. You are not a cursed Castillo. You are the future Mrs. Montgomery. I need to know that you're okay, and the only way I can do that is to be there for you. I need you. I need us. My heart yearns to hold you in my arms, run my fingers through those dark locks of hair, and kiss your tears away. I want to be there for us to grieve through this together. Please write back, or utilize your radio to contact me. I'll be here when you're ready.

Yours Forever,
Chris Montgomery

PS. I'm not giving up without a fight. You are the woman I want to walk through life with.

Folding the letter in thirds, I placed it inside of an envelope and set it aside. I would drop it off in a few days when I went back to check on her.

Three days later

I woke up early on a Friday morning, grabbing clean clothes from the closet. I dressed myself, slid my kicks on and collected my backpack and the envelope. Downstairs, I grabbed an apple for breakfast and left for the Golden Gate Yacht Club before school started for the day. I traveled down the boardwalk on my way to the parking lot; and for a Friday morning, the place was a little more crowded than usual. Men in black suits and sunglasses blended into the atmosphere. I saw the first at the cafe in line waiting on a coffee. His partner sat at a nearby table. The second pair sat apart on the benches a few feet apart appearing to look alone, and the last pair stood outside the clubhouse.

I didn't stick around to figure out what they were doing and I couldn't have been sure that they were with the Castillos or the law was finally moving in to investigate Mr. Castillo's yacht club. I needed to know more so I knew how to protect my family and Lorelai, but there were higher stakes here; I was in danger of losing the only woman I could love. I needed to get to her and convince her that living apart was not an option.

Upon arriving and walking through the entrance of the Golden Gate, I made my way back to where I left Cakes and Pies a few days prior. The dock that she was anchored at was now empty.

"Son of a bitch!" I mumbled under my breath and turned around coming face to face with Marie Castillo.

"Where is she? Where's Lorelai?" She asked, looking just as confused as I was.

Twenty

Get Ahold of Yourself, L. Castillo

Lorelai

AFTER CHRISTOPHER VISITED late in the night, I found myself standing against the door of the cabin sobbing. Tears fell freely down my cheeks. I sunk to the floor, laying my head against my legs. The wail of my sobs grew louder. What was I thinking pushing him away? Perhaps I wasn't, and the thought that I hurt him made me feel like a horrible person if I had the capability of hurting a man that only loved and cared about me. I inhaled a deep breath as the thought went from a possibility of making this work versus standing my ground with this break up.

Get a hold of yourself, Lorelai. You never deserved a man like Christopher.

My heart fought reminding me that he became the only person I had to rely on for the escape from my family and their crooked ways of living. Perhaps I should've waited to make up my mind about the family business. I had my doubts that I, Lorelai Sienna Castillo, could stoop to a level of performing at organized crime. Then again, I did manage to make Chris fall in love and hurt him in the worst way possible.

Standing up after I collected myself, I walked through the main living space of the cabin, taking in the framed pictures of Christopher and I that hung on the walls, and sat on the shelves. Reminders of our memories, making this yacht not only a house, but a home for us. The realization that I threw it all away because I couldn't trust myself to rely on him to get us through these trying times made me angry.

Walking to the shelving unit, I picked the picture frames off one at a time and threw them at the island stationed in the kitchen, glass shattering on the floor. Rampaging through the cabin, I destroyed every last memory I had with Christopher as tears fell freely down my cheeks. I sobbed as I packed a bag knowing that I could not be there when Christopher came back. Leaving the bag on the bed, I marched out of the cabin with my purse over my shoulder, leapt to the dock and went down to the main boardwalk to the pay phone. Pulling out a number from my phone book, I inserted the quarter and waited as the other line rang.

"Hello?"

"Santino? It's Lorelai. Are you busy?"

He chuckled. "No, I'm not busy. What's up beautiful? Are you okay?"

"Not really. I need someone to talk to. Are you available?"

"Um. Yeah. Where are you at now?"

"The Golden Gate."

"Shit, really? I'm staying north of there a bit at Waldo Point. You should come up. I'll go talk with security and let them know you're on the way."

I inhaled a deep breath. "Yeah? Alright." I agreed. "I'll get ready and head up."

"Lorelai. Be careful, okay?" He sounded sincere.

"I will. See you soon, Santino." I hung up, and walked back to the yacht.

Pulling the anchors up, and untying the ropes, I started the engine, put on my proper lights, and headed out without a second thought.

Upon arrival to the security gate, the guard gave me a dock number and I made my way over. Making sure the cabin was locked and secure, I grabbed my purse and threw the anchors out once more. I found Santino standing on the dock. Inhaling a deep breath, I stepped off and walked to him throwing my arms around his neck. He pulled me into his arms tightly and kissed my cheek.

Pulling back, he looked at me. "Come on. We can go hang out at my place."

I nodded and took the hand he offered me, following him out.

We boarded the luxurious yacht, and he brought me to the main living space. Going to the kitchen to grab us each a bottle of water, he brought it over as he led me to the couch. Sitting down, he wrapped an arm around me. "You look upset, Lorelai. What's going on?"

I pushed some hair behind my ear. "It's everything. You know, opting out of the syndicate, not knowing what I'm going to do after high school, Armani's death and not having any answers as to what happened. I have Marie, and that's really it. Not knowing what I'm going to do after I graduate scares the living hell out of me." I was lying. Of course, I was; I couldn't tell him what was going on. He wouldn't understand and I needed this distraction.

"You opted out of the syndicate? That's too bad, but maybe I can ease your mind with answers about Armani." He rubbed a finger down my arm; and even though I once feared this man and his grimy touch, somehow, I felt comforted by him.

"Do you know what happened?" I asked as I looked up in his ocean blue eyes. One fact stood out about Santino, his eyes were captivating. His defined jawline could cut through metal. Despite his good looks, he was always dedicated to my father's business from the time he was recruited when I was still a preteen. He was around for a large part of my upbringing. I should be able to trust him without a problem, right?

He inhaled a deep breath. "I do. Armani and I were over at the Golden Gate Yacht Club, taking care of a case your Papino sent us on, when we discovered that another family along enemy lines moved in. Your brother was adamant about coming back to chase them out. A warning act from one syndicate to another could be anything from stealing a job, to taking out the second or third strings of the syndicate. Well, Armani decided he wanted to paint a real clear message, so he hacked their systems and wiped them clean. Every last piece of information in the Moretti database was lost, and one only completes this when they want an all-out war."

My lips fell open as I stared off. "Let me guess, he did it without my father's permission?"

He nodded. "You knew your brother well. I tried to tell him not to do it and leave it in the hands of your Papino, but he already had his mind made up."

I sighed, tears welling in my eyes. I tried to keep my breath even, thinking about my life around that time. I was so wrapped up into Christopher, and stubborn about keeping my nose where it did not belong when it came to the syndicate. I couldn't have been bothered to check in with my parents, let alone my siblings. I always thought Armani and Luciana had a solid head on their shoulders. So where had I gone wrong? Perhaps it was the entire forbidden dynamic with Christopher. He had a way of allowing me to escape with him. He took me into his arms and danced the dance with me. He made me forget I ever belonged to a family involved in organized crime. He made me feel like I mattered while my family made sure I was kept busy with a job that freed up their time to continue torturing people. The level of anger I had with them, and anyone that helped them, rose. I knew it would be useless to manifest this anger, so I let it go with the tears that fell down my cheeks.

Quickly wiping the tears away, I looked back to him. "I did, but I also know that my family wouldn't let something like this go without a consequence for the Morettis." I paused, and bit my lip. "So, what do you have up your sleeve, Santino?"

His hands cupped my cheeks, wiping the tears away. "Don't worry your pretty mind, Lorelai. The plan I have will make the Morett's pay significantly," he whispered. Inching his way in, he planted his lips against mine in a firm, lust-filled kiss.

Twenty-One

A Turn Of Events

"I DON'T KNOW." I said, stress filling my tone. "I wish I knew. Did she contact you, Marie?"

She shook her head. "No. She told me she was here; but when I didn't hear from her, I became concerned."

I sighed. "We need to find her. We should go back and check the boat house rentals. Maybe she went back home."

Marie nodded, placing a hand at the back of my shoulder. "We'll find her, but you need to stay calm."

I shook my head. "I wish it were that easy, Marie."

"Did something happen between you two?"

I sighed. "It's a long story, we shouldn't talk about it here."

She nodded, eyeing me carefully before she guided me down the docks. We left the Golden Gate. I couldn't bring myself to tell her how bad this was, though I had a feeling she felt the immense tension in the air.

Walking into the Castillo Yacht Club, we were on our way to check the rentals when Luci stepped out in front of us, stopping us in our path. She wore a black and white plaid dress suit, with a red scarf wrapped around her neck. Her skin appeared more pale than normal with dark makeup around her eyes, and red lipstick covering her lips.

"I need to talk to both of you, now." She was direct and stern as she turned us around. "Don't ask questions, just walk."

In my peripheral vision I saw Marie give me a wide-eyed glance. I knew that this was a turn of events that occurred in the last forty-eight hours; and Luciana confirmed this when she walked ahead of us, leading the way through the Black Diamond arches. Landing at the back of the docks, there were six large yachts anchored in a line up. The first time I was back here, I was blindfolded and couldn't take in the detail. While we waited for Luciana to punch a code in, I noticed the docks connected to the back of turquoise buildings and breathed a silent shaky breath in through my nose. None of this felt right; but when the door opened, Marie wrapped her arm around mine and dragged me in with her and kept me close as we followed Luciana through one code secured door after the next. This place had some serious lockdown devices.

"What are you doing?" I whispered.

"Something doesn't feel right." She matched my tone of voice.

"That's because it's not…"

Luciana turned around stopping us in our tracks. "Enough with the whispers." She reached what looked like a control room, rows of leather office chairs in stadium seating faced a forty-foot wall covered with screens. "Christopher, care to tell me where Lorelai is?"

I sighed. "I-I'm not certain. We broke up about four days ago." I said, looking down.

"What happened?" She asked, her tone still stern.

Fear struck me that if I didn't tell her, she would hurt me or throw me to the wolves.

I sighed. "Everything we say stays in this room, right?"

"Sure," she smirked. "Spill it, Montgomery."

"Lorelai was pregnant, she had a miscarriage; and I firmly believe after Armani's death, and the incident with your father, that losing the baby was the straw that broke the camel's back."

Luci inhaled a deep breath, pinching the bridge of her nose. After a moment, she looked at me, and then Marie. "Okay. I have some news, and it's not good."

I clenched my teeth. "Okay. What is it about?"

"My brother's murder." She walked across the bottom floor. "I suggest you have a seat."

Marie dragged me with her up the steps to the third row of chairs and we both sat in the dead center waiting for Luciana to continue.

"It all started when my Papino went out of town and put Santino in charge. In my opinion, that was mistake number one. I tried to tell my mother that it was a mistake; but as usual, what my father says goes." She paused. "Anyway, I went along with Armani and Santino to the Golden Gate Yacht Club because we had a few fees to collect; and while we were there, we ran into trouble. Emanuele Moretti, the son and immediate second string to the Moretti Syndicate and his band of brothers approached us, trying to tell us to remove ourselves from their territory. Armani made sure to let them know they weren't crossing into our territories, that it was their family that moved into our territory and Santino backed him up. Well, Emanuele didn't like what they had to say, so he shoved past Santino and let us know they weren't going anywhere. Armani and Santino got fired up, and Santino insisted that Armani step up and put them in their place. He guided him through a blackout, meaning Armani single handedly hacked and wiped out their entire system. During the blackout, Santino sent Armani in, freed their hostages, dislodged the security bugs and the day before Papino returned, Armani came up missing."

Marie grasped my hand in hers and when I looked over to her, tears streamed down her cheeks. I rubbed the back of her hand with my thumb, covering my lips with my pointer finger and the edge of my thumb, staring off. The realization that all of this happened in the vicinity that Lorelai and I were hiding hit hard. I felt Marie's eyes on me, she felt the tension hit just as hard. Here I was trying to protect Lorelai, and her brother's murder could have occurred mere feet from where we stayed, another secret I would have no choice but to keep from the love of my life. The bottom line was that it was for her protection. I would continue protecting her at all costs.

Silence filled the room for a few minutes before a door opened and a soft tap of shoes crossed the floor. The elbow planted into my leg slipped and I nearly hit my head on the table as Armani Castillo Sr.

came into view. "Is this true, Luciana?" Fuck. He heard the entire story.

Luciana crossed her arms, the hard, facial expression falling. "Yes, "Papino."

He looked up to see Marie and I sitting in the chairs. "What the hell are they doing in here, Luciana? You know they aren't supposed to be here."

Marie stood up and walked down to face Luciana and Armani.

"Lorelai is missing."

"She's what?" Armani spat.

"She's missing, Uncle. Cakes and Pies is nowhere in the vicinity."

Silence resumed as each of us stared off in a different direction. I looked up so I could see them in my peripheral vision. The entire atmosphere in the vault became very cold and dark, and I questioned the impossible. Could the man that saw me as his very enemy overcome his stubborn mantra to rescue the daughter that chose me after he told her no? Could he get past the fact that I had protected her? Or would he point the blame on me?

Twenty-Two

The Offer

Lorelai

THE WEEK SPENT with Santino proved to be just what I needed. He took me to Matteo, who had the papers for the emancipation finalized. I was a free woman, finally. High school was still there and I had to attend, but I had to do it and avoid Chris. Acting as if he didn't exist would break me into a thousand pieces, but it's what had to be done in order to keep on track with graduation. Upon returning to his private yacht, we took trips down memory lane telling stories about my brother. He told me stories of when my Papino put him in charge to train Armani for the syndicate, and that he was there for his ritual and welcoming dinner. I learned that when a Castillo joined the family business, they were also required to give a speech proving that they studied the handbook. Armani, being the detailed man that he was, wrote and gave scenarios for how he would orchestrate and carry out assignments. In Santino's words, Armani was built to be a Castillo. I halfway believed him, as I told him about the protective side he had over Luciana and myself when meeting us at the bus stop, or the spur of the moment adventures he took us on throughout Marin County and San Francisco. Armani was the reason I knew the Bay Area as much as I did. He was the reason I woke up on time for school and ate properly.

While I never regretted the time I spent falling in love with Chris, I missed my brother. The grieving period of his passing hit me hard; and while I kept a strong face in front of Santino, my heart broke when it finally hit me that making memories with Armani, Luciana and I were no longer possible.

Friday morning, I walked out to the deck where Santino had breakfast and coffee waiting for us to sit down and eat. I felt nauseous, and pushed my food around my plate for a few minutes.

"Santino?"

"Yes, darling?" he replied with a smug smirk on his face.

"Do you think vengeance will ever come to the person or persons that were responsible for Armani's murder?"

His facial expression grew carefully neutral and he cleared his throat. "I do, actually. I'm sure that they will all be put in their place very soon," he soothed, and put his hand across the table, placing it on top of mine. "What do you say we take today and go out on the water? It seems like you need it."

I smiled at him gently. "I would like that. Thank you, Santino."

Santino was right. A day out on the bay soaking up the vitamin D was exactly what I needed. He respected my space, and his past creepy tactics to pursue me seemed to have disappeared from his agenda. I made a mental note that I would have to go back to Cakes and Pies to clean it up and go back to being on my own.

Looking over, I saw him sit up after falling asleep during our sunbathing session. "I have a surprise for you."

I smiled at him gently. "A surprise? What kind of surprise?"

He stood up, offering his hand. "Come with me."

I took his hand and followed him into the luxurious interior of his yacht. He took me to the bedroom, and pulled out a bag hanging over the door frame. "I thought we could go out for dinner tonight, so I

I bought something a little extra special for the occasion."

I narrowed my eyes at him with a careful glance and lifted the bag up, unveiling a gorgeous silk evening gown. I had to admit, the dress was smitten-worthy and a bag of jewelry hung from the hanger. "Santino, this had to cost a fortune. I couldn't possibly accept this."

He stepped back before he approached from behind, his hands cupped over my hips. "This is the kind of life I would give you all the time if you were mine, Lorelai." He spoke above a whisper against my ear. "Let me take you out, just for tonight."

I bit my lower lip, and looked back at him. "Just for tonight," I whispered back. "Don't get any other ideas stuck in that head of yours."

He lifted his hands in surrender and he smirked. "Scout's honor." I sighed quietly as he rubbed his hands over my hips some more. Being here with Santino brought certain reminders to my head. He would ultimately keep me connected to my family if I followed through on allowing him to pursue me. I had fought like hell to disconnect myself from my parents and the dark roads I could be led walking down that road. Part of me wanted to run as far away from Santino as possible. I knew that I needed time and space away from everyone to deal with the losses that fell upon me. But another part of me thought, what if he could make me happy? The thought made me cringe. Closing my eyes, I inhaled a deep breath and decided I wouldn't get ahead of myself.

His hands slid away from me as he placed a sweet kiss to my cheek. "Get dressed, and fix your hair and makeup. I'm going to get ready and make sure our reservations are secure."

I felt the tingle of his lips linger as he disappeared from my line of sight. I shook my head, and tried not tell myself that he was slithering his way in because I came to him. I was the one that had the power in my hands now. I tried to convince myself that he wasn't taking advantage when I was in a vulnerable state of mind, that he was a close connection to our family and felt the loss of Armani no longer being a part our world, that he could help the grieving period I was going through. Armani was the reason I came here in the first place and Santino was able to give me the answers I was looking for.

As early evening approached us, I finished with my hair and makeup and pulled the bag open to reveal the black and white mermaid gown. Black sequins were stitched down the front with a pattern of white flowers and poufy, ruffled side shoulders. My lips fell open. What would it say to Santino if I accepted these gifts from him? Pulling the dress off of the silky, upholstered hanger, I unzipped it and stepped into it. Zipping the side of the dress, I looked in the mirror and realized the dress matched my hair. I looked flawless, while my self-conscious said something completely different. I sighed. Santino would think I finally caved in to his wants and needs. I let him chase me for so long; and what I really needed right now was someone that understood the pain I felt with the loss of Armani's imminent murder, and Santino was there for my family through that. He backed off of me, he let me go and this was me quite possibly coming back to him.

Stepping away from the mirror, I turned toward the bed, pulled out the black strapped heels, and sat down just as there was a knock at the door.

"Lorelai? May I come in?" It was him.

"You may." I sat unbuckling the straps and looked up as the door opened. He stood in black slacks, a white button up and a sweater vest to match his ensemble. Closing the space between us, he moved down on one knee and took the shoe from my hands. He began to place them on my feet, one at a time. He stood up and placed me in front of the mirror, pushing my hair to one side as he snapped the necklace and bracelet on, placing a kiss against my bare shoulder as he looked at me through the mirror.

"You look exquisite, Lorelai," he whispered.

My head fell to the side as he planted soft, gentle kisses over my shoulder to my neck, sending shivers down my back. I shouldn't have been enjoying this. I shouldn't have been falling into this trap he was forming around me, and yet I couldn't stop him from continuing.

He pulled away before I could say anything, leaving his lips close to my ear. "Are you ready?" He offered me his hand.

I turned to look him in the eyes and placed my hand into his, allowing him to lead me from the room as we left the cabin and moved to the cockpit, where he took us out on the water for a short ride to the Waldo Point Resort and Yacht Club. Once docked, he led me off the vessel and up to the hotel. We took the elevator to the top floor to the rooftop restaurant.

"Two for De Luca," he confirmed with the hostess, who led us outside to a private cozy spot with gas fire pits on each side of the table, warming the area.

Santino pulled a chair out for me. "Ladies first, always."

I smiled and took a seat looking up at him. "Thank you."

"It's my pleasure, Miss Castillo." He sure was being smooth. Perhaps he wanted something more than just dinner.

The waitress came, and Santino ordered a bottle of wine, sliding the waitress a fat tip after asking for two glasses. She slid the money out from under his fingers, eyeing him carefully. I watched the two talk with their eyes. A very unsettling lump grew rapidly in my stomach traveling to my throat. I didn't like this. I didn't like it all. Shoving the thoughts away, I focused on the soft, peace-filled music being played by a live band as the sun began to set. I watched Santino fiddle with his palm pilot out of the corner of my eyes from time to time before standing up and moving to the glass wall, staring off into the distance.

Swallowing the lump in my throat, I allowed Christopher to enter my mind for the first time in over a week. I couldn't imagine what he had gone through when I pushed him away. He was dealing with a dual loss, just as I was. He not only lost our child, he lost me. I pushed him away and ran, ran away from the only person that understood the pain I was feeling. If only I had taken the time to realize that I could rely on him and that maybe we could get through this together.

Tears choked me. I tried to swallow them hard, over and over again. My breathing felt constricted as the emotions and tears began to win. Looking back at Santino, he was still lost in that damn palm pilot. Turning back around, I thought back on this week. Sure, we spent time together but he was still under the rule of my father. He was still working for an organization that I had been against for as long as I could remember. Some time passed by as I watched the birds fly over the water, the music in the background allowing me to push all of my thoughts about my troubles away. I became lost in the bright colors off the ocean from the sun and the sky, as they cast a bright light toward the coast.

An arm wrapped around me from behind. I jumped slightly, feeling his breath trickle against my ear. "So, I've been thinking. Do you really feel that it's necessary for you to finish your senior year? You still have what? Eight weeks?"

I turned to look back at him. "Yeah, and I've come this far. I should definitely finish." I spoke quietly, trying not to let the repulsion show through.

"Eight weeks is a very long time. Let's hypothetically say you go out for your GED. Do you know what we could do with the next eight weeks?"

I shook my head. I wasn't sure I wanted to know what he was about to propose.

"I could sweep you away from Sausalito, bring you to Las Vegas to a penthouse suite in your name and the world would be at your fingertips." He husked against my ear. "You could do anything you wanted with your life, the opportunities are endless."

Santino had a way of taking me away from my own reality. He knew how to get inside of my head and make opportunities seem impossible to pass up. In past encounters, I was able to brush him off with ease. I closed my eyes as he turned me around, cupped my cheeks with dominant hands as he planted a deep, passionate kiss to my lips.

I poured so many emotions into that kiss as I tried to push the feelings that I was running away from to the side. We were both breathing heavy against each other's lips as he broke the kiss and stared into my eyes with his brilliant blue eyes. Those eyes were becoming the very weakness of my entire existence.

Sausalito could very well be present in the rearview mirror sooner than I ever thought.

"Okay. Let's do it." I finally agreed, sealing my fate.

Twenty-Three

Dark Operations

ARMANI'S FACE TURNED stone cold, I could envision the walls frosting, our skin paling, and our blue lips exhaling visible breaths of air. Fear creeped deep inside that he could have taken me back to the chamber and finished me, but perhaps he saw I would never hurt his daughter, or he feared her scolding and that was why he let me go. He had a large window of opportunities to kill me, or take me somewhere far away where no one would find me; and still, he kept me at the yacht club. He knew that doing anything to hurt me with a result of fatality would result in losing his daughter forever. Now here we were, almost on the same side, working for the same goal. To find Lorelai and bring her home to arms of safety, my arms of safety; and I swore when we did, I wouldn't let go as easily as I had the first time. There would be no time for a grace period, I needed her as much as I needed the breath in my lungs.

The screens ahead of us flashed on and brought my attention to Armani as he pressed certain buttons to pull up different angles on the surveillance cameras. Men in suits were arranged around the hotel in lines going down the docks throughout the resort. The public eye had not noticed a thing because they were spread out; but when Armani zoomed out, the lines formed were a shape I couldn't place my finger on right on the spot.

"Luciana. Get over here."

She walked to her father without another word.

"What do you see here?" he asked as if he was testing her.

"They're icing out the enemy, Papa," she responded without a hesitation.

Papa? Lorelai always referred to him as her father. Perhaps this was the protocol of the syndicate.

Armani looked up at her with pride. "Very good. What does icing out mean?"

"They form lines around the premises in the shape of a snowflake."

He zoomed back out, looking around at other cameras to show the various lines of undercover armed Castillo soldiers standing in the shape of a snowflake surrounding the premises. The lines started at the docks, went down the boardwalk, and through the resort; and from what I could tell, Santino had enough soldiers to make not just one, but two snowflakes.

"Can you identify that this vessel belongs to an enemy?"

Luci studied the live stream for a moment, taking the mouse she circled the black rose. "Right here. It's the Moretti Family, Papa."

"Excellent eye, Luciana." He grabbed a walkie talkie radio, placing the device up to his mouth. "This is Papa. I am ordering anyone involved in the ice out notion to ignore Santino De Luca's orders. Do not make me repeat myself," he snapped.

"Sir….I mean, Papa, I'm not sure I can do that." A hesitant, male voice came in through the radio.

Armani pounded a fist to the table. "Who ordered you to this location?" Armani barked.

Watching the operation in action really showed me how much control he had over his children and others that worked for him. He was running an army. I expected zero hesitation, and yet here this man was questioning Armani.

"Santino De Luca."

Armani chuckled lowly into the speaker, clicking the mouse at the computer and keys on the keyboard. The camera streams disappeared and the screens darkened. "You will no longer be hearing from Santino." He paused. "And the last time I checked? I had the final say in this operation."

"I understand, Papa."

"Great." He sounded a little less annoyed now, perhaps he anchored Santino's location, and had him exactly where he wanted him? I wasn't sure, but I'm sure I would find out soon enough. My stomach churned, and twisted into knots. My insides became a nervous mess as I worried about how all of this would play out for Lorelai, if she would stand up for Santino like she did for me. I stopped the entire thought process. She wouldn't choose him over me. She was afraid of him. I loved and cared for her. We had an undeniable chemistry and connection.

"Now, you're going to answer a question for me. What is De Luca's location?"

"He's having dinner at The Shipyard, Papa."

Armani's hand curled into a fist once more. "Perfect. You and your freeze out group stay put. I'm on my way."

I couldn't be certain what was going to happen next, but Armani had stormed in and dug to the bottom of the mystery where Lorelai was located and clearly formed a plan at lightning speeds.

Armani messed with the channels on the radio. "Amelia, we have a situation."

"What is it, love?" she said a moment later.

"I have to make a trip over to Waldo Point. I need you to send a team to the Golden Gate on a freeze out."

"I can do that right away."

"Thank you, my love. Tell them to wait for instructions."

"Will do."

He set the walkie down and looked to Luci. "Luciana, I need you to make sure Christopher and Marie stay safe, and we'll need them to come with us if we have any chance to pull Lorelai back in. We have to move. Now." He was on his feet and we followed behind him on Luci's hand gesturing commands. We went back through a vortex of darkened hallways, and stepped into an office, going through a hidden bookshelf. We came out inside of the Black Diamond Club. We boarded the Black Knight speed boat and sat down. Marie and I exchanged glances as Armani took off on the water.

When we arrived, Armani was stopped by security.

"I'll need to see your ID and proof of privileges at this club, sir."

Armani pulled out his ID. "Check your list under Castillo. I assure you, my name is on the list."

The security officer narrowed his eyes and handed back the ID. "I'm not sure there's a place to dock, but I suppose you could try the back rows."

"Noted." Armani snatched his ID back, and continued through the gate when it was opened. He found a spot and quickly placed the ropes on the dock and helped the girls out before he looked at me. "Let's go, Montgomery!"

I climbed out without as much as a hesitation and waited for further instructions. Armani walked ahead of us, leading us through the docks.

I saw the lines of men in suits standing on the docks on each of our sides. Armani went straight to the hotel high rise and led us up the elevator. My nerves heightened as sweat dripped down my face. The thought of Santino trying to get away with her, terrified me.

Taking the elevator up, we walked toward the restaurant; and just before Armani was going through the arched entryway, Santino came out holding Lorelai's hand. The second he laid eyes on Armani, he made a mad dash for the staircase, forcing Lorelai with him.

Armani ran after them, and I was right behind Armani without waiting on Luciana's cue. As we ran down the stairs, I heard my heart thumping in my ears as Lorelai yelled in distress at Santino to stop, and each time he would respond and tell her they had to go.

"Santino! Stop! I don't want this! Please, let me go," she pleaded once more.

I imagined Santino pulling her down the steps, his speed picking up. Glancing over the side as I rounded one of the railings, I glanced down the center and she was struggling to push him away.

Santino blatantly ignored her pleas. "Stop fighting it, or I will throw you over this damn banister!"

Anger built up in me, I could see that he had not only manipulated her, but perhaps he had bribed her with some kind of award and now his true colors were shining through. We must've gone down ten flights of stairs before a gunshot echoed through the stairwell.

I ducked down as I heard a ping from the bullet and saw that Armani was able to dodge it as well. Marie came up from behind me, staying ducked down and hidden. I glanced at her, and I was met with a fierce glare. I wasn't the only one ready to kill Santino. Her jaw clenched. She was ready for a fight and I knew that together, we would save Lorelai. There was no other option.

Armani got on his walkie. "We need back up. I need all hands on deck. Move in from the north and south end. De Luca is armed, attempting to shoot and make a break for it. He has Lorelai."

Armani looked at Marie and I, but never lost sight of his petrified daughter. He stood up and continued down and I heard a stampede of footsteps moving up the stairs from below. The syndicate army had made their way in and Santino would soon have nowhere to run.

By the time Marie, Luciana, Armani and I reached Santino, the army of security officers stopped him in his tracks. We came to a face to face confrontation with Santino, his hands gripping Lorelai with evident force. An obstruction snatched the breath from my lungs as Santino wrapped an arm around Lorelai's neck, placing her in a headlock. Reaching behind him, he pulled a gun out pointing the barrel to her head.

Armani's face went beet red with fury. They stood parallel, walking in circles on the platform

"Back off, or I will shoot her." He paused, in heavy breaths. "Call the army off and step aside," Santino spoke through gritted teeth.

"You know," Armani scoffed, "the longer you try to make it seem like you're in charge, the worse this will become when we leave here, Santino."

Santino narrowed his eyes and shook his head. "I'm so sick and tired of living under your goddamn thumb, Armani. I've done everything for you. Everything you've asked of me, every task, drug deal, I've meddled in innocent people's lives, and blood has been shed in buckets. The only thing I asked for in return is her. So, I'm taking what you promised me in the end. Once and for fucking all."

I swallowed the hard lump in my throat and shook from the inside out watching Lorelai's face drop in horror. Armani made deals at Lorelai's expense? Was this why he forbid her to see me?

Lorelai's tears streamed down her cheeks, as she stared up at me with a plea of sorrow. How could she think I was mad or even an ounce upset with her? All I wanted was for this to go away, for good.

Armani inched closer to the man holding his daughter at gunpoint, circling around like a hawk hunting its prey. "You lost that privilege, Santino, starting when you successfully sent my son to his death." He paused, and I imagined that he was giving Lorelai a look of apology. "You know what I'm capable of. Perhaps you should turn to Lorelai and tell her the goddamn truth about how her brother died."

Santino's jaw set into place, furrowing his eyebrows. The daggers remained and panic rose in his eyes. "I don't know what you're talking about, Armani."

Armani shook his head, pacing the platform, his hand at the back of his jeans. "So, you weren't the one that encouraged him to hack the Moretti's system and clear them out under his name, and our IP address?"

"Armani wanted them out as much as I did," Santino spat.

Studying Armani's hand gestures, he placed his thumb with his forefinger together, and the first five men lined up behind Santino. They grasped his wrist twisting the gun from his grasp successfully, placing the security back on the gun.

Santino's arms were brought behind him as the men in suits placed his wrists in handcuffs.

Standing to the side, I could see a wicked smirk curve over Armani's lips. "Let's try that again. This time, let's try the truth."

Security turned Santino to face Lorelai, and he looked down to the floor like the coward that he was. He sighed and bit his lower lip. "Your father was out of town and left me in charge. We found out about the Morettis moving into Castillo territory; and because I had to call the shots, I suggested we make it hard for them to stick around. Junior was all for it. He wanted to help, but I was the one who suggested he hack their system and completed the blackout. It wasn't long after the hack that he went missing, a few days, maybe a week." He paused. "I never stopped looking for him. I searched in every spot I thought they could've taken him. I never tried to move in on the yacht club itself, but I fear that's where they were keeping him."

Lorelai shook from head to toe as tears fell down her cheeks. She reached her hand back and slapped him across the face. "You were supposed to be looking out for him! He told me you would be there if or when this job got tough, and you turned around without thinking twice and led him to his death?" She bit her lower lip, sadness filled her eyes as she looked at the floor. "When were you going to tell me? After you dragged me away from the only place I called home? You made too many broken promises, Santino; and I hope you pay the most severe price of living with it!" She yelled, the sound of her stern tone echoing through the stairwell. She turned to Armani. "Killing him would be the easy way out." She muttered and moved past him.

She set her eyes on me, instant tears cascading over her eyes and fell down her cheeks. My own emotions heightened as I set sight on her standing within touching distance. She closed the space between us, throwing her arms around my neck and burying her face into my chest. "I'm so sorry, Christopher," she mumbled through sobs.

It took me time to embrace the moment. Taking in the touch of her body against mind; her whispered, repeated apologies echoed through my head as I shut my eyes and wrapped her in my arms, pulling her in further against me and burying my head into her neck needing to breathe her scent, breathe the moment. Words escaped my mind. I opened my mouth and nothing came out for a moment. "Don't apologize, baby. It's all going to be okay now, no matter what." I whispered against her ear.

Keeping Lorelai close, I looked on at Luciana and Marie watching us and pulled her tiny frame in closer. She was all mine and I'd be damned if anyone dared to take her from me again.

"Get him out of my sight, gentlemen. I'll be over to deal with him shortly," Armani barked. "And take the back entrance out. We want little to no attention on this." Armani snapped before turning toward us.

Pulling away only slightly, I kept one arm securely wrapped around Lorelai and turned around.

"Luciana…" He gestured for her to step forward.

Luci stepped around us while Marie stepped in on the other side of Lorelai and wrapped an arm around her.

"Take them back to the vault to ensure safety measures for now, and wait for me to come back." He pulled his wallet out. "And send your mother out for ice cream or coffee. Whatever you guys want." He handed her a few large bills.

A smile cracked through my lips as I witnessed the softer side of Armani come out to play. I almost couldn't believe my ears. He was insisting his daughter order in a treat which told me one thing. He knew Lorelai very well and he was at least somewhat satisfied with the outcome of this mess.

Twenty-Four

Tragic Events End with Dessert Buffets

Lorelai

UPON ARRIVAL BACK to my family's yacht club, I walked with Christopher and Marie's arms wrapped securely around my lower back. I was still on edge and shaking. Christopher gave me his jacket, which warmed me from the cold temperatures; but my nerves were still a wreck. Luci walked behind us as we made our way down the boardwalk. We stopped at the arch of the Black Diamond Club as one of the larger yachts exited the docks from within the premises.

Men dressed in black suits stood guard on the middle and upper levels of the vessel. More shivers traveled down my spine and into my legs. I had no doubt in my mind that Santino was present on the yacht, locked up under the highest security. What happened to him now was not a worry of mine, I knew my father would make sure he was taken care of in worse ways than any prison would treat him.

Glancing to my right, I saw Luciana standing on the other side of Chris. "Come on, there's nothing more to be seen here." She led us under the arches and down the docks to the back of the club.

We stopped at a ground level door to the middle, turquoise building and she led us in. She opened a door that appeared to be a utility closet door. Once inside, Luciana inserted a key and pressed the button next to a set of elevator doors. These buildings had more trap and secret doors than I ever knew about. I supposed that knowledge was exclusive to syndicate members only; and here we were, three non-syndicate members getting a taste of what it was like. In my personal opinion, I had enough to last me a lifetime.

Stepping off the elevator, we were inside the vault. Marie looked around as she stepped off and snickered. "That was a top-secret entrance, I can only imagine the quick escape routes."

Luciana looked back at her and smirked. "This is one of many, Marie."

"Yeah? Interesting." She paused. "So, when's the ice cream getting here? I think we could all use some indulgence after that."

"Lots and lots of ice cream. Gallons!" I sniffled softly, feeling Christopher's hand squeeze the side of my waist. Turning toward him, I placed a hand on his chest staring into his eyes. The moment felt so surreal and magical. "Hey, there."

He smiled and wrapped me in both of his arms, planting a gentle kiss against my forehead. "Hey, yourself," he whispered.

"We should talk," I replied. "But first things first. Ice cream and coffee."

He chuckled, planting another gentle kiss. "I agree."

Laying my head against his chest, I remained quiet. My nerves remained jittery, but knowing Santino was gone and being taken care of helped. The thought of Christopher working on the same side as Luciana and my Papino was a sight to break my focus on the tragic events.

I watched as Luciana disappeared from the vault, squeezing my arms around Chris. I couldn't manage much more than standing and holding each other. I knew I messed up by running from, not only my problems, but the relationship issues after the miscarriage. The fact that he was still here was a miracle and I would make sure he knew just how grateful I was.

When the ice cream and goodies buffet was delivered, I leapt from Christopher's hold.

"Hey! Where do you think you're going so fast?" he growled playfully.

I turned toward him, kissing his forehead. "The quicker it gets set up, the quicker we can indulge."

He chuckled and walked over to lift the large trays of ice cream off the cart and set them into the industrial buffet cart. I grabbed the toppings and brought them over, setting them up and taking the cellophane wrap off. I stole a maraschino cherry and walked behind Christopher, slipping an arm around his waist. "Lean your head back," I whispered into his ear.

He chuckled. "Oh god, what are you up to?" he grumbled, doing as he was told.

I dangled the cherry over his lips. "Take a bite."

He practically choked after taking the cherry off the stem. He stood up and turned toward me as he chewed the sweet fruit and smiled at me. "Get your sweet tooth buffet fix assembled, so we can go talk."

I nodded. "Good idea. Do you want anything?"

"Grab enough for me to take a few bites."

I nodded and watched as he took care of our coffee, grabbing the largest cup set on the table while I filled two plates with our ice cream and assorted desserts.

Luciana walked up beside me. "Lorelai…"

I turned to look at her. "Luci…" The last time we saw each other, harsh words were spoken and I wasn't sure where I stood with being on speaking terms with her.

She sighed. "I know you want some time alone with Chris; but I just wanted to tell you, I'm happy you're okay."

I inhaled a shaky breath, avoiding eye contact. "I'm not. I'm not okay right now, but I will be."

"I understand and I know you need time with Chris. I can show you down to the common area. It's secure and private."

"That would be great. Thank you, Luci." I whispered, looking at Chris. I inclined my head and we followed Luci out of the vault. She took us to the common room and left quietly.

We sat and ate in silence with the exception of the 'mmms' and 'so goods' leaving my lips after every other bite. Once we were finished, he placed the plates aside and pulled me back gently into his lap and wrapped me in his arms securely. I allowed him to and looked at him with gentle eyes. "I owe you an apology, Christopher."

"For what?" he asked, brushing his thumbs against my waist.

"For running away like I did. I know that you would've been there had I let you."

He sighed softly. "None of that matters right now. What matters is that you're safe, and that we focus on healing from these tragedies we both had to take head on."

I laid my head against the front of his shoulder. "How do you suppose we do that?"

I felt his hand rub up and down the side of my back. "Well, I think it'll take time, and seeking therapy would be an ideal starting point."

I closed my eyes. "Probably so, but I think it would be beneficial for both of us, as a couple and separately. How to cope and live our lives after a miscarriage, and a family member being murdered."

He moved some hair behind my ear and lifted my chin so we were eye level. "That, and not blaming ourselves for these losses."

I smiled weakly, tears filling my eyes. "It will definitely take time, but I believe in us."

He shook his head. "I've always believed in us. You heal on your time and terms. I'll be right beside you the entire way."

My emotions were running high as the tears flowed down my cheeks. "I know the way I reacted after the miscarriage was wrong. I hit rock bottom emotionally. I felt numb, and cold. My world was falling apart, fading away as I knew it. I was a mess, blaming myself led to believing I didn't deserve you in my life let alone as a boyfriend."

His lower lip popped out as he looked me in the eyes and cupped my cheeks. "I think you deserve the world, and I will give it to you."

More tears fell free from my eyes. "I love you, Christopher."

He chuckled, tears forming in his own eyes. "I love you, Lorelai Castillo." He brushed the tears away before he pulled me close. "I will love you for the rest of forever," he whispered against my ear.

I smiled, nuzzling against him as his hands moved to my back, rubbing up and down. His touch gentle, yet firm and comforting.

Thinking back on the events of the evening, a multitude of emotions filled me. Turning around to see Christopher coming to my rescue was pure bliss. Papino promised I would always be protected by the syndicate, even though I wanted nothing to do them. He was still there, making sure justice was served. Luciana too. Enemies transitioned to allies in a time of need, it was beautiful in a way. My father let his protective order go and allowed Christopher to be there when I needed him most.

I laid back into Chris's arms, exhausted after all the trauma I endured from Santino. Feeling his arms wrapped around me, I nuzzled my face into his chest, listening to the steady thump of his heart beat practically putting me to sleep. The room was quiet aside from breathing, he ran his fingers through my hair and pressed gentle pecks to my forehead.

A few minutes later, the door opened and shut, but I didn't move a muscle.

"Lor? Dad has returned, and he's requested you come back to the vault."

I sat up slowly and looked at Luci. "Okay." I looked back at Chris and offered my hand out to him.

He took my hand and we followed Luci back. Upon entering, we took a seat. My father was busy on the phone talking quietly for a few minutes before he hung up and turned toward us sitting in the office chairs.

"Lorelai. You're free to go. The area is cleared, and I had my personal security guard track your yacht down over at the Golden Gate. He's brought it back. You'll find it anchored on the front of the boardwalk."

I stood and took Christopher's hand walking down, standing in arm's length of my father. "Thanks, Dad. I appreciate everything you did tonight."

He reached out and pulled me into a hug, kissing the top of my head. "A Papino will always protect his Bambina. No matter what she does to go against his word."

I smiled, hugging him back before he pulled away and looked to Christopher. We stood in a moment of silence as Chris locked eyes with my father.

"You take care of my Lorelai," Papino practically whispered, offering Chris his hand.

My eyes widened in surprise as Chris shook my father's hand.

"You have my word, Mr. Castillo."

Exiting the front of the building, we walked hand in hand down the wooden dock to the boardwalk. As promised, Cakes and Pies was anchored out front. We made our way onboard and I unlocked the door before we made our way in to be met with the broken glass from the picture frames scattered everywhere.

"Whoa… What happened here?" Chris asked.

I turned to look back at him and bit my lower lip. "I kind of lost my shit the night you came to see me."

He looked at me with gentle eyes and sighed. "Do you want to talk about it?"

I bit my lower lip, sliding down to the couch after making sure it was clear of glass. "I was pissed off, angry at myself for sending you away. I was pissed off that Armani was dead. I couldn't wrap my head around the miscarriage. I was emotional, I didn't know where to turn and the picture frames were the easiest thing to throw."

Without a word spoken, he stood and walked toward the kitchen and grabbed a broom and started sweeping the glass into a dust pan. Stopping after a moment, "I understand that you were upset, rightfully so." He spoke standing at the edge of the kitchen. He stayed calm and never rose his tone of voice. "They're only picture frames. Those are replaceable. You're not."

I watched as he went back to cleaning up the mess, he pulled out the vacuum and thoroughly made sure not even the tiniest shard of glass was left behind.

Sitting there, I stared off and caught a glance at him every so often. He wasn't angry, concerned? Affirmative. In that moment, I knew that we made it through some tough waters and that the road ahead of us wouldn't be an easy one; but we were fighters, we were

Montastillo strong. We offered love and support when it was needed no matter what life threw at us; and one day when we had children, we would be able to pass on that strength to them.

Twenty-Five

Repairing the Broken Molds

Christopher

Six weeks later

I **PLACED A** hand on Lorelai's thigh as she read through a magazine in the waiting room at the psychologist's office. After Santino's disappearing act, it didn't take Lorelai long to agree to inquire about couples' counseling. Going into our first session, we started with why we wanted to seek couples' counseling; and, at the end of the first session, our counselor could see we had valid reasons to be there. Together, we decided that therapy once a week to start out would be sufficient while we worked through the healing process of the tragic events we went through.

The door opened and Marlee, our counselor, stuck her head out and smiled. "Lorelai? Chris, come on back."

Lorelai closed the magazine and looked at me. "Ready?" She offered her hand and I stood up taking her hand before walking in the back to Marlee's office.

Once sitting on the comfortable couch, I wrapped an arm around the back of Lorelai's shoulders.

"So? What's going on in Lorelai and Chris's universe?" Marlee asked as she sat down with a notepad.

Lorelai looked at me, then Marlee. "Well, we have some good news to start off with."

"Starting with good news is always a positive way to start. Let's hear it."

"After everything, we're both in line to graduate high school. In fact, commencement is this weekend."

A smile widened on her face. "That is a huge mile marker! Are you excited?"

"Absolutely. We're so over the study sessions and homework. I mean, senior year wasn't what I expected, but it was better than I ever imagined in some ways."

"How so?"

She placed a hand on my leg and looked back at me. I smiled as she began to speak after a short pause. "Well, I wasn't around to make memories with my friends or take in all the perks of being a senior, but I met Christopher and he's the best thing that's ever happened to my life."

"And why is that, Lorelai?"

"He brought a promise to my future. A love that I wasn't sure existed. He supports me in everyday life goals, and not just my dreams, but our dreams. We have plans for after graduation too, but I can't say anything yet because we're waiting on the official word."

Marlee smiled. "Okay, well I'm sure you'll keep me informed then?"

I smiled. "Of course, we will."

"What about you, Chris? How have things been since our last visit?"

I brushed my thumb over the top of Lorelai's hand and caressed it gently. Tough conversations often made her emotional. "We continue making growth and progress. We're always open and honest with each other. We have our hard days and nights. Uninterrupted sleep hasn't exactly been the easiest of tasks."

"What do you mean?"

I looked to Lorelai making sure it was okay I continued, and gave me a nod to elaborate. "She has nightmares about the night Santino was trying to force her to leave for Vegas. I'll wake up from her tossing and turning. She's an emotional sleeper, she'll wake up crying, having a hard time breathing, and realizing it was only a dream. I do my best to make sure she knows she's safe and that Santino isn't coming back."

"What do you do to comfort her other than verbally tell her she's safe?"

"I'll get her a glass of water; and if staying in bed isn't an option, we'll leave the cabin and go lie out on the deck and watch the stars until she's calm enough to sleep again."

Lorelai smiled. "And that's just one example. He's made other approaches, too. He'll hold me, and rub my back until I fall back to sleep. Or he'll bring me a warm cup of milk and read gossip magazines out loud and make me laugh until I'm in tears. Sometimes, he'll bring me to the kitchen, cook us a full breakfast, and we'll sit on the kitchen floor and eat together. He's very adamant about taking my mind off whatever it is that has me worked up."

Marlee wrote some key notes down, and smiled up at us when she finished. "It sounds like you're a strong support system. What about you, Chris? Have you hit any walls?"

I paused to think about it. "I think between the miscarriage and almost losing her, I've been trying hard to make sure it doesn't happen again. We're young, yes; but Lorelai is my forever and I remind her of that a lot. Lorelai mentioned plans for the future, and I think that's what I have been working on most. Making sure that we aren't living on the cabin of her luxury yacht; which is great, don't get me wrong, but it's not a place we should live when we want to start a family sooner rather than later."

"Ah! There it is. So future living plans. I think these are all excellent goals. Mental health and communication in your relationship is very important. What about plans for careers or college?"

There it was, the other million-dollar question. "I'll continue working with my father at the construction company. He's still booked up a year in advance between working within San Francisco and the surrounding areas, and Lorelai…" I smiled at her. "Why don't you tell her?"

Lorelai smiled. "I'm going to be going to work at the Montgomery Winery with his mother."

Marlee smiled. "Wow! That's very exciting. You're both going to be jumping into careers, successful ones at that. I think as long as you keep your goals in sight, you two will be just fine."

Lorelai smiled. "Me too. Christopher and his parents have been so good to me in the last month and a half."

"So, no more hostility there?" Marlee asked.

I laughed. "I think my parents have grown to love Lorelai more than they do me on some days."

Lorelai laughed. "That's because I don't walk away grumbling when they want to joke around."

I nudged her playfully with my elbow and chuckled. "I don't see the point in useless arguments."

Lorelai leaned forward, placing a hand at the side of her mouth. "He's just grumpy," She whispered loudly.

Marlee laughed, "Well that's wonderful, it's so great to see you two improving. Have you two considered taking a night to focus on romance? I know we talked about it a few times. I think you guys are in a good place. Maybe we can push our next session out by a few weeks and before you come back, I want you to plan at least two nights, whether it's going out or staying in, and then we'll talk about it next time."

Lorelai looked at me with gentle facial features. I knew that making love had become a hard act for her to embrace after the miscarriage. She feared that if or when she fell pregnant that we would have to embrace that pain over and over again. This had been talked about over the weeks of coming to therapy.

She smiled at me and took my hand in hers before looking at Marlee. "I did go talk to a doctor at Planned Parenthood a couple of weeks ago, and they did an exam and they couldn't find any reason for us not to try again." She paused and looked back to me. "I think I'm ready to take that step now."

I squeezed her hand and brought it up planting a gentle kiss against the back of it.

Marlee smiled, admiring our progress. "I'm not an expert in that area, but isn't it around seven weeks that you have to wait before you try again?"

Lorelai nodded and looked down.

"Lorelai," Marlee began. "You were under a lot of stress back then. Your lives are looking up in a whole different light. Stay positive."

She looked up with tears in her eyes and nodded. "I know. I'm ready to try again."

I smiled, squeezing her hand and leaned in to kiss her cheek. "It's okay to be scared, baby; but I know that we'll have the child we've been dreaming of."

She looked at me and smiled. "I certainly hope so."

The session continued, and Marlee dug a little deeper on educating Lorelai when to take tests, keeping her diet healthy and to start taking prenatal vitamins before we started trying again. I was pleased with how Marlee took an emotional situation and turned it into a positive hopeful mindset for my beautiful Lorelai. Me? I sat and envisioned that pregnancy glow she would gain, talking about plans for us and our future tot to be, and watching our child grow inside of her. Needless to say, I was the number one support system to making Lorelai a mother to my children. I knew her fears and anxieties, but I refused to give up on making her dreams come true.

When the session ended, we made an appointment for three weeks out and walked out to the car hand in hand. I opened the passenger door for her and saw that she was in safely before I leaned in and pulled the seatbelt out, pulling it around her thin figure and snapping it into place. "What do you say we stop at the drugstore and I'll buy those prenatals Marlee was talking about?" I asked, stepping back but stayed close.

She smiled, placing a hand on my cheek. "That sounds wonderful, Mr. Montgomery."

I leaned in, planting a gentle kiss against her lips. "I love you," I whispered against her lips.

She inhaled a deep sharp breath. "Mmm… I love you, baby. So much."

I smiled against her lips leaning in for another kiss. She held onto the kiss for another moment before I broke it and stepped out. We left as the sun began to set, made a short pit stop before heading back to the yacht club where I would make dinner for us, and we would continue prepping for the big celebration weekend ahead of us.

Twenty-Six

A Man on a Mission

Christopher

Spring
Two weeks later

GRADUATION CAME AND went as a large celebration. As a surprise, my parents offered us a room at the winery for a week. Our week was filled with relaxing and exploration in Napa. We spent time with my family and my parents gave a grand tour of the winery, backstage and front and center. The week went by too fast, but watching Lorelai's face light up with smiles and seeing her sitting comfortable back to her old self was a fresh breath of air.

Upon our arrival back in Sausalito, I took in a view of Lorelai through a peripheral vision, merely glancing at her. The cool sea air blew through her hair, she wore her favorite pair of sunglasses; and I realized that even though she was torn apart from the inside out, she never stopped smiling. Thinking back to when I first suggested therapy after the miscarriage, she took a few hours to think about it but never said no. And even when she walked away from our relationship for a time, she did it because she thought it was in my best interest. Watching her take on all of the emotions, and overcoming these struggles, I realized she was the strongest, happiest human being I ever had the pleasure of crossing paths with; and I… I was going to make sure I never had to live without her.

Pulling back up at the yacht club entrance, I put the car in park.

"You go ahead back. Maybe we can go out to San Francisco tonight?

There's a place I've been wanting to take you."

"Oh? What kind of place?"

"It's a little fancy, so dress up. I have to run an errand, but I'll be back soon."

She smiled at me and leaned over to press her lips against mine in a sweet kiss. "Okay, handsome. Don't be long, okay?"

"I promise I won't, love."

She pecked my lips a few more times, a smile lifting against her lips as she looked me in the eyes. "I'll see you soon."

After she exited, I found myself at the Castillo residence and rang the doorbell.

A moment later, an older version of Lorelai came to the door. She was lanky and had the same piercing blue eyes and smaller glamour features as Lorelai. "Christopher. How may I help you?"

I gave her my best polite smile. "Luciana? May I come in? I'd like to talk to you."

"Um, sure." She stepped aside and allowed me to step in. "Sure.

What's with the surprise visit?"

I sighed and turned to her. "Can we sit?" "Sure." She led the way to a parlor.

"What's on your mind?" she said as we sat.

I swallowed hard. "Well, I realize that your parents might not like me, or want me near Lorelai; but now that she's emancipated, I suppose that doesn't matter. It may sound silly asking this, but from what she tells me, you two are close."

She nodded. "We are and just because she emancipated my parents doesn't mean we won't continue to stay close."

"I understand and respect that, which is why I am here. I want to ask Lorelai to marry me, and I'd like your blessing."

Her lips fell open before she looked away from me, her fingers intertwining as her jaw moved into a firm set. "What makes you think I'd give you my blessing?" She spoke in a quiet, cold tone.

I inhaled a deep breath, wondering if I should have gone to Marie first. "You two are close. So, you care about what she wants, and who or what makes her happy, right?"

Remaining silent for a moment, she finally responded. "I suppose…" She turned slowly to look back at me.

"Then I have no doubts that coming here was the right thing to do." I wasn't afraid, I did team up with Luci and their father to bring Lorelai home. Perhaps nothing changed for them? "I love your sister with everything in me, Luci. There is nothing I wouldn't do for her and, if you give me your blessing, you have my word that I will take care of her the best way I can for the rest of our lives."

Tears filled her eyes and fell down her cheeks as she nodded, and quickly wiped the tears away as a moment passed us by before she said. "Then you have my blessing, Chris." Her words were barely audible, but I could feel that she meant every word.

I smiled at her gently. "Thank you."

There was a pause in the room for a moment. "Take care of her, Chris."

"You have my word."

She stood up and walked me back to the door. "Is that all you needed?"

"Actually, I was wondering. Do you know if Marie is home?"

"I don't, but you're more than welcome to go check for yourself, Chris. When you exit the building, go to your right. She's on the top floor in the next building."

"Thanks."

She opened the door and I made an exit only to enter the next building over.

Standing outside of the Castillo residence in the building, I rang the doorbell.

A moment later, Marie came to the door. "Chris! What are you doing here?"

"Sorry for just stopping by, but I needed to talk to you without Lorelai suspecting anything." I said, honestly.

"Oh… well." She smiled. "Please. Come in."

She led us to the kitchen, and we sat down while she got us both a glass of water. "So, how's everything been going since the Santino Chronicles exploded?"

I chuckled. "It's been slow going, but we're in a really good place. Therapy has helped a lot. We actually just came back from our vacation in Napa and I have the perfect way to end our week, which is why I'm here."

She smiled from ear to ear. "Christopher! What is it? Tell me!"

I chuckled and smiled. "I came here because I know Lorelai is your best friend, and it would only be fair to ask for your blessing before I ask for her hand in marriage."

She gasped and clasped her hands over her mouth, tears filling her eyes almost immediately. "Oh my god! Really?"

I smiled. "Really. I love Lorelai with all of my heart and soul."

She pulled her hands from her mouth as she studied my face. I believe she was trying to make sure I wasn't bluffing. "You're not joking?"

I shook my head. "I would never."

"Of course, you have my permission! You're Lorelai's world now, Christopher...," she whispered through her tears.

I smiled. "And she's mine. Thank you, Marie."

She nodded slowly and smiled. "I'm actually glad you came here today. I have something for you to give to Lorelai."

I looked at her with a raised brow. "What is it?"

She stood up. "I have to go get it. Sit tight."

She left the room and I sat in silence while she was gone. She walked back in a moment later with a bag and sat down. "There are two cell phones in here. They're already activated and ready to use. I had a feeling this day was coming soon, and I wanted to make sure she had a way to stay in contact."

I nodded. "I'll be sure to give them to her."

"The other one is for you. I'm trusting that you'll keep her safe."

I nodded slowly. "Thank you, Marie. I take that job very serious."

She stood up and showed me the way to the door before giving me a tight hug. I looked at her and nodded before I walked out and made my way back to the car placing the bag in the trunk before I made my way out to finish the other half of my errand.

Walking into the cabin of the vessel about an hour later, I looked around. "Lor?"

"In the bathroom!"

I made my way to the back to find her sitting in the corner in one of my button-down collared shirts, tears falling down her cheeks. "I know Marlee suggested that we go out on the town, but I can't Chris. I'm just…I'm having a really hard time right now. I miss my brother. I

hate that I had to divorce my parents just so we could be together. If it's not their goddamn way, it's the highway and I…" She broke down in sobs, burying her face into her knees.

I hated seeing her like this. She hadn't broken down like this in quite some time. Maybe being back here reminded her of it all, and that was the problem. Kneeling in front of her, enveloping her frail, trembling body in my arms, I pressed a tender kiss to her temple. I carried her into the bedroom, allowing her to cry against me. "I know, I know sweetie. It's not easy on you, but I'm going to get you through this. I would never abandon you, nor force you to do anything you didn't want to do." I spoke in a quiet, breathy tone as I sat on the edge of the bed.

She inhaled a deep breath a moment later, the shaking of her sobs calming once she was safe in my arms. "I know you wouldn't…" She looked up at me. "But you had and have every right to, and I would understand if you did."

I shook my head. "I would never. Listen to me. I have just what the doctor ordered to take your mind off of this."

She stayed quiet for a moment before she looked up at me. "Yeah? What is it?"

A gentle smile etched across my lips as I carried her to the kitchen and sat her on the counter. I grabbed a box of cereal and poured two bowls of Peanut Butter Captain Crunch, handing her a bowl before I set my own bowl on the floor. Grabbing a few candles, lighting them and set them down. "Come to the floor. Eat with me in the candlelight." I smiled up at her childishly.

She took in the scenery, the flame of the candles reflecting in her eyes before she sat in front of me cross legged. "So, what? Is this your new idea of date night?"

I managed to steal a bottle of wine from one of the rental houses, too. It's in the fridge."

She gasped as she scooped the bowl up off the floor. "You little rebel."

I chuckled. "They don't refer to me as the wine snob at home for no reason."

She giggled softly. "Honestly? When I found out you were raised around a winery, that was the moment I knew you were a keeper."

I laughed. "What? It wasn't my Prince Charming personality?"

"Well, perhaps. You have saved me, in more than one way."

I flashed her a bashful smile and a wink as we dug into the sugary cereal in silence.

Standing up, I placed our bowls in the sink, reaching my hand out for hers.

"Where are we going?"

"You'll see, love."

She placed her dainty hand in mine and I pulled her up on her feet, intertwining my fingers into hers. Using my free hand to reach out to the mounted radio under the cupboard, I turned it on before wrapping an arm around her lower back, swaying back and forth with her.

A smile rose on her lips, and without saying anything, I could tell she was smitten and taken away with the simple gestures.

I took a few minutes to let the mood settle in as we circled through the kitchen, and I twirled her under my arm before I brought her back in gently. Her chest landed against mine with a gentle thud as our lips collapsed against each other's in a slow, loving lip lock.

I broke the kiss a moment later, gazing into her eyes through the glow of the candlelight, and inhaled a deep breath.

"What's going through that head of yours, Mr. Montgomery?" she whispered.

I flashed a small smile at her. "Just thinking…" I paused. "About how you've managed to turn my world upside down in under a year. No matter how hard it's been to take what life has thrown at us, having you at my side seems to make our hardships pass with ease." She smiled wide, but stayed quiet.

I took both of her hands in mine, never breaking the stare into her eyes. "I couldn't picture having another bright, beautiful young woman at my side." I brought her hand up to my lips and planted gentle kisses against her knuckles before I lowered myself down on one knee; and I pulled the black volar box out of my pocket and opened it. "Lorelai Sienna Castillo, will you make me the happiest man in all of Sausalito and beyond? Take this ring and be my wife?"

Her hands clasped over her mouth and tears sprang to her eyes. "What? Are you serious? Christopher! Yes! Yes! Oh my god! Yes!" I chuckled softly, pulled the ring out and placed it over her finger. I looked up at her as I stood slowly, wrapping my arms around her and lifting her off her feet as our lips clashed in one deep, passionate kiss after another. Her dainty fingers found my scruffy cheeks as I spun her around slowly and she giggled out in sheer happiness.

Pulling away, I smiled at her admiring her engagement ring and planted gentle kisses to her jawline. "What do you say we take these candles to the bathroom and take a bubble bath?"

She smiled up at me. "That sounds perfect, Mr. Montgomery."

"Mmm… it does, Future Mrs. Montgomery."

She giggled as I pressed a few more kisses to her jawline. I separated myself temporarily to pick up the candles and led the way to the bathroom.

She started the water and poured way too much bubble bath into the warm water. By the time it was full, we had a floor and a tub full of bubbles. I chuckled at her continuous giggling as I undressed her with care and helped her step into the tub, before I undressed myself and stepped in behind her.

Wrapping my arms around her, I pulled her back and watched as she curled up on her side, placing one arm around my waist, placing her left hand on my chest to continue admiring the diamond ring I placed on her finger.

After a long moment of silence, she spoke. "Chris?"

"Yes, princess?"

"Thank you."

"For what?"

"Just being you, knowing exactly what I need when I need it."

I smiled and ran my sudsy fingers through her hair. "You're welcome, baby girl. I love you so much."

"I love you." She smiled and leaned up pressing a gentle kiss against my lips.

Twenty-Seven

The Smell Of Freedom

Lorelai

Three months later

WAKING UP ON the Friday before the wedding, I walked out to the kitchen and placed a hand on Christopher's back, leaning in to give him a kiss on the cheek. Two cups of coffee sat out

in front of the coffee pot, ready to go. "Is this for me, handsome?"

"No, it's for the ghost sitting on the couch." He turned toward me and leaned in to give me a kiss on the lips.

I scoffed and giggled returning his kiss. "Too bad. Ghost Rider is going to have to fetch his own."

He chuckled and kissed my lips once more. "Don't forget, we're meeting Luciana and Marie for breakfast today. Do you want me to join you outside for our morning coffee?"

"Yes. That would be perfect, Mr. Montgomery."

He kissed me once more. "I'll be up in a few minutes, soon to be Mrs. Montgomery."

I pecked his lips once more and smiled up at him. "I'll meet you out there, gorgeous."

He winked at me and I blew him a kiss with my lips before I disappeared.

Sitting down at our table, I thought back on the last three months. Our second summer together was a lot different from the first. We weren't sneaking around, but our wedding plans had definitely gone into full swing. Marie was at my side helping me make every decision. Luci kept her distance after the result of Santino's big exit. After telling Chris's parents about the engagement, Chris and I made the decision together on having our small, vintage themed wedding out in Napa at the Montgomery Vineyard. I met with Mrs. Montgomery on Saturdays down at the Clubhouse for breakfast to work on plans for the wedding. Checking off my list from location to catering, entertainment, themes/colors, ceremony styles, meeting with a pastor, my wedding dress, and dresses for Luciana and Marie, and the invitations had all been planned out. I wasn't able to find it in myself to invite my parents to the wedding. There was so much animosity between us about Christopher in the beginning, and I knew they had their hands full and I wouldn't be surprised if they were trying to keep themselves afloat, dodging bullets with the government.

With my trust fund being cleared, I tried to tell Mrs. Montgomery, from the first time we met to talk wedding plans, that I could help pay for the wedding. She wouldn't have it. The following day, Chris told me we had to go to Napa to meet with his parents and Nana and Papa for the "engagement party." His parents and Nana and Papa were overjoyed to find out I was joining their family and insisted to pay every penny for our wedding. There was no arguing, and Chris seemed to find it adorable that I was trying and picked on me later about trying to question them. Needless to say, I was sitting on the couch, crossing my arms with a frumpy face, and one eyebrow raised at my fiancé as he continuously teased me.

The time flew, and Chris and I were both working full time jobs; and we used the evenings and weekends to spend quality time together. The cell phones he brought home also allowed us to stay in touch during the busy work week. Chris was closer to the club and arrived home earlier than I did during the week. He told me the atmosphere of the club had been eerily quiet. The men in the black suits disappeared and the Black Diamond Club was still present, but the traffic going in and out had slowed down from what he witnessed.

The cabin door opened and Chris made his way to our table. We sat and drank our morning coffee in silence for a few minutes before I felt him reach for my hand, grasping it gently. "What are you thinking about love?"

I brushed my thumb over his, examining just how perfectly my hand fit into his. "About how much our lives have changed in a year. How my family, aside from Marie, have become like strangers to me, that last night was my last night I had to sleep on Cakes and Pies. Life doesn't feel the same, but I'm also not sad about it. I'm thrilled and ecstatic and… hopeful for our future as Mr. and Mrs. Montgomery."

He squeezed my hand and leaned over, kissing my cheek. "It's wonderful, isn't it?"

I turned my head and leaned my forehead against his, looking down into his piercing grey-blue eyes. "It is," I whispered.

He looked back at me for a moment as we shared a quiet peace filled moment before he reached over taking the coffee cup from my hand. He stood up before he pulled me to my feet and pulled me down into his lap, sending me into a fit of giggles. I placed my hands on his cheeks and pressed a sweet, gentle kiss to his lips. He wrapped me in his arms, groaning softly before he broke the kiss and reached for my coffee. "Almost forgot to give this back to you. I wouldn't want to be stabbed for holding your coffee hostage."

I tried to hold back a laugh and failed miserably. "What makes you think I would stab you?"

He raised an eyebrow toward me, and shifted his eyebrows back and forth before he grabbed his own coffee. "Do I need to answer that?"

I laughed, "Not if you know what's good for you, you don't," I teased.

He chuckled lightheartedly. "So, is everything ready to go for tomorrow tonight? The rehearsal dinner starts at six?"

"Yes, all of our bags are packed for the wedding and honeymoon; and all of our boxes are packed for the move, so we will have little to no responsibility after the ceremony."

"Besides actually moving…," he stated.

I smiled. "Exactly, which won't be hard since most of our belongings are already moved."

He smiles. "True. Perhaps we could take this love fest to the shower…"

"Mmmm…are you talking dirty to me, Mr. Montgomery?" I spoke above a whisper.

"Oh, definitely." He breathed out against my ear.

I tipped the coffee cup back and drank it down. "I need more of that. Not coffee…the dirty talk," I rambled out.

He tipped his head back in laughter, cradling me bridal style into his arms carrying me into the cabin toward the bathroom, where the dirty talk turned the volume up on the steamy shower for a few short minutes. He left me breathless and needing so much more, but we had a schedule to stick to for our big wedding weekend in Napa.

After we were showered and dressed, we walked hand in hand down to the boardwalk toward the cafe. We walked in to find Marie and Luci already sitting in a booth and sat down across from each other. I sat next to Luciana, while Chris sat next to Marie. "Hey. Sorry, were you guys waiting long?"

Marie smiled. "Nope. We sat down about five minutes ago," she said as the waitress came with four coffees.

My eyes widened at the glorious coffee sitting in front of me. "And ordered us all coffee? Best soul sisters ever."

Marie smiled. "Of course. I knew you'd make a scene if we didn't."

Luci rolled her eyes. "If you plan to have children, that coffee addiction is going to have to be cut down."

Lorelai smiled. "Then I guess I better sip this easy." "What?" Marie and Christopher spat off in unison.

I looked to Luciana, whose face also fell, as I reached into my purse. "Twelve weeks to be exact," I said, putting the sonogram down.

"Honey!" Chris gasped. "You didn't… say… anything!" He choked out and leaned over with Marie to study the sonogram.

"I wasn't going to until I knew we were almost out of the danger zone…" I whispered, tears flooding my eyes. "Next week, we'll be out of the danger zone. The doctor is really happy with mine and the baby's health, too."

Chris stood up and came to my side of the table, placed a hand under my chin and pressed his lips to mine like his life depended on it.

Marie squealed looking at the photo. "What a cute little peanut!"

Chris broke the kiss and looked around at everyone staring. "It's okay! Everything is fine! I just learned that I'm going to be a father!" he announced to the entirety of the cafe.

I giggled as everyone started clapping and cheering for us. "Christopher! Sit down!" I scolded him playfully.

He turned to me and scrunched his face in playful disgust. "I'm a proud baby daddy, okay?" he snapped and I shook my head.

"You better be!"

Luciana shook her head. "The world should be petrified."

I looked at her. "Why? Because we're fun and adventurous?"

"No, because that kid is going to have Castillo blood in it."

I furrowed my eyebrows. "What's that supposed to mean?"

She shook her head. "Nothing. I just meant, you can't push me away now because that child is going to be spoiled by his Aunt Luci."

I eyed Chris and Marie. "Right, of course. Well, let's order."

The waitress came by just on time to take our orders, and Luci looked at me. "So, Mom called me a few days ago."

"Yeah? How is she doing?"

"Good. She couldn't tell me where she and Dad were. She's leaving me and Marie in charge of the yacht club. We've been working closely with Mom and Dad's assistants to learn the ropes."

"What happened to staying in the family business?" I asked.

"Taking a mandatory break." She spoke quietly. "To learn the business."

I nodded. "Good. This place seems a lot calmer lately."

"It has been calm. It's weird not having Mom and Dad around though."

"It's only for the best though, right?"

She nodded. "Yeah." She paused, and looked at Marie. "Anyway, Marie. You said you were taking the dresses and decorations up to Napa? Is that already done?"

"Yes. I did it yesterday after work. Chris's parents were at the vineyards and showed me the bridal room. Lor, you're going to love it. The interior of that place is immaculate, and the views are gorgeous."

I smiled. "I can't wait."

"So, what's the plan? Are we heading up there after we leave here?"

"Well, Chris and I have to finish taking boxes over to his parents' boathouse. They officially moved to the new house and we're going to rent the boathouse for now."

"Rent is a loose term there. My parents aren't charging us much to stay. They were able to pay it off when they got the loan for their new house up on the hill."

Marie smiled wide. "Your lives are shaping up. I'm so happy for both of you. A wedding, a house, and baby Montgomery is on his or her way? You two must be so thrilled!"

I smiled wide. "We are. We're very happy."

"You deserve it and Armani would be so damn proud."

I sucked my lower lip in and nodded, looking at Luci. I was going to ask her if she agreed until I saw angry daggers being sent in Marie's direction, and bit hard into my lip. A dark, awkward silence came over the table for a few minutes before the food arrived and we all dug in to eat.

Luci asked for the check when the waitress came by, and gave her cash. "I hate to do this, but I need to go take care of a few things before I leave to drive up to Napa." I stood up slowly as she hurried out of the booth.

"Okay." I reached my arm out to hug her. "We'll see you up there." She gave me a quick hug. "See you," she said before she disappeared toward the door.

I sat back down, looked at her plate that she barely touched, and looked from Chris to Marie. "She's acting strange."

"You think?" Marie retorted. "She's been like that since we started training on the business. I think she's up to something, but I have no idea what."

The waitress came back and I gave her the money with the check. "Keep the change."

She walked off and Chris, Marie and I made our way out of the cafe. As we exited, a parade line of yachts had set out on the bay. I held Chris's hand, looking down to the end of the boardwalk to see that the entire Black Diamond Club had been unplugged and taken apart down to the sign on the archway.

Goosebumps raised up my arms and down my spine. Perhaps this was why Luci was acting so strange, the life she thought she was inheriting in honor of our parents' wishes was ripped out from under her and she was left running their boring, legal, nine to five business. I didn't understand it myself, but I knew that our home of Sausalito would be a better place because of it.

We walked down to the docks where the business used to be ran and walked through them before we sat down and dangled our legs over one of the higher docks. Chris wrapped one arm around me, and placed the other on the small bump of my belly and smiled down at me. "You're so sneaky, wife to be."

I giggled. "Am I?"

"Yes, but I love it. I would be okay if you surprised me like that for every child we have, or plan to have."

My smile widened as I looked up at him. "I think that could be arranged, Mr. Montgomery."

Marie nudged me with her elbow gently and I looked at her. "Yes?"

"I don't want to interrupt your love fest, but can we just take this in? We're sitting inside of the very place the Black Diamond Club used to be."

I inhaled a deep breath with her. "It feels… it smells like…

Hmmm…"

We sat staring off at the distant line of yachts disappearing from our view, and spoke in unison, "Freedom."

Twenty-Eight

Head Above Water

THE MOVING OF boxes and packing the car up for Napa was liberating, all the planning and waiting for the time to come was over. Marie rode with Lorelai and myself, while Luci insisted to meet us there. Arriving in Napa, Lorelai and Marie were taken to the Bridal Suite by Nana to settle in; and later on, we all met up for the rehearsal dinner. The night was filled with smiles and laughter, and each moment that passed was a memory embedded into my head. It was the night before we finally said I do.

My focus stayed on Lorelai the entire time, she was glowing beauty; and the free spirit in her was released like I had never seen before. This woman would be my wife in less than twenty-four hours and that was the only thought in my mind as we went through the dress rehearsal. By the end of the night, both of my parents were somewhat drunk and decided to walk back with my grandparents, laughing to their hearts content to their designated rooms.

I turned my attention back to Lorelai who sat on the swinging bench between Marie and Luciana, swinging slowly.

"Ladies…? Do you mind if I cut in to kiss my bride to be goodnight?"

Marie smiled, and looked at Luci. "Not at all. We'll meet you back at the room, Lor."

Lorelai smiled. "Okay. I won't be long."

Luci stood up. "Make sure she gets back to the room safe, Montgomery."

I saluted her. "Aye, aye Captain Luci."

She rolled her eyes and walked off with Marie. I turned to look at Lorelai patting the seat next to her on the swing. "Come to the swing, soon to be husband."

I smiled and walked to her and sat, pulling her into my lap, and wrapping my arms around her. She leaned in, planting a sweet kiss to my lips. I placed a hand on her cheek, and rubbed a hand up and down her back to the small bump on her belly, groaning softly against her lips. "Mmmm…You're going to make such a beautiful bride and I can hardly wait to see you at the top of the aisle tomorrow."

She smiled against my lips. "I can't wait to walk to you in my dress, join hands, and finally be Mrs. Montgomery," she whispered.

"Mmm…it is your day to shine while you transform from a princess to my queen."

"Mmm…Christopher…You're so sweet…"

I smiled, sweeping my arm under her legs and stood up to walk back toward the suites. Arriving outside the door, I set her back on her feet with ease, and wrapped her in my arms once more. "Go get some sleep, princess." I leaned in and pressed a sweet kiss to her lips. She returned the kiss, cupping my cheeks before wrapping her arms around my neck, resting her arms against my shoulders. I held onto the moment knowing the next time I kissed her, it would be at the end of the aisle and she would be my wife. My beautiful, imperfectly perfect queen, Mrs. Montgomery.

Breaking the kiss a moment later, I pressed my lips to her forehead.

"Goodnight, my handsome prince."

I pulled back and looked down at her. "Sweet dreams. Perhaps I'll meet you in dreamland."

She smiled. "Where we'll sit on the fluffiest clouds in togas creating rainbows for all to see."

I chuckled and grinned at her, cupping her cheeks. "I'll see you first thing in the morning, my love."

She lingered her hands away and turned to walk inside, looking back to me before the door shut. I bit my lower lip and made the trek back to my own suite, shutting the door quietly.

Changing out of my clothes into a pair of pajama pants, I prepped for bed and crawled into the high thread count sheets, staring out the window at the large moon casting its light down over the countryside. Closing my eyes, I knew it would be nearly impossible to sleep. I pictured Lorelai standing at the end of the aisle attempting to envision her dress and allowed the image to pull me into a peaceful sleep.

The next morning, I woke surprised that I slept as well as I did. Jumping out of bed, I went to the bathroom and stared at my reflection in the mirror. Today was the day I would make Lorelai Castillo my wife, and the first day to celebrate our eternal love for each other. Stripping my clothes off, I showered, making sure to take some extra time to clean up.

The rest of the morning consisted of eating breakfast with my dad and Papa Nick, and dressing myself in the tuxedo that my parents insisted on buying for me. Mom came through to fix my hair. Normally, I would've bitched and complained about it; but today, I let her because, even though she would always be my mother and care for me, Lorelai would be moving in as the woman that would be taking care of me from now on. She gave me pointers about marriage, and what it meant when my dad lost a war with her. Happy wife, happy life. What she said, and how she wanted it done was completely up to Lorelai now. I wasn't going to argue. I made sure my mother knew that was already how it was…and she wasn't surprised. When she kissed my cheek, she told me I was always a gentleman and to never change.

Once we were all dressed and ready to go, we left the suite and headed down to the outdoor venue which was being set up with chairs, pale yellow and pink rose bouquets attached to the end of them, with two large flower arches at the beginning and end of the aisle on the grassy knoll looking over the vineyard and Napa Valley Mountains.

Lorelai

Marie and I couldn't sleep most of the night. We sat up in our plush robes, reading through a pile of Hollywood gossip magazines until we couldn't keep our eyes open a moment longer. The next day, we showered and placed our robes back on while Marie ordered in food and set it up in the sitting area in our suite. We ate and talked about how quickly the summer flew by and couldn't believe we completed and survived wedding planning 101.

As we finished our breakfast, Marie went to work on my hair and make-up. I trusted her with my entire life and I knew she would meet expectations. We decided to go with a simple yet elegant French twist. Next, she applied my make-up which was already pre-planned as well.

When all hair and make-up preparations were finished, Marie helped me get dressed and brought me into the full-size mirror, pulling the train out, and stood on a chair to place the veil on.

I looked at the unrecognizable reflection in the mirror, and swallowed a lump in my throat, as the butterflies fluttered more than usual.

Someone knocked at the door before it opened. Luci walked in with another round of coffee. She stopped in the mirror's reflection, a soft, blank look over her face. "The vintage princess look works for you."

I smiled. "Thank you, Luci."

"I have something for you."

"You do?"

She nodded and walked over, already dressed and ready to go. "I thought as the co-maid of honor, I would cover the something old, something new, and something blue tradition and Marie agreed."

She went to sit at the table and I followed, watching as she pulled a small gift box out. Taking it from her, I opened it to find a royal blue oval shaped, diamond encrusted pendant necklace on a silver chain.

"Luciana…this is gorgeous. Thank you."

She gently took it from the box and stood behind me to place it on. "It was Mommy's. The setting is brand new though. She wore it when she married Papino and told me she wanted you to have it."

I stared the gorgeous piece of symbolic jewelry. My parents and family may not have been here, but they were still with me. I flashed a smile back at her. "It's perfect, I'll make sure to thank her the next time we talk."

She eyed me. "I'll tell her for you."

I nodded glancing back to the mirror once more to look myself over in the mirror once more before show time. My ensemble was officially complete, and I truly felt like a princess. All I needed now was my dashing prince.

Christopher

I took my stance at the top of the aisle. My father came down and gave me a hug. "Should I tell them we're ready?"

"Everything looks good. I think so."

The pastor nodded. "Your wife came to tell me the decor was finished, so whenever the bride is ready, Mr. Montgomery." Dad nodded and walked back to let them know.

Taking a deep breath, I waited with bated breath as several minutes passed. My parents and a few of our close friends here in Napa sat to witness our big day. The music we picked out before the Wedding March began. Marie came down first, wearing a pale pink bridesmaid dress, throwing petals down the path with grace. I smiled, chuckling a bit and winked at her as she approached the front, making a goofy face at me before she took her position on Lorelai's side.

The music stopped a few moments later, and the Wedding March began. Inhaling a deep breath, I held it for a moment as Luci made her way down the path. I locked my eyes on Lorelai as she stood under the archway of roses, tears filling my eyes as she graced her way down the aisle in a sleeveless A-line lace vintage floor gown, the skirt of the dress in layers gave the dress a perfect princess effect. Her make-up was done to perfection, her dark locks of hair pulled back in a classy updo with small curls hanging down her cheeks with a veil that traveled down most of her back. While her attire, hair and make-up were perfect, it was her smile and the way she locked her eyes on mine that blew me away.

I held my breath until she was in front of me and exhaled slowly. "You look absolutely breathtaking…" I whispered as she stood in front of me, and Luciana fixed her train.

She smiled with tears in her eyes. "As do you, my knight in shining armor." She turned to give the bouquet of roses to Luci who proceeded to take her place behind Lorelai and off to the side.

The music came to a slow stop, and I couldn't take my eyes off of Lorelai for a second.

"Welcome friends and family. We are gathered here today to welcome Christopher and Lorelai to join hands and hearts in their infinite love for one another. Over the past few months, I've visited with them here at the vineyard several times, getting to know each of them as a couple and two individual souls that each possess a strong passion for family, life, adventure and, most of all, love. They have chosen to each write their own vows. We'll start with you Christopher."

I smiled reaching into my pocket to grab the speech I wrote and unfolded it, holding one of her hands in mine. "From the day I laid my eyes on you at my front door, your beauty struck me into shock and your quirky personality threw me off track before you reeled me in with your sense of adventure. You never gave up on me. Even when we were told to stay away from each other, the electric pulse pulled us back in. Today, I make a promise to love and care for you however you need me; but first, I'd like to tell you a little story. As a little boy, I grew up watching four of the most important people in my life love and care for each other. My father woke up to clean pressed clothes, went to work while Mom stayed home to take care of the house, came home to a home cooked meal, a clean house, and worked some more to help my mother complete the other household tasks. There were never any serious arguments. Sure, Dad whined about it, but then my mother would pull him back to reality. While my father worked with my grandfather and built a family business name, our last name became well known because these men worked hard to take care of us financially, but they never stopped there. They maintained the house, fixing leaky pipelines, the cars if they broke down. They found a way to make it work again and they applied the same concept to the well-being of their wives. Starting today, and all the other days ahead of us as your husband, I will work hard to make sure we have a place to live and grow. I'll check my work problems at the door and care for you tenderly. We'll work together to solve the broken problems in our lives and strive as we overcome them. You are my Queen, and I will make sure you know it until I take my last breath."

Tears streamed down her cheeks as she smiled ear to ear. She inhaled a deep breath, cursing under her breath. I chuckled at her.

"Wow, I'm not sure how I can follow that, but I'm going to try," she said, a few laughs could be heard in the crowd. "Christopher, from the day I saw your family moving into the business my own family ran, my eyes focused in on you like a hawk. I knew I had to know you; and from the moment you looked me in the eyes, I knew you were a special young man with a big heart. I reached for your hand, unsure you would trust me; and we took off frolicking through Sausalito, making memories of the first few months we knew each other. I cherish those times so dearly because it was the beginning to our story. The story we will tell our children and our grandchildren in hopes that they too find their perfect soulmate. You were my warm blanket when I had nowhere else to go; and because we came out stronger on the other side, you will forever be my security blanket yesterday, today, and all of our days for the rest of eternity."

Tears welled in my eyes and slowly fell down my cheeks; and as I looked into her eyes, I was looking inside of her fiery soul. This woman had me entangled in emotions and love that grew an infinite size right in that moment.

Sniffles could be heard in the audience and there was a moment of silence before the pastor spoke. "Chris and Lorelai have chosen to participate in a candle lighting ceremony, which will take place now."

He handed me a large candle that was lit, I reached for Lorelai's hand as we walked in to the first candle. Soft music started playing in the background as she placed her hand over mine, and we walked from one candle to the next in the circle until all the candles were lit. Each candle we lit had a word on it, love, cherish, compromise, honesty, health, wealth, sickness, and infinity.

Standing back in front of the pastor, we blew the candle out together and I handed it back to the pastor that set it aside.

Luciana brought the rings up, presenting them to the pastor.
"Who gives permission for this man to marry this woman?"

"I do," she said before handing the rings off, while Marie stepped up to fix Lorelai's train.

"Lorelai, go ahead and take Chris's ring, and hold it at the tip of his left ring finger…"

"Do you, Lorelai Sienna Castillo, take Christopher Nathaniel Montgomery to be your wedded husband, to have, to hold, through sickness and health, for richer or poorer for the rest of your life?"

She locked her eyes on mine once more. "I do." She slid the ring down my finger.

I took her ring, and held it. "And Christopher, do you take Lorelai Sienna Castillo to be your wedded wife to have, to hold, through sickness and health, for richer or poorer for the rest of your life?"

"I do," I said, sliding the ring down her finger.

I smiled widely at my wife, my bright and beautiful wife, as she tilted her head up at me with a smile that went to her sparkling eyes.

"You may now kiss your bride…"

I slid both hands over her arms, cupping her cheeks as I leaned down and planted a gentle loving kiss to her lips. Her hands moved to my arms as she returned the kiss with passion. The energy between us felt like fireworks exploding in the skies, one of the large golden-brown ones that fell in slow motion like palms on a palm tree.

I broke the kiss, looking into her dazzling blue eyes, and brushed my nose against hers playfully. "I love you so much, Mrs. Montgomery."

She giggled, and pecked my lips over and over again. "I love you, Mr. Montgomery."

Lorelai took her bouquet of flowers back and we walked back down the aisle as husband and wife, down to the road where a white horse and buggy carriage waited to take us on a ride through the vineyard.

After helping her in, I wrapped her in my arms and kissed her as the driver took off. As nervous as I was about losing this woman not all that long ago, we went through so much to get to this very moment; and it was more than worth fighting for. Lorelai Sienna Montgomery was now my wife, my queen. She was perfect in every imaginable way and now she was mine to love and protect.

Two Weeks Later

The honeymoon was over and we were back home settling into the boathouse and unpacking. Rummaging through an unpacked tote, I found a wrapped box with no indication as to who left it. "Hey honey?"

Lorelai was in the kitchen making us lunch. "Yeah, babe?"

"Come here. I found a present."

"A present? Who's it from?"

"I'm not sure." I looked at her as she sat next to me.

"What are you waiting for? Open the mystery present!"

I chuckled and looked at her. "We should do it together."

I set the other end on her leg and we each took a side to open. Pulling the box open, there was a wooden plaque inside that was engraved with 'The Montgomery's' on it.

She narrowed her eyes at me. "Who would wrap up a family name and conveniently stick it in our house?"

I chuckled. "I don't know. Should we go hang it?"

"Hey. There are scratches on the back of it. Look." She turned it around to show me and continued. "What if some creep snuck in here while we were sleeping?"

I laughed and smiled at her. "Then I guess I'm a creep sneaking into my own house."

"Christopher!" She yelled and followed after me as I grabbed a nail and a hammer from my tool box.

I continued laughing, and walked to the door and opened it. "Are you going to come document this monumental moment with your awesome photography or continue making fun of me?"

She ran upstairs. "I'm not making fun of you!"

I looked toward the stairs. "Yes, you are!"

She came back downstairs. "You think you're funny and you're really, really not, Mr. Montgomery!"

I chuckled. "I am too! You don't know funny when it's in front of your face."

She ignored me as she set up the camera and looked at me. "When you're ready, Mr. Montgomery."

I placed the nail to the center of the door after measuring the width, plotting it in the center and nailed it in. Looking back at her, I smiled brightly. She rolled her eyes and took the picture.

"Can we hang it together?" She asked, excitedly.

"Of course, get over here."

She walked around, and I gave her one half of the ribbon and together we hung it over the nail.

I turned her toward me and wrapped her in my arms, rubbing her lower back. "It looks perfect, Mrs. Montgomery."

"It does. Should we take a picture outside? We can use it for Christmas cards."

I leaned down and kissed her gently. "That sounds perfect, my beautiful, crafty wife."

She moved the tripod outside, and I stepped out and closed the wooden door. She set the camera and came and stood in front of me. I wrapped an arm around her, placing my hand over the small baby bump, and her hand fell gently on top of mine like clockwork. "3,2,1…" Snap.

Epilogue

The Devil Within

Lorelai

APPROXIMATELY SIX MONTHS later, Spring had sprung and I was thirty nine weeks pregnant, and a wobbling duck as Christopher liked to refer to me. I accepted the playful insult, and went around the house quacking randomly. My husband thought it was quite funny, and I was always amused and surprised at how we grew as a married couple. He finally adapted to what I like to call a sense of humor.

I was waiting for him to come home from work; and I stood up to check on dinner and a warm liquid dripped down the inside of my legs just as the door opened. "Uh oh…Chris…"

"What's wrong, baby?"

"I think we're going to have to turn the oven off and forget dinner."

"Why?"

"I think my water just broke."

Chris quickly grabbed our hospital bag and led me to the bedroom to change my pants, helping me clean up before we rushed out of the house and went to the hospital.

12 hours later

I lay in my hospital bed, completely exhausted in a love drunk state of mind, looking down at Nathaniel Kingston Montgomery. He was healthy and perfect in every way possible.

Chris was standing and admiring our handsome little prince as someone came knocking at the door, and Marie peeked her head around the corner.

I smiled wide and gasped. "Aunty Marie… You're here…"

She smiled as she walked in with balloons, flowers and little gift bag. "Yes, she is. How'd everything go?"

I smiled down at the tiny human in my arms. "It was very slow going. I went natural and it sucked, but he was worth it." I paused. "Do you wanna hold him?"

"Absolutely!" She walked over, and I sat up and carefully handed him off, watching as Marie sat down and admired him in silence for a moment. "Oh my god, he's stinking adorable, Lorelai."

I smiled. "He really is. He's perfect. I already counted all of his fingers and toes, and kissed him a whole bunch."

She giggled. "I'm so happy for you guys." She sat and rocked him back and forth. "Have you seen or talked to Luci?"

I shook my head. "No. Not since the wedding."

Chris grabbed my hand and wrapped his fingers around mine. "We've talked about this. She made her choice."

Marie nodded. "I know. I haven't seen or spoken to her either, and I can proudly say I'm running the club just fine without her help."

I nodded. "Well, I know I'm not much of a help with that these days; but if she's gone, you should do something about eliminating her half of the ownership."

"I tried. My dad said we couldn't without further discussion."

I sighed and looked at her. "I'm sorry she did that to you."

She shook her head. "Don't be. You have a family of your own to worry about now. It's okay, Lorelai."

I smiled. "Two handsome men and a little lady."

She laughed. "Exactly." She kissed Nathan's forehead. "You're too cute for your own good, little man Montgomery." She stood, and placed him back in my arms. "I should get back, but call me when you come home okay?"

"I will. I love you, Marie."

She leaned down and hugged me. "I love you too, sister." She pulled away and walked toward the door. Chris and I sat there watching as she left.

Chris sat on the edge of the bed and smiled down at me and our little miracle rainbow baby. I smiled back at him and placed my free hand on his leg. Life was officially complete with the arrival of Nathan. I decided to quit my job at the winery, and his parents were completely understanding. Chris would be home with me for the first six weeks before he went back to work. Life was good. No scratch that, life was fantastic. I had an amazing husband and a little boy that I already adored, and I couldn't wait to see where the road of life would take us.

Luciana
Four Years Later

Christmas Eve was upon us. People everywhere were gathering together to celebrate this joyous holiday with friends and family, my family included. I walked through the penthouse with a glass of whiskey over the rocks. Walking through the crowd of people, I eyed Anthony standing by the snack table popping an olive in his mouth, and narrowed my eyes at him before I slipped down the double black glass staircase to the wall of portraits.

I looked at him as he came up next to me. "Ready for the next chapter of your life to begin?"

He smirked. "I was born ready."

With a stone-cold face, I unlocked the sliding wall behind my father's portrait and we made our way through the dark secured hallways. Walking into the vault, I grabbed a plate sitting on the buffet table. "Help yourself. We're going to be here a while."

I made myself a plate of food and sat down at the control station; hitting the power switch, the screens lit up. The front and center screen popping on first.

"Who are those people?" he asked.

"Oh…Um…that's my sister and her little shithead of a husband. She chose him over our family…"

Anthony raised an eyebrow. "So, why are you watching them? What did they do?"

"She cut me off." I snapped and moved the camera in on a little boy that appeared to be around four years old. "That's my nephew…Nathan." I moved the camera again and zoomed in a bit on the identical twin baby girls digging into what appeared to be mini birthday cakes with a number one on them. "And these are my nieces,

Hannah and Hayley. Identical twins."

"Hmmm…so is this just a basic surveillance?"

"Pretty much. She thinks I left Sausalito, but I'm making my return sooner than she thinks." I said in a simple monotone. We sat back to eat our Christmas dinner, while the other cameras around the boathouse popped up around the main screen.

Turning the volume up, we listened in to the family eating and celebrating the girls' birthdays as the doorbell rang.

Chris stood up to answer the door with a Santa hat over his head. A never before seen identical image of myself stood in the doorway, soaking wet from the rain outside.

I watched as Anthony leaned forward squinting his eyes. "Who is that at the door?"

I zoomed in a bit when a concerned Chris stepped back to look at Lorelai.

Anthony's mouth fell open as he looked from the screen over to me and back at the screen, his eyes widened in a baffled state.

A dark laugh escaped my lips. My puppet master strings were in place and the games were just beginning.

The End

Coming Soon

Now that the Black Diamond club have made their big exit, follow the Montgomerys as they make their home in beautiful Sausalito.

Join Lorelai and Chris as they venture through the ups and downs of raising their hormonal teenagers who come forward to tell their own story.

A message from a familiar face:

The monitor scratched loudly.

An all too familiar face moved across the unsteady screen. She wore a red hooded pea coat; her dark hair fell around her face. Luciana cleared her throat as an evil smirk broke through her jungle red lipstick. "Hello world. I don't know if you can hear me…the system over here is faulty, so I must be quick! Lorelai thinks she got her way when she stole the family's money to keep her mouth shut and ran off to marry Chris. She doesn't know that there are secrets the syndicate has kept from her with good reason."

The scribbles started cutting the young woman off.

"I don't have much time. Just know that you haven't seen the last of me. Lorelai will pay for turning her back on our family!" She leaned forward as her bright blue eyes looked into the screen and paused as she stared into the camera. "That's a promise." The screen scrambled and went black.

Acknowledgements

The journey to get here has been quite a long process, almost two decades to be exact. I have so many people who have had my back, scooting me along the pathway to publishing. First and foremost, I want to thank my editor, Jessa Dahmes. Your left field entrance into my life as a new author was a pleasant experience and I can't wait to see where this journey takes us! Thank you for being kind, patient and animating this manuscript to its full potential!

Jill Horle. My sister by friendship because God knows if we were blood related, we would've sent our parents to the looney bin. Thank you for being there from the beginning of this journey. You were the first to see the potential of this dream coming true and you never gave up on rooting me on to achieve this goal. Thank you for being the amazing woman you are!

Kitka Buchanan. You were there when I hit the brick wall. There was a time when I didn't think any of this would be possible. With your kindness, and heart of gold, you slipped me away from that brick wall with little to no scrapes and bruises when it came to transitioning this dream to a reality.

To my Mother, who gave me life and constantly told me what a crazy imagination I had. You have been my endless supporter. No matter the hard times, I am forever grateful for you recognizing that I had a creative talent.

JM Walker, I've sat and fangirled over your beautiful book cover designs, and I couldn't be more ecstatic and thankful that your talents get to be the headliner to my book babies.

Sunshine, you are truly a ray of light! For all the late-night chats throwing ideas at you and making your ears bleed with my endless banter and questions regarding all things Montgomery Beauty. You are not just my best friend, but my sister. If it weren't for you being my rock to break the anxiety, I wouldn't be where I am today.

Katlyn Webb. Girl. Our friendship bloomed into something fiercely beautiful! You too were the rock I didn't know I needed. Thank you for giving me and the Montgomery Fuckery timeline a chance and for being in my circle of support. It means absolutely everything to me.

To my PA, Jordan Hummel. My gosh, you are a blessing I didn't know I needed. You've kicked it in the ass thus far and this is just the beginning. I can't wait to see where this road takes us!

KJ. My British soul sister whom I am also forever thankful for. You gave me a giant push of motivation in more ways than one. Let's face it. We would be here for centuries if I had to list the reasons your name made this cut.

Kirsty Eyre, Heather Garcia, and my childhood best friend, Megan – All of you ladies have had a huge influence in helping me get where I am today.

And not lastly, or mostly, I want to send a big fat thank you to Jared Padalecki for launching the Love Yourself First campaign and being the amazing, kind, moosey human being that you are. It was because of Love Yourself First that I kicked myself in the ass to get here.

There are so many other names, reasons, and memories I could list here; but it would probably take another novel to do it. You people know who you are, and I'm beyond thankful and humbled that you are there to back me up and run with me on this crazy journey.

About The Author

Stephanie was born and raised in Cleveland, Ohio. She lives, breathes, and drinks in fangirling over her favorite celebs, her dog, and being a self-appointed social media snob. She's got a wild imagination by nature, which drove her to write. Steph tries to stay true to the phrase, "Love Yourself First." LYF is what inspired her to publish her first book. When she's not slaving over creating words to form a story, you can find her feeding her caffeine addiction, traveling or spending time with her friends and family.

Where can you find me?

Facebook Author Page

https://www.facebook.com/SassySalvatoreWritesWords/

Facebook Fan Group – Salvatore's Syndicate Suite

https://www.facebook.com/groups/448910852168867

Amazon Author Profile

https://amzn.to/2RkAwkj

Instagram

https://www.instagram.com/author_stephanie_salvatore/

Twitter

https://twitter.com/SassySSalvatore

Spotify Username: stephanieryan8587

Playlist: Sausalito Nights Soundtrack , Abhorrent Bloor Soundtrack

https://www.pinterest.com/stephanieryan87/montgomery-beauty/

Made in the USA
Coppell, TX
06 June 2021

56953010R00135